"In a tornado, everything gets whipped around," the lieutenant said. "It could have been anything flying in the air that knocked him down."

"But that's precisely what I mean," Jessica said. "All those pieces may have been swirling around the room upstairs, but when the floor gave way, they fell straight down through the hole."

"What are you suggesting, Mrs. Fletcher?"

"I'm not suggesting anything. I'm just wondering what exactly hit him."

"I think your imagination is getting the better of you, Mrs. Fletcher. Wes Newmark's head was cracked open like an egg, and half a house was sitting on top of him. The bottom line is that if he'd taken shelter, he'd be alive today."

"Why do you think he didn't take shelter?"

"I have no idea. Maybe he was a stubborn son of a gun. Maybe there's no logical explanation. Why do *you* think he didn't take shelter?"

"I think he may already have been dead."

Other *Murder, She Wrote* mysteries

MAJORING IN MURDER

A *Murder, She Wrote* Mystery

A Novel by Jessica Fletcher
and Donald Bain
based on the
Universal television series
created by Peter S. Fischer,
Richard Levinson & William Link

A SIGNET BOOK

SIGNET
Published by New American Library, a division of
Penguin Putnam Inc., 375 Hudson Street,
New York, New York 10014, U.S.A.
Penguin Books Ltd, 80 Strand,
London WC2R 0RL, England
Penguin Books Australia Ltd, 250 Camberwell Road,
Camberwell, Victoria 3124, Australia
Penguin Books Canada Ltd, 10 Alcorn Avenue,
Toronto, Ontario, Canada M4V 3B2
Penguin Books (N.Z.) Ltd, Cnr Rosedale and Airborne Roads,
Albany, Auckland 1310, New Zealand

Penguin Books Ltd, Registered Offices:
Harmondsworth, Middlesex, England

First published by Signet, an imprint of New American Library,
a division of Penguin Putnam Inc.

First Printing, April 2003
10 9 8 7 6 5 4 3 2 1

For Zachary, Alexander, Jacob, Lucas, and Abigail

Prologue

"Watch out, Mrs. Fletcher," a voice called to me as a Frisbee came sailing toward my head. I ducked quickly, the books I'd been carrying spilling to the ground. The red disk passed overhead, bounced on the grass, and rolled on its edge another twenty feet away.

A young man, in a baseball cap with the brim to the back and a navy blue sweatshirt with SCHOOLMAN COLLEGE in bright yellow letters across his chest, ran to assist me. "Are you all right?" he asked, picking up the books that had fallen and returning them to my arms.

"If I'd had one hand free," I said, lifting my briefcase in my right hand and cradling the books in my left, "I might have caught that thing."

"You're welcome to join our game, Professor," he said, sprinting to retrieve the Frisbee and tossing it to a girl who was waving her arms in the air. "We're just killing time till the buses leave."

Across the road, in front of the new gymnasium, four coach buses idled, their front doors open. A banner proclaiming GO, TIGERS was draped on the windshield of one. A large crowd, mostly students, milled about, many wearing blue-and-yellow sweatshirts and holding matching pom-poms and foam tiger heads mounted on sticks.

"What's happening over there?" I asked.

"We've got a scrimmage in Wabash today."

"You get that big a crowd for a scrimmage?"

"Sure. That's Indiana basketball. The season doesn't officially start till next month. But we got into the play-offs last year and we're gonna do even better this year." He leaped into the air to snag the Frisbee his friend had thrown back.

"Well, good luck," I called over my shoulder as I crossed the road that separated the athletic fields from the rest of the college campus. Behind me, the Frisbee game continued on a section of grass leading to the black oval where Schoolman's track-and-field team was practicing sprints. From beyond the track and the baseball diamond that adjoined it, I could hear the whine of a combine as it moved along the field, threshing grain in neat straight lines.

This part of Indiana was flat, the perfect geographical configuration for farming. Fields of corn, soybeans, and wheat, as far as the eye could see, surrounded the small college. The only relief to the horizontal plane was an occasional line of scraggly trees marking the junction where one crop ended and another began, and the college itself, a cluster of two-story limestone buildings and Victorian houses, down the road from a small village.

I'd come to Schoolman College to teach a course on writing murder mysteries. Harriet Schoolman Bennett, dean of students and the granddaughter of the founder, was an old friend. We'd served together on the mayor's committee to combat illiteracy when I'd taught at Manhattan University in New York City and she'd been earning her Ph.D. at Columbia. That was before Schoolman suffered the financial consequences of declining enrollment, and Harriet had come home to rescue what she'd wryly called "the family business."

Schoolman was a small liberal-arts college in a state that boasted large universities. Situated midway between Purdue and Notre Dame, it struggled in the shadow of its larger and more sophisticated rivals. Recently, however, its fortunes had begun turning around, thanks to its writing curriculum. Harriet had instituted the program five years ago to gain much-needed publicity and to shore up the student base. Contacting her connections in the academic world and buttonholing old friends to help out, she'd attracted a series of bestselling authors to come to Indiana to teach. Each semester, a different well-known novelist led a course in creative writing. And she planned to expand the "famous names" program to include journalists, poets, playwrights, and biographers. My course was entitled "The Mystery Genre in Publishing Today," and Harriet had promised that I'd find the bucolic college campus a stimulating environment, both for teaching and for working on my own manuscript.

I'd been here for less than a month, and so far had found it just as promised, an idyllic and peaceful setting, all the problems of the world miles away, out of sight beyond Indiana's amber waves of grain. I was looking forward to a semester of teaching and writing, to soaking in the academic atmosphere, debating with students, sitting in on my colleagues' classes, attending the guest lectures, musicales, and impromptu events that constituted small-college life, and, of course, rooting for Schoolman's basketball team.

But it was not to be. The ivory tower was not the sanctuary it seemed. Beneath the tranquil surface, there was a storm brewing.

Chapter One

I'd seen a green sky before, but nothing like this. The color was not the green you picture when you think of grass and trees. It wasn't mint green or hospital green or even olive green. It was more like the color of the ocean when it pushes into the bay and up the river, when the bottom is murky and an oar dipped in the water roils up the particles of silt into a muddy cloud. It was that color green.

I climbed the steps of the Hart Building, debating whether to return to my apartment or go inside and wait out the approaching storm. The quad, usually alive with students, was eerily empty. Only the soft rumble of thunder and the rustle of leaves in the oak trees in the square broke the silence.

"I don't like the looks of this, Mrs. Fletcher." Professor Wesley Newmark, chairman of the English department, stood on the top step studying the darkening sky. The wind elevated the few strands of sandy hair he'd carefully combed over his bald pate.

I followed his gaze. "What do you see?" I asked.

"You ever been in a tornado?"

"I thought we were north of Tornado Alley."

"Those borders are very flexible in Indiana. Wind is coming from the southwest. From the back of the building. Probably why we aren't seeing anything." He squinted at me as a gust of wind spit droplets on the lenses of his glasses. He pulled a handkerchief from the pocket of his gray tweed jacket with leather elbow patches. "You'd better get inside. If the alarm goes off, take shelter in the basement." He wiped his glasses and replaced them on his nose. "I've got to get to my appointment. I'm late already." He started down the steps, hugging his bulging leather briefcase with both arms to keep the wind from catching it. A strong gust pulled the sides of his jacket back, exposing a wrinkled white shirt flapping over his generous stomach.

"Where are you going?" I called out, but the wind carried my voice in another direction. He didn't answer, or if he did, I didn't hear him. He hurried down the stairs and ran across the quadrangle in the direction of Kammerer House, where the English department had its offices.

I opened the door to the Hart Building. It was Saturday morning and most classes had finished for the week. A few students sat cross-legged on the floor of the hall, their books piled beside them, half-empty coffee cups in their hands. I recognized two of them and smiled as I passed. Across the hall from my classroom, a television set played to an empty faculty lounge. A message flashed on the screen: *Tornado Watch till Four p.m. This Afternoon."*

Oh, my. A tornado was not the kind of stimulation I'd had in mind when I'd agreed to come for the fall term.

It had been cloudy, but not threatening, when I'd left my small but cheerfully decorated one-bedroom apartment to walk to campus. One of four carved from a large Victorian house, the apartment was a model of efficiency, every piece of furniture in the combination living room/dining room serving a multiple purpose. The sofa could pull out to a guest bed, the side tables contained drawers or cupboards for storage, and the chairs were on wheels so they could be easily moved to wherever they were needed. The table by the bay window would make a lovely place to serve dinner, but it functioned as a desk for now. Usually I would have worked from home, but I'd been driven out by the sounds of a rock band practicing next door, an occurrence, my neighbor assured me, that happened only once a month, when it was his turn to host the musicians.

The classroom offered a quiet sanctuary in which to work on my next manuscript; at least it would have if my thoughts didn't keep drifting to the impending storm. After an hour of fussing with my outline and trying to dictate notes into my minicassette recorder, I decided the time had come to leave. Perhaps the band had gone home by now. Outside my window the rain had stopped, but a charcoal-gray sky promised more to come. I packed up my papers and mentally calculated how long it would take to reach my off-campus quarters. I hurried down the empty hall, pushed open the doors, and stepped outside.

A pinging noise and the sharp feel of hail hitting my scalp made me shrink back under the narrow overhang and raise my briefcase over my head. This was a novel experience. I couldn't remember the last time I'd been in a hailstorm, and certainly not one with golf ball–size ice pellets. I watched fascinated as the hailstones bounced down the stairs and rolled onto the path. Across the quad, between two buildings, was a small parking lot, and I heard the hail strike the hoods of the cars. The unmusical percussion jarred me from my reverie. *Oh, dear,* I thought. *There's going to be a lot of damage from this storm.*

The door opened behind me, and Frank, a maintenance man at the college, grabbed my elbow.

"Professor Fletcher, you can't stay out here," he said, tugging me back into the building. "Everyone's already in the shelter. Come quickly. There's not a lot of time. I'll take you to the—"

A series of short horn blasts interrupted his instructions. Spurred by the alarm, I ran after him down the deserted hall to the emergency staircase. The thunder was louder now. Or was it the wind? I was having trouble distinguishing the source of the sound. The loud roar was deafening, punctuated by the clatter of breaking glass and crashing debris. I felt the building shake, and the hairs rose on the back of my neck.

We raced down the flight of stairs to the basement and through an open door into a concrete bunker illuminated by bare lightbulbs screwed into wall fixtures. A dozen people were huddled on benches or sitting on the floor.

"Oh, good, you found her," someone called out. "What about Professor Newmark?"

"Couldn't locate him," Frank called back as he and another man hauled the iron door closed and shot three dead bolts just as something massive slammed into the metal from the other side.

"I saw him over an hour ago," I said. "He said he was late for an appointment across campus."

I felt a hand on my arm and turned.

"Come. There's room on this bench." A woman slid over to make space for me to sit.

The concrete walls muffled the blast of wind, but the iron door creaked and rattled on its hinges as if a giant were throwing his weight against the panel to break it down. A moment later the lights went out. Only a red bulb above the door remained illuminated, casting a feeble light. The rest of the shelter was steeped in darkness.

"Talk about just in time," yelled a voice I recognized as one of my students, Eli Hemminger. "Like to keep us in suspense, huh, Professor?"

"I prefer to save these kinds of hairbreadth escapes for my novels, Eli," I said, shivering as I realized the danger I'd been in. "But this is more like a thriller than a mystery."

We lapsed into silence, awed by the demonstration of power beyond our concrete walls. In the dim light, there was nothing to do but concentrate on the fury of the storm and wait for it to subside. Eventually the bellowing wind passed over us, and the door, dented but still locked, stopped creaking. I heard the faint static of a radio as someone attempted to pull in a signal.

"Frank, don't you have a flashlight?" a voice from the back of the bunker called out in the dark.

"Yeah. Hang on a minute. I'll find it."

He flicked on the flashlight and panned the beam around the confined quarters. "Everyone okay?"

A chorus of assents came back to him. The simultaneous response seemed to break the tension, and a buzz of conversation filled the close quarters.

"I'm Rebecca McAllister, by the way," said the woman next to me as she put out her hand. "I teach the American Lit class."

From what I could see in the dim light, she was a tall woman, probably in her early thirties, with the pale looks of someone who spent a lot of time indoors. She had gathered her long brown hair into a twist on the top of her head, held by a plastic comb, and wore jeans and a suit jacket that didn't quite fit. The jacket was too large.

"How do you do? I'm Jessica Fletcher."

"Oh, I know all about you. There was a write-up in the student paper about your coming. I have a copy if you haven't seen it."

"I haven't and I'd like to."

"I heard the department had a reception for you. I'm sorry I missed it. I just got back on campus."

"I'm sorry you missed it, too," I said. "It was lovely."

"Why were you so late getting down here?" she asked. "Didn't you know the tornado was coming?"

"No," I replied. "When I came in today, I saw a message on the TV in the faculty lounge that a tornado watch was in effect till four. But a watch only means the possibility of a storm, not that one is imminent."

"The watch was changed to a tornado warning half an hour ago."

"Was there an announcement? I didn't hear anything."

"The public-address system is down, but the warning must have been flashing on the TV screen."

"I'm afraid I didn't see it. I was working in my classroom and didn't realize anything was wrong until I stepped outside."

"How horrible. You could have been killed." She turned to Frank, who was working to get the door open. "Frank, why didn't the alarm go off earlier?"

"There's a short in the system somewhere and I couldn't get it going. Finally gave up and went to search for stragglers. The wind must've jiggled the wires and set it off."

"That should have been fixed a long time ago, along with the PA system," Rebecca said.

"Tell that to President Needler," Frank said, grunting as he pulled on the dead bolts. "He's the one holds the purse strings. George, take over for me here."

Turning back to us, Frank raised his voice to be heard above the noisy chatter. "Okay. Listen up, folks. Please keep your seats. I'm going to ask you to pretend we're on an airplane, and I'm the flight attendant."

"You don't have the legs for the job, Frank," Eli shouted.

"I don't know, Eli: I look pretty good in tights," Frank replied over giggles around the room.

"Cool! We can't wait to see."

"Kidding aside, there was no all-clear siren, so I'm guessing the tornado tore it down," said Frank. He pulled a pamphlet from his hip pocket and held it up. "Once the door is open," he continued, speaking loud enough to be heard in the back, "we're going to follow the safety manual to the letter. Understood? I'll go ahead to make sure there's nothing dangerous on the way out of the building. There may be a lot of damage, so prepare yourselves. I have to report in to the Campus Security Office and could be a while. I'm counting on you not to move from your seats until I come back and say it's okay to leave. Once we're outside, you can try your cell phones, but keep in mind the towers may be down. Be patient. We're uninjured. We'll need to look for those who haven't been as lucky. I know you want to help, but the best way to help right now is to sit tight till I get back."

Rebecca, who'd been watching George wrestle with the bolts, leaned forward. "Frank, what happens if you can't open the door?" she asked in a loud whisper.

"It may take a bit of time if there's debris blocking it, and I may need some extra muscles to help out. But we'll get it open."

"But if you can't?"

"Don't panic *now*," Frank said, laughing. "The storm is over. Everyone in the state knows we had a tornado out here, and they'll send help. Campus security will be counting heads and they'll find us. Okay?"

"Okay," she said, not sounding as though she meant it.

After a short tussle, Frank and George managed to draw back the bolts that held the dented door closed and pushed it open. Faint light from above seeped into the concrete chamber, accompanied by the drumbeat of rain hitting a hard surface. There was a collective sigh of relief. The two men disappeared into the stairwell and we waited. At first everyone was quiet. But as the realization that we'd escaped harm percolated around the room, people began to talk. I heard some chuckles from the back and knew that Eli was cracking jokes again.

I turned to Rebecca. "Aren't we lucky this room was here?" I said. "Was it built as a tornado shelter?"

"It looks that way, doesn't it?" she replied.

"If you'll excuse my interrupting your conversation," said an elderly gentleman sitting across from us, "I couldn't help overhearing your question, Professor Fletcher. I'm Archibald Constantine, by the way." He pulled himself forward, leaned on his cane, and thrust out his hand to me. "I teach sociology."

"How do you do?" I said, shaking his hand.

He winked at Rebecca. "Professor McAllister, I hope you had a good summer. Did you get your paper finished?"

"I did, Archie."

"Nice to make your acquaintance," he said to me, sitting down again. "This bunker you were asking about was not originally intended as a tornado shelter."

"It wasn't?" Rebecca said.

"No. The Hart Building was built in the late fifties at the height of the Cold War. This was supposed to be a fallout shelter." He peered into the gloom at the back of the room, squinting over his half glasses. "There are cupboards down there for food and emergency supplies," he said, pointing a gnarled finger. "Several years ago I found some olive-green canisters that had been left behind—saltines, I think they were."

"What did you do with them?" Rebecca asked.

"Gave them to Needler. He likes old things. I imagine he has them stashed away somewhere."

"Old crackers. Yuck! I hope he didn't try eating them."

"Those containers must be collectors' items these days," I said.

"He could probably get a good price for them on eBay," Rebecca said. "I'll have to mention it to him. Of course, if Harriet Schoolman Bennett hears about it, she'll confiscate them and put them up for auction herself."

"Why do you say that?" I asked.

"Dean Bennett's been conducting a fire sale ever since she came back, getting rid of old textbooks and supplies. She's got plenty of money for a brand-new gymnasium, but every time I turn around, something else has been sold out from under me. It's worse than the time my husband had his tag sale, and roamed through the house looking for things to add to his dollar table. For months I was looking for my bread-baking stone, only to learn that my neighbor, Lillian Kaplan, bought it from Ed for fifty cents."

"Yes, but she's putting us back on the map," Professor Constantine said, running a hand through his thatch of white hair. "We were about to go under." He looked at me. "She's got a good head for numbers, Harriet does. And her idea to bring attention to the college with celebrity professors seems to be working, too. I like her." He smiled.

"You like her because she hasn't made any drastic cuts in the sociology department," Rebecca put in. "She just hasn't gotten around to you yet, Arch."

"Don't you like her?" I asked her.

"Oh, she's nice enough," she said, seeming to realize I might be a friend of the woman under discussion. "I'm just grousing because the English department's share of the budget's been cut down to the bone, and I can't get any of the new texts I want. Don't listen to me. Get Archie to tell you more about the bomb shelter." She leaned back against the stone wall and folded her arms in front of her.

I turned to Professor Constantine. "Do you talk about the shelter in any of your courses?"

"I do," he said, looking around. "I teach a class in twentieth-century life. We take field trips here. Occasionally I get small groups of students who want to stay here for a few days, experience living together in a fallout shelter. This place was designed for eight or ten people to live in for a week or so; there's a rather elaborate ventilation system in place. In the fifties they stocked it with cans of water, food rations, first-aid kits, and a Geiger counter so they could check for radiation and know when it was safe to leave."

"Concern about nuclear weapons was a big part of our society then," I said, "but it would seem to me that Indiana is pretty far away from where you would expect bombs to fall."

"Perhaps," he said, "but like most states, we have military bases. And the Newport Chemical Depot, west of Indianapolis, was used to manufacture a potent nerve agent. If our enemies had known that—and it's likely they did—it would have made Indiana a tempting target."

"In that case, you'd have to have quite a lot of these shelters if you were going to accommodate everyone on campus," I said.

"Precisely!" Constantine exclaimed, beaming at me as if I were a prize student. "The whole scheme was completely impractical given the size of the student body, even at that time. I've got maps of the campus dating back to the fifties, showing where the shelters were to be located and the tunnels connecting them. This is the only one I've seen that even looks finished. It was designated for the college president and administrative staff."

"Where was everyone else supposed to go?" I asked. "They couldn't just save themselves."

He waved a hand in front of his face. "No, of course not," he said. "The idea had been to build a series of these in each of the buildings, but they proved to be enormously expensive, and as you may imagine, their construction raised a great debate over who would qualify to take shelter in them during an atomic attack. Eventually the college decided to scrap the project entirely. But there are concrete shells in most of the basements, so they have become tornado shelters, hopefully effective ones. Of course, over the years some of them have been used for storage; they may be a tight squeeze these days. We haven't had a tornado in Schoolman in more than sixty years."

"Just our luck to be here to experience one," Rebecca said, squinting at an oversize watch she wore on her wrist.

"I think we're about to see how we weathered the storm," the old man said.

I looked up to see Frank in the doorway. He held a clipboard in one hand and a first-aid kit in the other. "All clear," he said.

Chapter Two

It was raining lightly when we emerged from our shelter and stepped out onto the landing in front of the Hart Building. The wind had calmed and the thunder was rolling away in the distance. Off to the east, flashes of lightning could be seen against the sliver of horizon visible between those structures still standing. I took a deep breath. The air was bitter with the tang of mud. The smell reminded me of wet dog.

The quadrangle was a vastly different sight from the one I'd seen earlier. The tall oaks that had barely begun to shed their autumn leaves still stood in the square formed by Schoolman's academic halls and administration buildings, but were stripped bare of both leaves and small branches. What remained were skeleton trees, blackened as if they'd been victims of a fire, and draped with torn papers, shreds of fabric, and other fragments of rubble in a macabre decoration. The grass, what was left of it, was littered with more papers, splintered wood, and other bits and pieces that the wind had picked up in classrooms and offices, pulverized, and flung outside.

Eli put his hands on top of his head and whistled. "Wow! It looks like Times Square the morning after New Year's Eve in New York."

"How would you know?" said Tyler, one of his

classmates. "You've never been outside of Indiana your whole life."

"I've got a television, don't I?" he replied.

As we gazed out at the devastation the tornado had wrought, the square slowly began filling with students, faculty, and staff from other buildings. Members of the Emergency Committee had pulled white T-shirts over their rain slickers—the large red cross on the front and the back a symbol of their office—and had fanned out across the campus. They were directing foot traffic toward the triage area for any who'd been injured, or to the Student Union, where a crisis center had been established for everyone else. I knew this because when I'd agreed to spend a semester at Schoolman, I'd read the pamphlet on emergency procedures that had arrived in my mail at home in Cabot Cove, along with a stack of other instructions and forms to fill out.

"It's actually not as bad as I thought it would be," Frank said to no one in particular. "All the classroom buildings are intact; only a couple of the houses we converted into offices took a bad hit. Of course, most of the cars got dented, but it could have been a lot worse."

He was probably right. Except for a bank of windows in the Hart Building and bricks torn loose from the façade, the building was in surprisingly good condition; the basic structure had withstood the forces of the tornado.

He looked back at the people who'd followed him outside. "Okay, folks, before you do anything, please check in at the Crisis Center. Then call your families to let them know you're okay. Please stay out of any other building until it's been cleared for safety."

"Why don't you take my arm?" I said to Professor

Constantine. "We can help each other down the
stairs." The steps in front of us were littered with wet
papers and I was concerned he might slip.

"My dear, it would be my pleasure," he said, gripping my elbow. "Is this your first tornado?"

"My first and I hope my last," I said, slowly de-
scending. "We get our share of nor'easters where I
come from, but not tornadoes, thank goodness."

"I've seen a few tornadoes in my day," he said as
we reached the sidewalk in front of the building.
"They can make a mess, as you see here. But they're
usually confined to a relatively narrow geographic
area. The real danger comes from their unpredictabil-
ity. You never know where they'll touch down."

Harriet Schoolman Bennett jogged over to where
we stood and called up to the people still on the landing. "Everyone all right up there?" At the nods, she
continued, "Some of the phone and electrical lines are
down, but the cell tower was spared. If you've got a
cell phone, please share it so people can notify relatives they're okay. We've set up a triage station in the
Sutherland Library. If you come across any walking
wounded on your way to the Union, bring them to
the reading room." Her cell phone rang and Harriet
held it to her ear with one hand, extending her other
to assist a woman coming down the steps.

The group slowly dispersed, picking their way
around the debris. Eli took over for Harriet, stationing
himself on ground level and holding out his arms to
help others.

"Harriet, is there anything I can do to help?" I
asked.

"Sure. Come with me. We can always use an extra
pair of hands. Frank, I want to see you, too."

Frank and I joined Harriet, walking rapidly to keep

up with her pace as she turned back toward the building that housed the Student Union. She waited till we
were out of earshot of the others.

"Frank, what happened to the alarm? I didn't hear
it till the storm was practically upon us."

"I'm sorry, Dean Bennett. The wiring is just too
old," he said. "It's been giving me fits for weeks now.
I told President Needler, but he said there wasn't any
room in the budget for repairs, that I'd have to fix it
myself. I'm a pretty good electrician, but this system
is beyond what I can do. We need an electrical engi-
neer to take a look at it, and that could cost big
bucks."

"Call in an expert as soon as you can," Harriet told
him. "I don't care how long it takes or how much it
costs. We can't afford to lose lives because our warning system fails."

"Have there been any fatalities?" I asked.

"Not that I know of," Harriet replied. "I had a
telephone team call in to all the buildings when the
tornado watch was upgraded to a warning. Hopefully
everyone got the message and took shelter in time."

"I rounded up everybody who was still in the Hart
Building and got them down to the shelter," Frank
said. "But I nearly missed Professor Fletcher here."

"What?"

"But he found me, as you can see," I said. "Professor Newmark had warned me that there might be a
tornado on the way."

"Was he with your group in the basement?" she
asked.

"No," I replied. "He was leaving for a meeting, but
he recognized the signs of an impending storm and
told me to take shelter. Where were you?"

"The library. The downstairs stacks are underground. It's one of the safest places on campus." Harriet pulled open the door to the Student Union. "We were lucky in one thing," she said. "The basketball team was playing Wabash today, and a large contingent of the student body and faculty went over there to cheer them on. Thank goodness the tornado never made it that far. I told Coach Adams to get everyone's name and see if the college could put them up for the night. We don't need more people to worry about for the time being. I'm not going to feel comfortable until I've accounted for everyone on and off campus."

An animated crowd was milling about inside the lobby, where tables had been arranged on either side of a center aisle to funnel people into the adjacent cafeteria after they had signed in.

"Everyone, we need to clear this area," Harriet shouted over the commotion. "Make sure the Emergency Committee has your name—it's very important— and then wait for instructions in the dining room."

"Dean Bennett, Dean Bennett," a young man called to her, shouldering his way through the throng. "The police are here and they're looking for you."

"Tell them I'll be right out. Frank, can you get these people inside so we can report back to the Emergency Management folks if anyone is missing? We also should start assembling cleanup crews and see if we're going to need overnight shelters."

"I'll get right on it," he said.

Harriet's phone rang and she pulled it from her pocket. "What? How did you get this number?" she asked, raising her voice to be heard over the noise of the crowd. "I don't have time for that now. I don't care what your problem is. No, I don't know when." She snapped the phone closed.

I looked at her with raised brows. The strain of the

situation was showing. Although I knew Harriet to be aggressive, occasionally to the point of being abrasive, I'd never witnessed overt rudeness on her part.

"Who was it?" I asked.

"A reporter. I don't know how they got my number so fast, but I can't stop what I'm doing to talk to the press. I've got enough to do."

"That call won't be the only one, Harriet. The TV stations must have broadcast reports about the tornado. News accounts may be the only way some of the families will be able to find out about their friends or relatives. Don't you have a public relations person who can handle the press for you?"

"I forgot all about her. Frank! Frank!" She looked around till she spotted Frank herding a group of students into the cafeteria. He looked back at her. "Have you seen Roberta Dougherty?" she yelled.

Frank pointed to a table down the hall where three people were conferring, their heads bent over a sheaf of papers and a yellow pad.

Roberta looked up when Harriet approached. A slim woman in her late twenties, she was dressed in a blue pantsuit. Her cell phone was clipped to her lapel. She ran a hand through her auburn hair to tame curls that looked as if she'd just gotten out of bed.

"Dean Bennett, Mrs. Fletcher, I'm so glad to see you," she said, rising from her chair. "We're working up a statement to give to the press."

"Good, I just had a call I had to defer," Harriet said smoothly. I smiled at the spin she put on her rude response to the reporter. "What does the statement say?"

"They want to know about casualties and damages. So far, according to the Emergency Committee, we've got three hundred forty-seven unaccounted for," she said, referring to her yellow pad.

Harriet gasped. "That many?"

"That's a preliminary number."

A young man ran up to the table and slipped a piece of paper into Roberta's hand. "No, make that two hundred ninety-two—thanks, Leroy," she said as he ran back to the sign-in table. "The number is changing every minute. We're waiting for Coach to send in the names of all the folks who went over to Wabash. We're only, what?"—she consulted her watch—"a little over an hour since the tornado came through. We're in pretty good shape with the numbers."

"All right. Did you get the names of the people in the library?"

"Not yet. That's where the injured are, right?"

"Yes," Harriet replied. "The building was untouched. Amazing, considering that Kammerer House next door is practically a pile of sticks. I'm going over there in a little while. I'll have them send in a report. Do you want me to read that?" She pointed to the paper in Roberta's hand.

"Sure, but I was going to have it typed. Should the statement come from President Needler?"

"No, he'll be too busy." Harriet scanned the statement Roberta had prepared and nodded. "We don't have a damage assessment yet, but this is okay. Take any media calls. Just stick to this and you'll be fine." She handed the paper back to Roberta. "Give me your cell phone number so I can forward any press calls I end up getting."

Roberta tore a sheet from her yellow pad and wrote down her number. "I could call the news services and give them a report, kind of handle them in a group. Okay with you?''

"Do whatever you think is right," Harriet replied. "You're the college spokeswoman."

Roberta grinned.

"I'll talk to you later when I have more information," Harriet said over her shoulder, pulling me back down the hall.

"Where is President Needler?" I asked.

"Who knows? He was here this morning, but right now he's among the missing."

"Could he be with the basketball team?"

"It's possible but unlikely. He's not exactly a fan, but he recognizes the importance of basketball in Indiana. Everybody does. The state is crazy for the sport. The season doesn't officially start for a month, but they're already scrimmaging. Basketball's like a religion in this state. Seems like the season is twelve months long."

"He would have let someone on campus know if he was going to the game, wouldn't he?"

Harriet looked to the ceiling. "Don't count on it. I've never been able to figure out that man. Sometimes he's the classic absentminded professor, and other times he's a brilliant administrator. Working with him has been awkward. While I'm the dean of students on campus, I'm also on the college's board of trustees representing the Schoolman family."

We waded back into the crowd surrounding the sign-in tables. The numbers hadn't dwindled, but maybe it was because more people had come in. Harriet found Frank again.

"I sent George to do an inventory of damages," he reported. "It looks like the tornado touched down on three buildings, hit the quad, and bounced up again.

We should know in a couple of hours about the dormitories and the off-campus housing, but I'm expecting everything there to be fine. In the meantime, the kitchen guys have hooked up the generator. In a pinch, we can use the cafeteria as a shelter."

"Wonderful! I'll go over to the library now. That's where I'll be, but call me if you need me."

"Harriet, don't forget about the police," I reminded her.

"I did forget. Thanks, Jess. You'd better come with me. I seem to be a bit scattered today."

"For good reason," I told her.

We retraced our steps outside and walked around to the back of the building where a couple of black-and-white patrol cars were idling, the volume of their radios turned up so the officers could hear them from a distance. Two uniformed policemen and a police-woman were on the road, setting up flares and red cones to divert traffic away from the college. A fourth in plainclothes, a cell phone to his ear, waved Harriet over.

"Sorry it took us so long, Dr. Bennett," he said, folding his phone and dropping it into his coat pocket. "We had to clear the road in a couple of places."

"Well, I'm glad you're here now." Harriet introduced me to Lieutenant Bill Parish. "Bill's mother and I went to high school together," she told me.

"Do I know you from somewhere?" he asked me. "Your name sounds familiar."

"Jessica is one of our celebrity authors," Harriet said before I could answer. "She writes murder mysteries and is here for the semester to teach our students about the genre."

"Oh, yeah. I knew I knew that name. You picked a tough time to come," he said. "It's rare to get a

tornado in the fall to start with. I don't ever remember
one hitting Schoolman, and I grew up here."

"I understand the last one was more than sixty years
ago," I said.

"That long, huh? Well, I hope it goes sixty more
before we get another." He turned to Harriet. "The
hospital has been alerted and we've got an ambulance
and a passenger van on the way," he said. "Where
are the injured?"

"We're using Sutherland Library as a triage center.
It's on the other side of the quad. I'll take you there."

"I know where it is."

"We're going there anyway."

"Did the storm do a lot of damage?" I asked him
as we crossed the quad.

"Schoolman got the worst of it," he replied.
"Mostly trees and telephone poles down. Haley's Market lost its front window, and everything inside was
overturned. If I didn't know the storm did it, I'd be
out looking for kids on a tear. There wasn't a box of
cereal or a piece of fruit left on the shelves. Everything was broken and spilled on the floor."

"Anyone hurt?" Harriet asked.

"Nothing serious, but the ER has a pile of people
waiting to be seen."

"How'd they do on the other side of town?"

"The twister took out a swath of corn about two
hundred feet across over at the Wasserstrom farm, but
it missed the barns, and Dick reported only one cow
lost. Mrs. Hampton's house was badly damaged, but
at least she wasn't home at the time. I heard from
Adam Finch that she's up visiting her sister in
Elkhart."

"Thank goodness for that," Harriet said. "Maybe

we can see if there's anything we can salvage for her before she gets back."

"I asked the mayor to send someone over, told her to have them especially look out for any photographs."

She patted him on the shoulder. "You're a good boy, Bill."

"Thank you, ma'am," he said, smiling at her.

The "boy" Harriet was complimenting was a man in his thirties with a thinning crew cut and square features.

We reached the library, and Lieutenant Parish held the door open for us. Inside, several members of the Emergency Committee were administering first aid to those who'd been injured in the storm. Less than a dozen people were scattered in chairs around the graceful reading room, which boasted a beautiful stained-glass skylight that arched overhead. The light filtering through the colored glass cast mosaic patterns on the carpet.

Elizabeth St. Clair, the college's nurse and head of the Emergency Committee, greeted Harriet brusquely. "Where's the ambulance? I've got wounded here."

"On its way, Betty. The road was blocked, but they should be here any minute."

A short, stocky woman, with wiry salt-and-pepper hair stuffed under a baseball cap and a stethoscope looped around her neck, Betty nodded sharply and consulted her clipboard. Harriet had told me on the way there that Betty St. Clair had been a field nurse in Vietnam; her military training was evident in her bearing and in the report she handed Harriet.

"We've set up a triage system and divided the injured into three groups based on the seriousness of their condition," she said.

"How many?" Harriet asked.

"Eleven so far. Over there are a couple of bumps and bruises, and a few who are just shook up and need to sit quietly for a bit," she said, pointing to a small group gathered in the back of the room near the computer terminals. "If you can send over a counselor, that would be helpful."

"I'll see who I can spare."

"I gave everyone's name to the Crisis Center. We're patching them up and releasing them unless they tell us they want to see the doctor. So far, two of them do. I told them it may be a while till we can even get them over there. There are others we'll be moving out first."

"Which ones are those?"

"Next to the stacks," Betty said, cocking her head toward the side of the room where tall bookcases were lined up, one behind the other, like a row of dominoes standing on end. "I've got a sprained ankle, a wrenched shoulder, and a stomach pain," she said, ticking them off on her fingers. "Last one's probably psychosomatic, but we'd better check it out. One youngster banged his head, can't remember how, needs stitches. I've got a butterfly bandage on the wound till the doctor can see him. My urgent cases are up front—two fractures, one compound with possible internal injuries."

I walked to where the more seriously injured were being tended. They were stretched out on two of the reading tables, each wrapped in a gray woolen blanket with another folded and placed under their heads. A young woman was one of them. The side of her face was badly bruised, but I recognized her as a student in my morning class.

"Hello, Alice," I said. "How are you feeling? Is there anything I can do for you?"

"Oh, Professor Fletcher," she said, tears welling up in her brown eyes. "I can't believe what happened to me. It's so awful."

"What did happen, Alice? Couldn't you make it to the shelter in time?"

"I was running to get there and I tripped and fell down the stairs."

"How awful."

She nodded. "My heel got caught in something and I went flying. They had to carry me into the shelter. Everything hurts."

"I imagine it does," I said, smoothing her hair away from her brow.

"Mrs. St. Clair says my ankle is broken."

"The doctor will fix you up."

"Will you sign my cast?"

"I'll be happy to. Is there anything I can do to help you now, Alice? Would you like me to call your family?"

"I think Mrs. St. Clair did that already, but there *is* something you can do."

"What's that?"

"Do you see my shoes anywhere? They took them off, and I don't know where they are. I know I can't wear them now, but I don't want to lose them."

I looked around. Under the table was a shopping bag with a folded jacket inside. I groped under the jacket, felt the heel of a shoe, and pulled out a pair of black suede pumps with four-inch high heels. "Are these yours?" I asked.

An ecstatic smile spread across her face. "Thank goodness. I spent a month's allowance on those shoes. I would have died if I lost them."

You almost died wearing them, I thought. It would be hard *not* to trip in a heel that high, especially attempting to run. But I said only, "They're right here," and replaced them in the bag, which I set on the table near her feet.

Behind me, Harriet was talking to the other injured person, the college's bursar, Philip Adler.

"Betty says you've got a bad break, Phil. Can you tell me how it happened?" she asked.

"Got trapped under a beam when the storm blew away the roof."

"Why weren't you in the shelter?"

"Never got there. Working," he said, gritting his teeth.

"Working! What could be so urgent that you'd jeopardize your life to keep working at it?" Harriet scolded. Then, seeing his discomfort, she immediately added, "I'm sorry, Phil. We'll have you at the hospital in no time." She stroked his arm.

"I was going over the budget and waiting for Wes Newmark," he said, grimacing against the pain. "He'd said he had something important to discuss with me. But he never showed up."

"Whatever it was, it's not important now," Harriet said. "We'll get you taken care of, and then we'll worry about the budget."

"I'm sorry, Harriet."

"Don't you be sorry. And I'm sorry I yelled earlier. Just worried about you, that's all."

We heard a siren blaring, and a moment later an ambulance pulled up to the side entrance of the library.

"At last," Harriet said, looking to the door. "Here are the EMTs, Phil. I'll come see you in the hospital as soon as I can."

Lieutenant Parish escorted three emergency medical technicians to where Betty St. Clair stood, and she began directing them to the tables. Dragging chairs out of the way, they wheeled a portable gurney to the side of Phil's table and, after checking the splint Betty had used to stabilize his leg, deftly transferred the injured man onto the padded surface.

Alice was assisted into a wheelchair. Those who'd sustained other injuries waited to be helped into a passenger van, the only vehicle the hospital had left to transport patients to its emergency room.

Lieutenant Parish bade us good-bye and Harriet and I walked outside. The air was now crisp and the sky had cleared, the sun starting its downward arc.

I took a deep breath. "You'd never believe a storm came through here, looking at that sky," I said.

"That's what it's like in Indiana," Harriet replied. "The weather is so changeable."

On the quad in front of us, some of the staff, dragging green plastic garbage bags, had already started cleaning up. We walked slowly in the direction where the storm had done its worst. Others had preceded us, and there were groups of students strolling down the walk and lingering in front of the blown-out buildings like visitors to a tourist attraction. Police officers, aided by campus security, were stringing yellow tape around the perimeter of three properties and hanging Keep Out signs every fifteen feet. A photographer from the college newspaper was shooting pictures of the devastation while a student reporter took down the comments of the witnesses.

Kammerer House, where the English department had its offices, was badly damaged; only the front wall was left on the second floor, and there was a gaping hole where the ceiling of the first floor had given way and debris had poured through. Milton Hall next door, which housed the office of campus services, was worse, the back of the building entirely gone, and only part of the facade still standing. Beyond them, the bursar's office was minus a roof, and the front porch had disappeared.

I looked up at the second floor of the bursar's office. Harriet's gaze followed mine and she shuddered. "I don't know what Phil was thinking, staying at his desk. People can be so foolish."

As we turned and started back to the library, a security guard left his post and hurried up to Harriet. "Dr. Bennett, may I see you for a moment?"

"What is it?"

"I need to show you something."

"Can't it wait?"

"No, ma'am. I don't think so."

We ducked under the yellow tape and followed the guard around to the back of Kammerer House. He picked up pieces of siding and roofing and threw them aside, clearing a path so that we could get closer to the remains of the building.

"It's there," he said, pointing through a missing window.

"What's there?" Harriet replied, leaning in to make out what he'd seen.

"There. Under the file cabinet," he said, his finger and voice trembling. "Can you see it now?"

"I can see it," I said, moving closer, being careful to avoid the shards of glass that littered the ground. A dented file cabinet was overturned, covered by several feet of rubble, the other end lying on an upended chair. Behind the chair, on a crumpled piece of carpet with a dark blotch, I made out the top of a head. Strands of sandy hair, stained red, dangled from the bare scalp on which a cleft an inch wide exposed the white bone of the skull. I didn't need to see the gray tweed sleeve, nor the leather elbow patch, to know I was looking at the battered body of Professor Wesley Newmark.

Chapter Three

It would take several hours to extricate the body of Professor Wesley Newmark from the collapsed portion of the building. By good fortune, his was the only fatality of the day. To ensure it stayed that way, the local fire and police departments cooperated in developing a plan to lift the wreckage of Kammerer House that had fallen through the ceiling to gain direct access to the end of the room where the body lay. Until then, the file cabinet could not be shifted or the office chair removed without possibly causing a further cave-in.

There was no doubt that Wes was dead, but the "rescuers" were intent on reclaiming his body as quickly as possible. No one argued their decision, and as afternoon moved into evening and the air took on a decided chill, the observers grew more numerous, keeping a quiet vigil that seemed to spur on the men who were setting up the rigging.

Spotlights commandeered from the drama department, along with emergency lighting from the fire department, had been hooked up to a generator to allow the work to continue after dark. The Red Cross brought in volunteers to serve coffee and doughnuts. An ambulance stood by to transport the body to the hospital morgue.

Earlier in the day, a news helicopter had hovered

overhead. Later, a crew from an Indianapolis television station arrived to record the recovery effort, and became disgruntled when it became obvious it would be a while until the body was removed.

Wes had been a bachelor, and in the absence of President Needler, it was Harriet's unhappy responsibility to call his closest relative, a sister in Alaska, to relate the news of his death. That call, made in the privacy of her office, had been one of only two times she'd been away from Kammerer House. The other time had been the forty minutes she'd spent helping relieve some of the pressure on Roberta Dougherty, who'd been juggling press calls and demands for interviews all day. To accommodate the small legion of reporters that had descended on campus, Harriet had agreed to an impromptu press conference in the Student Union cafeteria.

Roberta provided Harriet with the official college statistics, which she announced to the press: one dead, eleven seen by the college nurse, six transported to the emergency room, one hospitalized.

Roberta handed around a sheet with the statistics that had been compiled.

"We estimate there's about two million dollars in damages," Harriet said. "As you can see, three houses that served as offices were severely damaged, and several larger buildings will also need repairs. The cleanup has already begun. We will be resuming classes as soon as the students who were visiting Wabash return to their dorms. We're very grateful for that community's generosity in providing accommodations for the night for our basketball team and the fans who accompanied them to the game."

Harriet deviated from her prepared remarks. "I want to add that while we are all relieved that School-

man escaped the scores of casualties that could have
accompanied a storm of this magnitude, even the loss
of one affects us deeply. We are all distraught at Professor Newmark's death. I knew Wes for many years.
He was a lovely gentleman, a dedicated scholar, be-
loved by his students and admired by his colleagues.
I speak for the entire faculty, staff, and student body
when I say he will be greatly missed. And I know we
all join in extending our heartfelt sympathies to his
family. We plan to hold a memorial service. At that
time, all Schoolman offices will be closed and classes
canceled so everyone may join in paying their respects
to our departed colleague and friend."

"Where is President Needler?" a reporter asked.
"Why isn't he here?"

I saw Harriet's hand tighten around the paper she
was holding, but I don't know if anyone else sensed
her disquiet.

"Lowell Needler was a good friend of Professor
Newmark and he was greatly distressed to learn of his
death," she said, laying the paper on the table in front
of her and smoothing out the wrinkles as she spoke.
"He asked me to express his regrets at not coming to
speak with all of you. In addition to his personal grief,
he is also grappling with the logistical burden of planning how Schoolman will address the damage from
the tornado, meeting with various departments, and
working to ensure that the college returns to normal
as quickly as possible."

I wondered why Harriet felt it necessary to cover
up for President Needler. It was curious that he was
not on campus, but there could be many practical reasons why he wasn't on hand. I had the impression that
it wasn't so much his absence that embarrassed Harriet as the fact that she didn't know where he'd gone.

Still, why not let him take the consequences? Anytime I'd ever seen someone try to stonewall the press, it invariably backfired. If President Needler wasn't where he was supposed to be, he would have to explain eventually.

"Dr. Bennett," a reporter shouted before Harriet could make a graceful exit, "we heard the college's emergency warning system was out of order. Do you think that contributed to the injuries and to Professor Newmark's death?"

Harriet blanched, but quickly regained her equilibrium. "On the contrary," she said, "Professor Newmark cautioned another of our professors to take cover because of the impending storm, so he was certainly aware of the potential danger. We did have difficulty with the alarm signal initially, but we don't rely on one warning system alone. We have backup emergency systems in place. They were activated. Everyone was alerted well in advance of the storm. Plus, the primary alert system did come on before the tornado hit the campus. All in all, I'd say the college did an exemplary job of protecting its students and staff."

"Dr. Bennett, what are the other warning systems?"

"Dr. Bennett, is the college still in financial trouble? Where will the money come from to make the repairs?"

"Dr. Bennett, is Schoolman making plans to upgrade its buildings in light of the damages?"

"Dr. Bennett, can the school stay open while repairs take place?"

The shouts came from around the room. I knew Harriet was impatient to get back to Kammerer House, but she admirably stayed to answer the questions.

While Harriet dealt with the press, I left the cafeteria and wandered down the hall to get a drink of water. As I leaned over the fountain, I saw movement in the nearby stairwell to my right. I looked up to see a figure disappear up the stairs. I'd glimpsed him for only a second, but I was certain I'd recognized the tall stature and distinctive mane of white hair of President Lowell Needler.

The stairwell was empty by the time I stepped inside. I climbed to the second floor and opened the doorway to the hall to see him rounding a corner. A moment later I heard a door slam. Was the college president just returning to his office now, for the first time since the tornado? Did he know a press conference was taking place? Harriet had been making excuses for him all afternoon, but was he even aware of what had occurred on campus? If he wasn't, his appearance downstairs would be shocking for him and humiliating for her.

I'm not sure why I followed the president to his corner office, but I did. His whereabouts certainly weren't any of my business. I barely knew the man, my only direct contact with him having occurred when Harriet introduced me to him in his office, at a welcoming ceremony, and a few chance encounters lasting seconds. His absence in the midst of a devastating storm was Harriet's problem. I thought of my dear friend back in Cabot Cove, Dr. Seth Hazlitt, who was fond of telling me that I had more natural curiosity than a dozen Maine coon cats, and would probably get in trouble because of it one day.

I was poised to leave.

Instead, I knocked.

No answer. I knocked again. There was a pause and then the door swung open.

President Needler looked surprised. No, bewildered

was more apt. He stared at me. His coat was draped over one shoulder. There was some kind of grime on the back. It looked like cobwebs. He ran a large hand over the stubble on his chin. "Mrs. Fletcher," he said in a hoarse voice.

"I don't mean to bother you, President Needler, but—"

"I wasn't expecting you," he said. "Is there a problem? I trust everything's going smoothly with your classes."

"Yes, quite smoothly."

He turned and wandered back into his office, his gait that of a man not sure where he was or where he was supposed to go. I followed. He turned suddenly, saw that I was right behind him, and said, "Won't you come in? I've only just gotten in myself."

"I hope you don't mind my intruding," I said. "It's just that—"

"No, no intrusion at all," he said, taking a hanger off the coat tree behind his desk. "Been a bit of a rough day, eh?"

"Yes," I said. "A tornado is a unique experience."

"Of course. You're from back east. You don't have such things there, I take it." He waved in the direction of a chair. "Please sit down." He hung up his coat and took a seat behind his desk. The answering machine on the credenza behind him was blinking. He eyed it warily.

"Harriet Schoolman Bennett has been looking for you," I said. "Have you seen her yet?"

"No. No. Just got here, as you can see." He glanced down at his hands, then popped up from his chair. "Excuse me a moment, won't you?" He went to a door that led to a washroom, closed it halfway, turned on the faucet, and washed his hands.

I looked around the room. The office was decorated in traditional academic style, with two walls lined in bookcases, a green leather sofa beneath a picture window, and a large mahogany desk and credenza against the fourth wall, on which were framed photos and certificates. Sets of leather-bound volumes filled most of the bookshelves. Some books with decaying bindings were laid on their sides. Here and there were mementos of trips or experiences: a pair of pewter tankards, a whittled wooden fisherman, a personalized gavel. Two green canisters, probably the ones Professor Constantine had found in the fallout shelter, stood side by side on a lower shelf.

"That's better," he said, smiling and retaking his seat.

I noticed that he had washed his face as well, and run a comb through his snowy hair.

"You have an impressive book collection," I said. "Some of them look quite delicate. Are they very old?"

"First editions," he said proudly, his face brightening, "just about every one of them. That tan book on its side, the one with the spine missing, is the first volume published of Elizabeth Barrett Browning's poetry. I bought that when I was in college myself. That's when I started my collection. Made a lot of mistakes in the beginning but I learned."

"What kind of mistakes did you make?"

"Oh, nothing irreversible. Letting friends borrow them. Big mistake. People are careless with books, even ones that aren't theirs. I learned well. I don't lend them out anymore. That's what a library is for. Go borrow books from there, I tell them."

"Did you lend someone the Browning book?"

He went to the shelf and picked up the book in question. "No, I bought it like that. That was another mistake. It's not worth very much because the condition is so poor, but I keep it in hopes of replacing it with a better one. A good one will go for almost five hundred dollars." He stroked the cover and gently replaced the book on the shelf. "I may keep it anyway. It has sentimental value to me now." He selected a dark green leather slipcase and pulled out the book. "Now, this one is another story. This is a first edition of Mark Twain's *The Prince and the Pauper.*" He opened the cover carefully. "I'm not sure it's ever been read. It's in pristine condition. You'd pay more than a thousand dollars for this in today's market."

"So much?"

"You can buy a lot of first editions for under a hundred, but the real thrill is in finding the rare ones. Charles Dickens goes for a lot. Chaucer, of course. I heard an edition of *The Canterbury Tales* went for over forty thousand in an auction last year."

"Where do you buy your first editions?"

"There are antiquarian book dealers and specialized auctions. I use them sometimes, but there are no bargains there. I haunt antique shops and secondhand bookstores."

I was surprised we'd ended up in a discussion of rare books, but was enjoying it, and he seemed to be, too. The tornado and the destructive path it had carved seemed only a memory, unworthy of being injected into the conversation.

"Have you ever tried the on-line auction sites?" I asked.

"Rarely. They make it easier to find what you're looking for, but unfortunately, they also make collecting of any kind more popular. These days there are a lot of people buying up first editions. Makes it tougher for me to fill in the gaps in my collection."

"How interesting."

"It is to me," he said, putting the Twain back in its place of honor on the shelf, "but I'm sure you didn't stop by to admire my books. Why don't you tell me what it is that I can help you with."

"The, ah . . . the tornado," I said. "Everyone was looking for you, especially Harriet. Had you been over at Wabash with the basketball team?" I asked, not sure it was my place to pry but not terribly concerned about it.

"I beg your pardon?"

"Wabash. The basketball team had a scrimmage there today. A lot of people went to see them play and missed the storm. I thought perhaps that's where you'd been."

"Ah, that was certainly good fortune, their being away at a nasty time. No, no, I wasn't there, but don't let it out. I'm not much of basketball fan." He lowered his voice and winked. "You could get in trouble for admitting that in Indiana."

There was an awkward pause while I tried to formulate my next question. Finally I asked, "President Needler, have you heard about Professor Newmark?" I hoped I wouldn't have to be the one to break the news to him.

"Poor bugger. Yes, I heard. Is that what you wanted to tell me? You looked so worried there. That was very kind of you. But you needn't have been concerned."

"Since you haven't been here, I couldn't be sure you knew." I paused, drew a breath, and asked, "Where were you?"

If my question annoyed him, he didn't show it. He said absently, "Had to go off campus for a bit," and leaned back in his leather chair. "But bad news travels fast. Isn't that the saying? Hard to avoid news of that nature."

"There's something else you should know."

"Oh?"

"There's a press conference taking place right now. Dean Bennett is downstairs in the cafeteria talking to reporters. They were asking for you."

He sat up. "What did she tell them?"

I gave him a summary of Harriet's comments, including her response to the inquiry on his whereabouts.

"Clever girl," he said, leaning back again.

"I thought you'd want to know," I said.

"I appreciate your sensitivity," he said, smiling at me. "Sounds like Harriet's handling everything in her usual efficient manner. She certainly doesn't need me downstairs to muck it up." He stood up. "And as she correctly surmised, I must tackle the new difficulties we face occasioned by this storm." He came around the desk and put a hand on the back of my chair. "As you can see, I have a lot of calls to return. I hope you'll excuse me now." He appeared to have snapped out of the fog he'd been in. His voice was stronger now, his posture decidedly more erect. He thanked me profusely, escorted me to the door, and all but pushed me into the hall. I heard the snick of the lock when he closed the door behind me.

What a strange duck, I thought. *I wonder where he's been all this time. I asked him outright, but he obviously wasn't about to tell me.*

Harriet was still outlining the college's insurance coverage and assuring the press of the soundness of

Schoolman's remaining structures when I returned to the cafeteria.

"While we have been fiscally stable, this kind of unexpected expense will definitely put a strain on our resources," she said. "Nevertheless, we fully expect to meet our obligations. Please make sure to include that in your story if you plan to cover the impact of the storm on the college's finances. I'm afraid that's all the time I have, ladies and gentlemen. Thank you all for coming."

Harriet hurried out of the building by a side door and I followed, quickly filling her in about the return of the college president.

She stopped short. "You talked to him?"

"Yes. He's upstairs in his office. Do you want to go back?"

"I don't have time now, but I'll kill that man when I see him," she said as we crossed the quad on our way back to Kammerer House. "Where the heck has he been? Did he say?"

"No."

"He left me high and dry with so many decisions pending and no support from him."

Waving to the security detail that was keeping the curious off the premises, Harriet and I slid under the yellow tape and trudged around to where the center of activity was concentrated. The street behind Kammerer House was closed to traffic and filled with emergency and police vehicles, their red, yellow, and blue flashing lights imparting a strange illumination to the scene.

Lieutenant Parish greeted us. "We're just about ready to pull him out," he said.

"Has the college chaplain arrived?" Harriet asked. "I sent for him."

"Yes. He's over there with the fire chief," Parish said, pointing to Pastor Getler, a small, round man with a neatly trimmed beard, standing next to a strapping fellow in a blue uniform, and another tall man in a white jacket holding a clipboard.

Getler saw us, excused himself to the men, and came up to Harriet, gathering up both her hands and startling her with a light kiss on the cheek. "It's a sad day, Dean Bennett, a sad day indeed. My heart is full for the poor soul, taken in his prime. I wept when I heard the news. And how are you?" He peered into her eyes. "Did you weep for Wesley Newmark? It's all right to cry, you know."

"I'm very distressed about Wes's death," she said. "Look, I know it's a bit early to discuss this, but we're planning a memorial service for him next week. Vernon Foner wants to give the eulogy. You'll be available to offer a prayer, of course."

"Naturally. Be happy to put together the whole program."

"That's not really necessary," she said. "The English department has asked to plan the memorial, and I told them to go ahead. Wes wasn't observant, but I think he would have liked a prayer to be included in any service for him."

"Well, if my expertise is not needed . . ." He released her hands.

"Nevertheless, we would welcome your prayers. I'll call you as soon as we've arranged a time."

"It will be in the chapel, I assume."

"Yes, in the chapel."

"Well, that's appropriate. But the chapel by its very nature is a place for religious ceremonies, you know." He took a deep breath, and looked as if he were about to launch into a lecture.

I stepped forward and thrust out my hand. "I don't believe we've met," I said. "I'm Jessica Fletcher."

Harriet flashed me a grateful look, and added, "Yes, Pastor Getler, Jessica is a visiting professor, one of our celebrity authors."

"Ah, the famous mystery writer. Heard a great deal about you," he said, taking up both my hands, "and I've read one of your books, too."

"I'm flattered," I said.

"Of course." He squeezed my hands and smiled weakly. "Can't remember the exact title right now, something about murder."

"Yes, that's usually the case."

"Silly me," he said. "It'll come to me, I'm sure. Anyway, I look forward to talking to you sometime when we can sit down and get to know each other better."

"It will be my pleasure," I said.

"We must talk more." He gave my hands a final squeeze before letting go and turning back to Harriet, his expression sober. "I'll expect to hear from you. Unfortunately, right now I have a sad duty to perform."

He strolled back to where his two companions still stood.

"Heaven help me," Harriet said in a low voice. "Now I'll have to persuade Vernon Foner to write a eulogy."

"But I just heard you say he *wants* to give a eulogy," I said.

"I had to say something or Getler would have taken over the whole service and no one else would have had a chance to speak. Verne was the first name that came to mind. I'd better talk to him tomorrow. It'll be awkward if Getler sees him before I do."

"Now, don't go borrowing trouble, Harriet."

"Can you believe the ego of that man?" Harriet muttered. "He's insufferable. I have to deal with him, but I'd avoid him at all costs if I were you."

"But he's read one of my books," I said with a straight face, " 'something about murder.' I didn't know I had a book with that title."

Harriet snorted and covered her mouth with both hands. "Don't make me laugh, not here. If I laugh, I might start crying, and I don't want to give Getler an excuse to comfort me."

We turned to watch while one of the firemen tested the stability of a jack, the scene instantly sobering. "We're good to go," he yelled.

EMTs from the local area wheeled over a pallet on which a dark green body bag lay unzipped.

Two other men crawled through an opening in the wall that had been enlarged from the original window. Once inside, they carefully dislodged the upended office chair that was blocking the way. It fell on its side with a loud clang, one wheel rapidly spinning. The men pushed the chair toward the opening, where others outside quickly grabbed it. Reaching the body, they checked to be sure nothing would further hinder its removal. They drew Wes's briefcase from beneath his body and flung it out of the way. It landed next to a bush outside. Then, inch by inch, they backed out, dragging the lifeless form of Wes Newmark with them, pausing only when a fragment of wallboard snagged the cuff of his trousers and threatened to topple the whole mare's nest. Once free of the passage, they stopped again to turn Wes over, fold his broken eyeglasses, which had been caught under his body, and lay them on his chest. They placed a sheet on the ground, onto which they laid his body, cradling his head as if to protect him from further injury. They wrapped the sheet around him and gently lifted him into the green plastic body bag.

The man in the white jacket, who'd been talking to the fire chief, walked over to the pallet. He pulled a stethoscope from his pocket and listened for any signs of life.

"Is that the medical examiner?" I whispered to Harriet.

"That's Brad Zelinsky," she replied softly. "He's the county coroner."

"Is he a doctor?"

"Yes. He works at the county hospital."

"Do you need to identify the body for him?"

"No, Brad can do it. He's one of Wes's poker buddies."

I don't know why it should have surprised me. Small communities like Schoolman, and Cabot Cove, my hometown in Maine, share similar traits, among them a certain intimacy. In a small town, everyone knows each other, even if it's only by sight, enough for a smile and a wave. That knowledge sets us apart from the larger communities beyond our borders. What we sacrifice in privacy, we gain in comfort and security. People who move to a small town from a big city sometimes find that off-putting, preferring to keep their lives private and to choose friends from a small segment of the population. Wes Newmark had struck me as a private sort of person, not the kind to socialize much with anyone. But then Schoolman College as a whole wasn't very large. If he'd lived here a long time—Harriet had said she'd known Wes for many years—I suppose it would be foolish to think an English professor wouldn't have friends off campus as well as on.

I studied Dr. Zelinsky as he finished his examination and ticked off several boxes on his clipboard. He must have been over six feet tall, but his stooped posture made him appear shorter. I gauged him to be in his late fifties. His brown hair was tousled, and as I watched him, he ran his left hand through thinning locks, leaving a clump standing on end. He scribbled his signature on the bottom of the form, touched Newmark's shoulder, shook his head, and walked away.

Pastor Getler leaned over the body. I could see his lips moving but couldn't hear his words. Only the crackle of the police radio broke the respectful silence that accompanied his prayer.

The quiet continued during the rapid breakdown of the recovery site. The ambulance sped away with the deceased, its siren and lights extinguished. The fire trucks backed down the street, onto the main road, and drove off into the night. The police in their patrol cars followed shortly afterward. The lights from the drama department and fire department were dismantled, and the crowd that had waited to witness the liberation of Professor Wesley Newmark's body dispersed.

I walked over to the building and picked up Professor Newmark's briefcase. It was empty except for several pencils rolling around in the bottom, along with a few paper clips, rubber bands, and a plastic calculator. I handed the briefcase to Harriet. "His sister might like to have this," I said.

"That's very thoughtful of you, Jessica. Are you sure it's his?"

"Yes," I said. "He was carrying this when I saw him last, but it was bulging, presumably with papers. Now it's not."

"Just look at the quad," Harriet said as we walked around to the front of the building. "It's covered with papers. Whatever he had in this briefcase is probably somewhere out here."

"I hope not," I said.

"I'm going to hunt up a cup of tea before I go home," she said. "Will you join me?"

"That does sound good."

"Do you think the Red Cross left us any of their doughnuts?"

"If we're lucky."

"It's ironic," she said as we headed for the Student Union. "Because of Wes, we got a big boost in the cleanup from the fire and police departments. They filled three Dumpsters tonight. Tomorrow that job is ours."

"And you can't just hire a crane and cart all the debris away," I said. "You have the files and records from three departments to salvage."

She moaned. "That's right. Which means it will take twice as long to clear everything away. Plus we used the basement in Kammerer House for storage. There must be dozens of file cabinets down there."

"That's strange," I said.

"What's strange?"

"If Kammerer House had a basement, why didn't Wesley Newmark take shelter down there? Was it kept locked?"

"No. There was no need to lock up old records."

"Phil Adler, your bursar, said he was expecting a visit from Wes."

"And Phil got hurt waiting for him," Harriet said. "Foolish man. When I see him at the hospital, I'm going to ask about the nature of that appointment."

"I'd like to join you when you go, if you don't mind."

"Of course I don't mind. You're more than welcome."

I didn't want to alarm Harriet, but all evening I'd had a feeling that something wasn't right. Two men had braved a tornado, and one of them had died. What kept them in their places? What worry was greater than the need to take cover from the storm? And when it was upon them, why didn't they run? I'd heard the roar of the wind and felt its breath on my neck. Yet I'd made it to shelter in time. Why hadn't they?

And that briefcase. Where *were* its contents? Briefcases usually contain papers of one sort or another. I hadn't seen any papers inside Kammerer House. Surely if the tornado had emptied the briefcase, wouldn't there be at least a few papers left inside it?

No, something was wrong. And I wanted to know what it was.

Chapter Four

Vernon Foner, tieless, in slacks and a sweater, stopped at our breakfast table the next morning, and Harriet seized the opportunity to designate him to assess the English department's needs and to report back to her as soon as possible.

"Does this mean I am acting department head?" he asked.

"This means simply that I'm asking you to assess the department's needs," she replied directly and strongly. "An acting department head will be appointed later. President Needler is swamped, as you might imagine, and has asked me to coordinate for him," she told him.

"Please assure him that he can count on me," Foner promised cheerfully. "I'll have a preliminary report for you this afternoon. By the way, if no one has already reserved it, the Langston Apartments in Sutherland Library would make excellent temporary quarters for the department. Did I tell you I saw similar rooms in Italy this past summer? It really is a shame to keep them closed when they could be enjoyed by people and serve a valuable function at the same time."

"I'll keep it in mind."

No one questioned Harriet about the assumption of duties that usually fell to the president, believing her

story of his immersion in the problems of the college
caused by the storm. But, in fact, she'd assembled a
core group of trusted advisers and was shouldering his
responsibilities as well as her own, and accomplishing
it with a steely resolve. I didn't doubt for a moment
that she was very much in charge, and up to the task.
Since Needler's return, he'd locked himself in his office, according to Harriet, and allegedly was occupying
himself by phoning alumni to ask for donations to a
cleanup fund he claimed he was in the process of
establishing.

"At least if he generates some income with these
calls, we could say his time is well spent," Harriet
confided to me over breakfast. "But I'm afraid he's
turning off some of our most generous contributors."

"Do you think he's unbalanced?" I'd asked. It
seemed a logical question, considering Harriet's tone.

"It's hard to tell with him, Jess. Some say he's brilliant. Others view him as eccentric, to be kind. All I
know is that when the school hired him, he brought
with him all sorts of credentials that promised to add
some needed sheen to our image. I talked with his
secretary this morning. She assures me I'll be thrilled
when I see the bottom line of the alumni fund."

"Was he always like this? I mean . . . well,
eccentric?"

"Now and then, but I don't think the board would
have hired him if we'd had any idea he tended to
isolate himself during a crisis."

In addition to Foner, whose ambition, I decided,
was written on his sleeve, two other people stopped by
our table and walked away with assignments. Harris
Colarulli, a postdoctoral fellow in the science department, and his wife, Zoe, an associate professor of English, had come over to offer condolences. Zoe was

due to attend the English department meeting, but
Harriet asked Harris to meet the buses returning from
Wabash with the basketball team and the fans. He
was to compare the returnees with the college's lists,
double-checking that everyone was accounted for. Zoe
would help him when her meeting adjourned.

"Keep it up," I said to Harriet after they'd gone,
"and everyone is going to steer clear of you."

"You're right," she said, managing what passed for
a laugh. "But this is the best way to get things done.
As soon as people ask if they can help, say yes, and
give them something to do."

"Ladies and gentlemen, if we may come to order."

Vernon Foner stood at the front of the classroom
and looked up from three piles of paper he'd laid
neatly side by side on the lightwood desk in front of
him. He'd changed for the meeting, having abandoned
his casual attire at breakfast in favor of a gray three-
piece suit and pastel pink tie, very corporate, very
much a leader's outfit. He tugged on the hem of his
vest, checked the knot in his tie, and ran the tips of
his long fingers down a list he'd prepared for the meeting. His apparel was considerably more formal than
that of the rest of the faculty, who wore casual clothes.

I walked to the front of the room and sank into a
seat close to him. I was feeling the effects of a long
evening spent on the telephone, assuring my worried
friends back home that I was just fine, followed by a
long, sleepless night spent trying to push out of my
mind the image of Wes Newmark's dead body.

The door opened and a wail came from the back of
the room. "Oooh, Rebecca, I can't believe he's gone."
Letitia Tingwell, the department secretary, threw herself into Rebecca McAllister's arms and sobbed.

Rebecca patted the woman on her back, and several others came to help her into a chair. The graduate assistant, Edgar Poole, grabbed a box of tissues from a table and placed it in front of the weeping woman.

Foner peered over the top of his half-moon glasses. "We really have a great deal to accomplish and not a lot of time."

Rebecca glared at Foner. *Verne,* she mouthed in his direction, her gaze flying to the ceiling in disgust.

Foner pursed his lips and sucked on the inside of his cheek. One foot tapped impatiently. He looked over at me. "Can't be helped, I guess," he said.

"They're upset," I said, leaning closer. "You can understand that."

"I'm just as sorry as the next one that Wes died. But he did, and we've got students to teach and a department to run."

"Don't you think you can spare them a few minutes to grieve? After all, it may be the first time they're seeing each other since they heard the news."

"I'm not screaming for order, am I? But I will if we don't get started soon. I've got a lot of things to do. Dean Bennett wants me to write a eulogy for Newmark. Of all people to ask, I can't believe she asked me."

"Why's that?"

"Wes and I weren't great friends—that's no secret— not that I would've wished him dead. But Dr. Bennett should have asked Manny Rosenfeld or Larry Durbin. They knew him a lot longer than I did."

"Why didn't you suggest she ask one of them instead of you?"

"You don't turn down a command performance from a Schoolman. It's actually an honor that she wants me—a pain in the neck, but an honor. I'll do it, and I'll do a great job." He looked out at the faculty of the English department as they began to find their seats. "He'll sound like a saint by the time I'm done," he muttered to himself.

Mrs. Tingwell's sobs had subsided into hiccups. She dabbed at eyes ringed with mascara and lustily blew her nose. She wasn't the only emotional person. Two others were red-eyed, and a few sniffles were heard around the room.

"I know that we're all upset at the loss of our colleague," Foner said. "And we will have an opportunity to express our grief more formally—President Needler has asked us to plan a memorial service, which I will get to in a moment—but right now we need to discuss several urgent administrative matters. Edgar, hand out the agenda, please."

Edgar grabbed a pile of papers and walked around the room, placing one in front of each person.

"As you can see, there's quite a bit on our plate. And the administration has announced that classes will resume tomorrow."

"Verne, how long do they expect the cleanup to take at Kammerer House?" Rebecca asked. "If the cabinets survived the storm, we may be able to recover some files."

"We would be severely handicapped if we relied on such an outcome," he replied, staring at her until she turned bright red. "Think about it, Rebecca. It may be months till any papers are recovered. What you need may be hanging in a tree at this moment. No, I don't think we'll follow that scenario." He turned to the green board on the wall behind him and picked up a piece of chalk. "Let's go over the assignments and see what alterations need to be made."

There were now eight of us in the English department, six faculty, seven if you counted the graduate assistant, plus Mrs. Tingwell, a stout woman somewhere in her fifties, who was fond of flowered dresses with lace collars. She had been put in charge of orientation for the visiting celebrity professors and had been kind enough to take me under her wing, making sure the small refrigerator in my faculty apartment was nicely stocked when I arrived, and introducing me around campus. She'd been the department secretary for thirty years, she'd told me—"I know where all the bodies are buried"—and even though Wes's tenure had been considerably less than that, she'd been devoted to him. "I know a good man when I meet one."

Foner cleared his throat and swallowed, his prominent Adam's apple bobbing up and down above his pink tie. "Mrs. Tingwell," he said, "I am assuming we can count on your good offices as we always have to man the department office, wherever it may be set up."

"Of course, Professor Foner," she said, her voice quavery, her eyes filling with tears. "Are you the official acting chairman now?"

"I am the unofficial acting chairman," he replied.

"Self-appointed, Verne?" Professor Lawrence Durbin asked. He was the department's Shakespeare authority, a bear of a man with unruly red hair.

"President Needler has yet to name an acting chairman, so for the moment, yes," Foner said, sliding a finger under the knot of his tie and stretching his neck from side to side. "Nevertheless, Dean Bennett requested that I assess the department's needs, and I take that to mean I am acting as chairman."

"I see you've dressed up in corporate mufti today," Durbin said. "You must be lobbying for the job."

Foner stiffened. "I have to report to administration

this afternoon. There may be some board members present. I don't see that my attire concerns you."

Durbin's laugh was low and rumbling. He said in stentorian tones, " 'Some men are born great, some achieve greatness, and some have greatness thrust upon 'em.' "

Foner glared at him: "Meaning what?" he asked.

"Shakespeare, Verne. *Twelfth Night.* You remind me of Malvolio. Don't despair over a lack of breeding or talent. There's always luck." The bearlike, red-headed Shakespearean expert laughed again and turned away.

Zoe Colarulli waved the sheet of paper Edgar had distributed. "Could we get down to business? You have me down for teaching Wes's Readings in Contemporary Literature, Verne. Don't you think you should have discussed this with me first? I have a full load, what with the Introduction to Language Arts and my composition classes. That's at least sixty-five students. I don't see how I can handle any more. Rebecca's classes are smaller. Why can't she handle some of this?"

"Now, just a minute. I have as many students as you do, Zoe," Rebecca said. "Don't try to pass your responsibilities off on me."

"Yes, but mine are composition classes, and that requires more work."

"I work just as hard as you do," Rebecca said, glaring at the younger woman.

"Ladies, please, don't stress yourselves. That's what we're here for," Foner said smoothly, "to determine who does what. Nothing is set in stone. We're going to be democratic about this."

"Vernon, I would like to add something, if I may." The speaker was Professor Emmanuel Rosenfeld, a soft-spoken man in his sixties. He'd been at School-man longer than any of the others, including Mrs. Tingwell, and had served as department chair earlier in his academic career.

"Go ahead, Manny."

"You have a very ambitious agenda here, for which I compliment you," he said. "But we'll be here all day if we debate the merits of each of these items."

"You're right. That's why—"

"May I suggest that for each agenda item, you designate a volunteer to take charge of the problem and come up with the resolution? Then we can all reconvene at four-thirty and you'll have your report for the administration. Does that sound good?"

Under Professor Rosenfeld's gentle prodding, the responsibilities were quickly parceled out, and the meeting broke up with a new sense of purpose. Mrs. Tingwell and Edgar retired to a corner to put together a preliminary list of supplies the department would need, Edgar writing down her tearful instructions with his left hand, while reaching for the tissue box with his right. Professors Colarulli and McAllister took on the dilemma of who would teach Wes's classes. Larry Durbin proposed to investigate which files still existed and which missing ones needed to be replaced. Manny Rosenfeld had offered to chair the memorial service.

"May I help with arranging the memorial service?" I asked him.

"I would be very grateful for your assistance, Mrs. Fletcher."

"Please call me Jessica."

"And you must call me Manny. We're excited to have a celebrity on campus. Is this your first time teaching?"

"Actually, it's not," I said as we walked outside together.

The air was cool enough for a light jacket, but the sun warmed our backs as we walked across the quad, which was once again filled with students. The grass had been cleared of heavy debris, and some of the refuse hanging from the trees had been pulled down. Workmen on ladders were plucking pink tufts of insulation from one of the oaks, where it had caught in the cracks of the rough bark. Others with pointed sticks were batting or poking other tree-borne scraps to dislodge them from the remaining branches. We stopped to watch the work.

"In the spring, those trees will have new shoots and leaves, and we won't see a trace of what happened here," Rosenfeld said. "And by next fall, when they shed those leaves, their bare branches will look normal again."

"It's wonderful, the earth's powers of regeneration."

"It is, but my poor friend Wes will miss it. Fall was his favorite season. He loved the feeling of anticipation when the students came back to campus. He loved their enthusiasm and how they challenged him, never letting him get away with pat answers."

"What a lovely memory. He sounds like a wonderful man. I wish I'd known him better. We'd met only a few times."

"Wes was basically a good guy, but a hard man to know, quiet, private, worked hard, kept to himself. A bachelor. No one really close to him. Our only social interaction was the monthly poker game in town."

"He must have enjoyed that."

"He was good at it, I'll tell you that. It's a low-stakes, friendly game, fifty cents, a dollar. We don't let anyone play too deep. If a guy is down thirty bucks, we make him stop playing. But I don't ever remember Wes losing. He was always serious, concentrated on his cards. I often wondered if he enjoyed himself or just came to avoid being labeled antisocial."

"He probably looked forward to those evenings more than you know."

"I hope you're right. He'd changed quite a bit these last three or four months."

"Oh? How so?"

Rosenfeld frowned, as though trying to put words to what he was thinking. "Wes always was a bit paranoid, but it got worse recently. He seemed unusually on edge, anxious, distrustful. I've no idea why."

"Obviously something heavy weighing on his mind," I offered.

"Yes. I keep thinking there were still things he would have wanted to do. Travel, or read something new. I've got a pile of books I've been meaning to find time for. I picked one up for the first time last night."

"That's what death does," I said. "It reminds us to appreciate life, not to take it for granted. But it's a harsh way to learn that lesson."

"It's ironic, really. You get up in the morning, shave, dress, go about your business, and a storm comes up, dumps a house on top of you, and kills you."

"Yes, it is ironic," I said.

But was that what had happened? I was still disturbed about the way Wes Newmark had died. What was it? I knew I'd better come up with an answer soon or I was in for another sleepless night.

Chapter Five

"Dr. Zelinsky, pick up five-one-six-six," a voice said over the public-address system. "Dr. Zelinsky, pick up five-one-six-six."

Harriet and I walked down the corridor of New Salem County Hospital on Monday morning, bright orange visitor badges clipped to our collars, our plans to visit Schoolman's bursar, Phil Adler, the previous day having been scuttled by her campus responsibilities.

"I hate hospitals," Harriet said, jamming her fists into her jacket pockets.

"Lots of people do," I said. "They don't bother me."

"I used to think it was because my husband died in a hospital. I was there for months, sleeping on a lumpy cot. Every time I went home to change and returned there, I would feel sick to my stomach. I thought it must just be that hospital and that situation, but this is a different hospital, and I don't like this one either."

"What do you think bothers you?"

"The smell," she said. "It's faint, not strong. They keep this place very clean, I know. But there's always this slight odor."

"A mixture of institutional food and antiseptic?"

"That's it exactly," she said. "It gets me every time."

Adler's room was in the corner at the end of the hall. Harriet knocked on the partially closed door and pushed it open. He was reclining against two pillows, with his leg in a full cast, supported by three more pillows. He looked older than when I'd seen him last, his hair mussed, and with gray circles under his eyes.

"Are we disturbing you, Phil?" Harriet asked.

"Not at all," he said, raising a bandaged hand. "Come on in. Can't offer you much in hospitality, but you're welcome."

"You remember Jessica Fletcher, don't you, Phil?"

"Sure. Our celebrity professor."

"How are you feeling?" I asked.

"Not great," he said. "There's quite a lot of pain, and the pills last only so long."

"I'm sorry you're uncomfortable," I said. "Would you like us to call the nurse for you?"

"No, thanks. Won't do any good. The nurse they assigned me is a bad-tempered one."

"I heard that," said a nurse, bustling into the room and setting a tray on the table next to his bed.

"I meant you to," he said.

"And don't I know it." She picked up his wrist and timed his pulse. "Well, sweet talk won't get you anywhere," she said, poking a digital thermometer in his ear.

"Would you like us to leave the room?" I asked.

"Not necessary," she replied. "He'll be happy to hear it's time for his meds. Maybe it'll make him a nicer host."

"How long will Phil have to stay in the hospital?" Harriet asked.

"I'm not the doctor, but I'm guessing he'll be here close to a week," the nurse said. "They put the bones back together but they can't suture the skin till they make sure there's no infection. He's also got two cracked ribs and a bruised spleen that the doctors are watching." She handed him a paper cup with two pills in it, and poured a glass of water from a bedside carafe.

"Thank you."

"You're welcome," she said. "I see your manners are showing this afternoon. That's a nice change from this morning." She picked up her tray. "He can use some cheering. Have a nice visit, ladies." She was out the door.

"I guess I've been complaining a lot."

"You've got reason," Harriet said. "I brought you something from Mrs. Grace in the kitchen." She dug into her bag and came up with a foil-wrapped parcel.

"What is it?"

"A piece of the apple crumb cake she served at breakfast this morning."

Adler took the package with a wan smile and placed it on the rolling table next to his bed. "Please thank her for me." He was silent for a moment. "I heard about Wes," he said in a low voice.

Harriet sighed. "You did? I wasn't going to tell you," she said. "I thought I'd give you a little more time to recover."

"Brad Zelinsky was in this morning with that policeman, Parish. They told me. I was waiting for Wes," he said, looking from Harriet to me. "That's why I got caught in the tornado. By the time I decided I should run, the storm was over the house and I was under a beam."

"What was the appointment about?" I asked.

"I don't know," he said, picking at a loose end of his bandage. "He just said it was urgent, that he had things to discuss with me and I shouldn't leave the office."

"Then you don't have any idea what he wanted to talk about?" Harriet asked.

"None. Parish asked me the same questions."

"Considering your position at the college," I said, "do you think it would be safe to say Wes Newmark had some question for you having to do with budget or finances?"

"You can't be sure. Maybe he knew some student who needed financial aid. Or maybe he wanted to borrow my car. He did that once last year when his old Chevy broke down. How do I know what he wanted? He didn't say anything except, 'Stay there; I need to talk to you.' "

"Were you good friends?" I asked.

"Not really. We had the occasional lunch together in the cafeteria, and I sat in on his regular poker game a couple of times—Brad invited me—but I can't say we were good friends."

"Who were the regulars in that game?"

"For heaven's sake, Jessica, what could that possibly have to do with the appointment?"

"I'm just curious, Harriet. It's not important."

"Why do you think Wes didn't keep his appointment?" I asked Phil.

"Who knows? Maybe he couldn't find whatever he wanted to show me. Or maybe he was running late and the storm overpowered him like it did me. Hard to keep an appointment when you're lying under a pile of furniture."

"It's really strange," Harriet said softly. "He never told me he was meeting with you, but whatever he

wanted to discuss must have been extremely important
to him."

"Well, I don't know what it was," Phil said, "and I
guess we'll never know." He leaned back on his pillow
and closed his eyes. "I think the pills are kicking in,"
he said.

"One last thing, Phil," I said. "*When* did Wes make
the appointment with you?"

"I can't remember."

"We'll leave you in peace," Harriet said, pulling on
my arm. "Is there anything I can bring you the next
time I come?"

He shook his head, eyes still closed. "If I think of
anything, I'll call," he said, his speech slightly slurred.
"Thanks for stopping by."

"I want to check in with the social-work department
before we leave," Harriet said after we'd closed Phil's
door behind us. "He's going to need assistance when
he leaves the hospital. With that cast, he won't be able
to dress himself, much less get around. I want to alert
them to the problem."

"I thought he was married," I said. "He wears a
ring."

"Was. His wife left him last year. I don't think he's
gotten over it. The office is this way," she said, steer-
ing me around a corner. "She was one of those self-
centered glamour girls, long blond hair, high heels and
jeans. A city girl. And she had a difficult time adjusting to small-town college life. I never cared for
her. She complained all the time. I can't say I was
sorry when I heard she went back to Chicago. Apparently she has family there."

"Harriet, would you mind if I stopped somewhere
else while you see the social worker?"

"No, of course not. I'll only be fifteen minutes or so. Where shall we meet?"

"How about right outside the auxiliary gift shop. If you're delayed, I can browse their shelves."

"That sounds perfect," she said. "I'll meet you there in fifteen minutes."

I went to the reception desk in the lobby and asked where I could find Dr. Zelinsky.

"Would you like me to page him for you?" the lady in the pink uniform asked.

"No, I don't want to interrupt him if he's busy or with a patient. Does he have an office in the building where I can leave him a note?"

"You could leave a message for him with the pathology lab. It's on the basement level. Turn right when you exit the elevator."

I followed her directions and came to a glass door on which PATHOLOGY was etched in block letters. I pushed the door open. A pair of lab technicians bent over microscopes looked up. "Can I help you?" one asked.

"I'm looking for Dr. Zelinsky," I said. "If he's not here, I can leave him a message."

"Let me see if he's available. Who shall I say is asking for him?"

"We haven't met. My name is Jessica Fletcher. I'm a visiting professor at Schoolman College."

"Have a seat," she said, pointing to an office chair. "I'll find out if he can see you."

A moment later, Dr. Brad Zelinsky emerged from an office in the back.

"How do you do," he said, extending his hand. "I've heard about you. How can I help you today?"

"I wonder if we could speak privately for just a moment."

Chapter Six

"I'm sure your fears are unfounded, Mrs. Fletcher," said Dr. Zelinsky as he opened the door for me. He'd kindly given me ten minutes, and that was all I'd needed to make my point.

"I hope you're right," I said. "It's just a feeling. I can't quite pinpoint what it was that triggered my thinking."

"People die in tornadoes every year. Most often it's just a tragic accident, but there are always numskulls who ignore the warnings. They figure, 'It'll never happen to me.' And we've got Phil Adler upstairs as another example of this kind of stupidity. You can quote me on that."

"I'm not planning to write anything about this," I said.

"Just a figure of speech," he said. "I gave Phil a piece of my mind this morning. He didn't like it, but he couldn't run away, and that's his own fault. I told him we've got enough problems taking care of sick patients in this hospital without throwing in healthy people who are just too dumb to take shelter when they're supposed to." He drew a handkerchief from his pants pocket and wiped perspiration from his brow. "Sorry, didn't mean to get so hot on the topic."

"I understand," I said. "And as I told you, I'm

really relieved to hear that you'll be conducting an autopsy."

"Got to do a postmortem whenever there's an accidental death. That's the law."

"Or one under suspicious circumstances."

Zelinsky smiled. "You're sure a persistent one," he said. "Yes, that's true, too. But as I said, I don't see anything to support that theory right now."

"But if you do—"

"If I do, I'll call you," he said. "Or you can call me. You have my card?"

"Yes." I patted my jacket pocket.

"The autopsy results are public information, so there won't be any trouble if I read you the report."

"I appreciate that, Dr. Zelinsky. When do you think the autopsy will take place?"

"Well, seeing as I'm the one doing it, it can take place whenever I have the time. I'll probably get to it today, tomorrow at the latest. Don't want the body hanging around. I expect I'll be getting a call from Markham's Funeral Home anytime now. That usually pushes me along."

"By the way, I understand you were a regular in Wes Newmark's poker game."

"Who told you that?"

"Harriet Schoolman Bennett."

"Ah, the small-town grapevine. My secret is out. I'm a closet poker player," he said, smiling.

"Who else played in that game?"

"Any particular reason you want to know?"

"I'm helping to arrange the memorial service. I want to make certain all his friends are invited."

"Well, there's me; Wes, of course; Phil on occasion; Lowell; Larry Durbin; and Manny Rosenfeld. Harriet even sat in once or twice."

"Lowell? Would that be President Needler?"

"Yeah, although he's a lousy poker player. Loses every month. We had to put in the thirty-dollar-limit rule for him. Otherwise he would have gone broke." He glanced at his watch. "Look, I have to get back to work. Nice meeting you."

I thanked him, left the laboratory, and found my way to the gift shop on the main floor. Harriet hadn't arrived yet, and I perused items for sale while I waited for her. There was a large selection of toilet articles, powder, cologne, toothbrushes and toothpaste, and other personal items a patient might need but not have brought to the hospital. Toys and games, for adults as well as children, took up several shelves, as did silk flower arrangements, displayed next to a sign that read REAL PLANTS AND FLOWERS ARE NOT PERMITTED IN THE CARDIAC UNIT. In one corner was a large display of books and magazines, and I wandered in that direction, stopping along the way to admire a hand-crocheted bed jacket made by a hospital volunteer, according to its label.

"She's such a talent, that one," said a blond lady in a pink apron, who was marking prices on a box of teddy bears. "We have other things by her, too. If you need any help, just sing out."

"Thanks," I said, "but I'm just looking."

"You're not from around here, are you?" she asked, pulling off her eyeglasses and letting them dangle by a gold chain attached to the earpieces.

"How do you know?"

"I could say that I can tell by your accent, but that would be stretching it a bit," she said. "Truth is, I know by sight most everyone who lives around here, and yours is a new face, even though you do look familiar. You wouldn't be one of those Hollywood people, would you?"

I laughed. "No. I'm from Maine," I said. "Just visiting for the semester at Schoolman College."

"We had a movie crew here once. Looking for 'small-town ambience,' they said. Turned the place upside down, blocking off traffic on the streets, closing the local bakery while they filmed inside. People were excited at first, but when they couldn't get their morning pastry they got mighty annoyed, I can tell you. By the way, I'm Eunice Carberra. I live here in New Salem."

"It's nice to meet you," I said. "I'm Jessica Fletcher."

"The mystery writer?" Her face lit up at my smile. "We've got some of your books. I knew you looked familiar. Would you mind signing them?"

"I'd be delighted," I said, following her to the book corner.

"I could put up a little placard," she said, handing me two of my books. " 'Signed by the author.' I can't wait. Let me get you a pen."

I browsed the bookshelf while she rummaged in a drawer next to the cash register.

"We've got some nice books on Indiana, if you plan to sightsee on the weekends," she said, giving up on the drawer, pulling a pen from a canister on display, and bustling over to me.

"Are you sure?" I asked, looking askance at the colorful pen. It had a little figure on top with blue hair. She nodded. I wrote my name in shocking pink ink and gave her back the pen and books.

"I'm going to make the sign right now," she said, returning to the register.

I scanned the shelves and noticed children's books on Abraham Lincoln and Johnny Appleseed; both had been Indiana residents at times in their lives. There was also a picture book on Amish quilts. I pulled it down and flipped through the pages, pausing at a pretty design in blue and yellow.

"There's quite a large Amish population in the state," Eunice said, seeing what I was reading. She carried over a roll of tape and a small card on which she'd hand-lettered her message. "Most of them live up around Nappanee, about an hour from here." She placed my books on the shelf, front cover facing out, and taped the card to the shelf above them.

"I don't drive," I said.

"Too bad," she said. "It's a lovely ride. They still farm the land with horse-drawn plows—"

"Jessica, there you are," said Harriet, interrupting the story. "I'm sorry I'm late. The social worker was on the phone when I walked in, and we barely had any time to talk by the time she got off. Hello, Eunice."

"That's all right," I said, replacing the book on the shelf. "We were having a nice conversation."

"I'm sorry to pull away a potential customer, Eunice, but we've got to get back to campus."

"I'll forgive you, Harriet," Eunice said, winking at me. "Just bring her back another time."

We climbed into Harriet's Volvo, left the hospital grounds, followed the main street through the town of New Salem, and minutes later were passing fields of corn and soybeans that flanked the road to Schoolman. Most of the crops had been harvested, but here and there were blocks the farmers were still cutting. Harriet was occupied with her own thoughts and drove fast. Even though we could see for miles ahead,

I was grateful there were no vehicles on the road other than several telephone trucks parked on the shoulder while their crews checked the overhead lines. We saw few signs of the tornado along our way. Whatever poles and trees had succumbed to the storm had already been removed. It was only when we drove onto the college grounds that the effects of the twister could be seen, as if it had chosen Schoolman as its main target and ignored the surrounding countryside.

The college was alive with the sounds of construction equipment when Harriet pulled into her parking space on the side of the Student Union and shut off the motor. Across the quad, a small crane hoisted rubble from one of the damaged buildings and deposited its load in a dump truck, while a dozen men dismantled what parts of the house they could reach and carted the pieces to a Dumpster in the driveway. Hammers, saws, and drills contributed to the cacophony as Frank and his workers completed repairs on the Hart Building. I was struck by how quickly the human community recovered from disaster, cleaning up, patching up, and moving on. Oddly, it reminded me of a time in my childhood when I'd accidentally stepped on an anthill and watched as its inhabitants poured forth, working together feverishly to mend the damage. We were not so far away from the insect kingdom in our response to calamity.

"I have a favor to ask," Harriet said when we'd gotten out of the car. "Wes's sister is expected sometime today. It's a meeting I dread." She paused.

"Would you like me to be there when you see her?"

"I know it's an imposition."

"It's not an imposition. If my presence will make it easier for you, I'm happy to do it."

"I've been leaning on you so much these last few days, I feel as if I've taken unfair advantage of our friendship."

"Don't think that for a minute. We're all grateful for support during hard times. This is a time when I can help you, and I'm happy to do it."

"You'd figure since I'm a widow, I would understand her loss and be able to say the right thing. But I get just as tongue-tied as the next person when it comes to dealing with the bereaved. And in this case I feel guilty about Wes. I'm responsible for his death."

"Why? You had no control over the storm."

"I keep thinking that if that darn alarm had gone off earlier, he would have saved himself. I should have known Needler wouldn't release the funds to fix it."

"Harriet, Wes Newmark knew a storm was coming. As you told the press, he even warned me to take shelter."

"I know, I know. Still, I keep thinking there must have been something I could have done."

"Well, there wasn't. Don't torture yourself."

"In addition to not having saved him, I'm angry at him for dying. Isn't that ridiculous? Guilt and anger. What a combination."

"That's very common, Harriet."

She sighed. "The college was just getting up to speed. All our programs were starting to take off. And now this. We're still struggling financially, but that will resolve itself—at least, it would have if we hadn't gotten hit with all these extra expenses. I should be mourning Wes, but I'm furious that he died and we have all this inconvenience instead of concentrating on building up the college funds."

"Harriet, you're being too hard on yourself. It's perfectly fine to feel these things—normal, even natural.

It's how you act upon them that's the key. And your behavior has been absolutely appropriate. You're arranging a memorial service. You're meeting with his sister. You've got the cleanup well under way, and you're having all the necessary repairs taken care of. Seems to me you're doing everything right."

"Do you really think so?"

"Yes, I do. Feel better having gotten it all out?"

"Yes, now that I've told you how horrible I am."

We both laughed.

"Enough self-flagellation for one day," I said, happy to change the subject. "What time are we meeting Wes's sister?"

"She wasn't sure when she was arriving, so I suggested that we get together at Wes's place at four."

"Shall I meet you there?"

"That would be fine. It's called La Salle House. Do you know where it is?"

"Yes. He hosted a department tea for me there. It's a lovely house."

"That's one of the ways we reward our department heads. We can't always match the pay of other colleges, but we provide beautiful accommodations. Wes lived there for fifteen years."

"He never married, I take it."

"He never mentioned it if he did. Letitia Tingwell may have hoped to change that, but now we'll never know if she could have succeeded."

"The department secretary?"

"Yes. She was devoted to him. As loyal as they come. He would ask her to tidy up after his parties, take his clothes to be laundered, things like that. She performed a lot of personal, wifely duties beyond what her job description entails. I always thought he took advantage of her, but she pooh-poohed me when I mentioned it. If there was more there than a typical boss-secretary relationship, they never demonstrated it in public. In fact, I'm not certain he even noticed her that way."

"Maybe he took all those favors for granted as his right as a department head," I said.

"Wouldn't surprise me. Wes was a fine academician, very knowledgeable, but not exactly the sensitive type."

"I thought he was well liked. Wasn't that the case?"

Harriet clapped a hand over her mouth and shook her head. "Oh, listen to me," she said. "My mother used to say, 'Never speak ill of the dead.' Forget this conversation, please. I'm talking out of turn today."

"Harriet?" I paused, debating whether to share the substance of my conversation with Dr. Zelinsky. Harriet had given me an opening, but perhaps it wasn't the right time. She had so much on her mind; it would be unkind to burden her with my suspicions, especially since they were unconfirmed. There would be time to talk with her after the autopsy was completed.

"Jessica?"

"I'm sorry, Harriet. It wasn't important."

"What is it? I just poured all my thoughts out to you. You're more than welcome to reciprocate. You certainly looked serious just now, so whatever you were thinking must be important."

"What's Wes's sister's name?"

"Is that what put that look on your face?" She laughed. "Lorraine. Lorraine Newmark."

"That's all," I said. "I'll meet you at La Salle House at four. Why don't you relax till then, get some rest?"

"Rest? I don't know the meaning of that word."

Harriet went to her office, and I crossed the campus to where the heavy equipment was in operation. Construction machinery always seems to draw a crowd of sidewalk superintendents, and this site was no exception. Groups of students and faculty were standing around the perimeter of the bursar's office, watching the construction crew pull apart the building. One section of the lawn was covered with whatever the crew had been able to salvage. Desks, chairs, copiers, filing cabinets, wastebaskets, and office supplies were set out haphazardly, staff members examining them for damage, making the scene look like a dusty furniture showroom or a flea market. A moving van stood nearby to take everything salvageable off to temporary office space in another building.

I walked over to Kammerer House, where the demolition had been temporarily suspended, the priority given to setting up the financial department. I slipped under the yellow tape and walked around to the rear of the building, hoping the activity down the street would divert attention from my trespassing.

Little had changed since Professor Newmark's body had been removed. The black office chair that had blocked his corpse had been left on its side on the grass. I knelt down and peered into the house; the supports that jacked up the file cabinet and all the debris on top of it were still in place. Beneath it, a stain on the crumpled carpet marked where the body had lain. There was a smear that might have been blood several feet away, and another dark mark that clearly was a footprint. I stood up and looked at the hole in the ceiling where rubble from the second floor had tumbled through, and tried to remember the original arrangement of furniture and filing cabinets on the first floor.

"You're not supposed to be here, you know."

I jumped. "My goodness. You startled me."

Lieutenant Bill Parish frowned at me. "That yellow tape is there for a reason, Mrs. Fletcher. It even says to keep out. You're not setting a very good example for your students."

"You're right," I said. "I shouldn't be here. There was just something I wanted to check on that bothered me the other night."

"And what might that be?"

I pointed under the supports. "You see that filing cabinet on its side, Lieutenant? I think that used to stand against the wall."

"They usually do."

"Yes, but I don't see how debris falling from that hole in the ceiling could have toppled the filing cabinet in such a way as to hit Professor Newmark's head. And why would he be sitting in that spot? There's no desk over there."

"Maybe he rolled his chair over to the file cabinet to look at something in one of the drawers."

"But if he did that and the cabinet fell on him, it would have hit him in the front of the head, not the back."

"Maybe he turned around just when it fell over."

"But when the tornado tore a hole in the second floor, he would have heard it happen and should have had time to move out of the way."

"Maybe he was crouching down by the file cabinet to protect himself."

"But the cabinet fell into the room, not to the side."

"Well, maybe it was something else that hit him on the head."

"Exactly."

"In a tornado, everything gets whipped around. It could have been anything flying in the air that knocked him down."

"Yes, but then wouldn't there be papers and other objects strewn all around the room? I don't see any of that."

"I don't know how you can say that. Look at all the junk that fell in from upstairs."

"But that's precisely what I mean, Lieutenant. All those pieces may have been swirling around the room upstairs, but when the floor gave way, they fell straight down through the hole."

"What are you suggesting, Mrs. Fletcher?"

"I'm not suggesting anything. I'm just wondering what exactly hit him."

"Why is that important?"

"Don't you think it's important to know what killed him?"

"I think your imagination is getting the better of you, Mrs. Fletcher. Wes Newmark's head was cracked open like an egg, and half a house was sitting on top of him. There were plenty of objects that could have killed him. The bottom line is that if he'd taken shelter, he'd be alive today."

"I agree," I said.

"You do?"

"Yes. Why do you think he didn't take shelter?"

"I have no idea. Maybe he was a stubborn son of a gun. Maybe he thought he was infallible. Maybe he was one of those people who likes to tempt fate. Maybe he did it on a dare. Maybe there's no logical explanation. Why do *you* think he didn't take shelter?"

"I think he may already have been dead."

Chapter Seven

Lorraine Newmark looked lost. She wore a faded blue parka, brown corduroy pants, a matching turtleneck, and an expression of bewilderment.

"Is this where he lived?"

"Yes," I said. "The college provides housing for its department heads. It's lovely, isn't it?"

"This is nicer than anyplace we ever lived, anyplace I ever lived, anyway."

She stood in the center of the spacious, old-fashioned parlor. Leaded-glass windows looked out over a garden pond and, beyond that, the green expanse of the athletic fields where the lacrosse team was practicing. Inside, a brocade sofa, small, square pillows perched on either end, faced the elegant fireplace with its beautifully carved mantel and surround. One side table held a neat stack of hardcover books, the titles on their dustcovers all facing the same direction. Matching Chippendale side chairs flanked the sofa, facing each other across a low mahogany table. Nineteenth-century oil paintings hung on the walls.

"Would you like to sit down?" I said. "Harriet Schoolman Bennett will be here any minute. She sent her apologies for being late. Let me take your coat."

She pulled a paper from her pocket and shrugged off the ski jacket, which I carried into the front hall and hung in the closet. Her worn backpack leaned against the wall. When I returned, she was still standing where I'd left her.

"Please sit down," I said, deliberately taking the sofa to be the first to dent its perfectly smooth cushion, which Letitia Tingwell had plumped up not an hour before. She'd been cleaning the house when I arrived and had greeted me with the news of Harriet's delay. I was disappointed. I had wanted an opportunity to poke around before Harriet got there, but Mrs. Tingwell's presence prohibited any snooping. She'd left only moments before Wes Newmark's sister had knocked on the door. I thought they might have passed each other on the front walk, but if they did, they hadn't stopped to exchange greetings. I'd introduced myself, expressed my condolences, and ushered her into the only room I was familiar with, having been the guest of honor there at an afternoon tea at the start of the semester.

"Was it a difficult trip for you?" I asked. "I know you've come all the way from Alaska."

She sat gingerly on one of the side chairs and looked down at her dirty sneakers. "Not really. Mrs. Bennett arranged for the flights and the car from Chicago."

"Have you lived in Alaska a long time?"

"About twenty-two years."

"When was the last time you saw your brother?"

"I don't know. Probably just before I moved up to Juneau. We weren't close, you know. We kept in touch—Christmas cards and all—but we really didn't have a lot in common. I never got to go to college. My father said it wasn't important for a woman." She looked embarrassed. "Not that it isn't nice for a woman. I would have loved to go, but there wasn't enough money for both of us. Besides, Wes was the brain in the family. . . ." She trailed off.

"What do you do in Alaska? I've always thought it must be a beautiful place to live. The scenery is spectacular."

"It's nice if you don't mind the cold. I don't. I work in one of the logging offices, keeping books for the manager. It's not exciting, but it's steady work, and they give you benefits. Not too many places up there do."

"Have you thought at all about funeral plans for your brother?"

"Not really. I figured I'd see about it once I got here." She hesitated and squirmed in her seat. "I don't have a lot put by for a big funeral. Maybe Wes has some savings I can dip into. I'm his only relative, so I guess I'm his only heir."

"Did he give you a copy of his will?"

She looked shocked. "No! I hadn't even thought of that."

"I'll be happy to help you with the arrangements, and I'm sure Harriet will make sure everything goes smoothly until his will is probated. Are you staying in this house while you're here?"

"Mrs. Bennett said I could, but I didn't know it was so fancy."

"It's just a house," I said.

"Hello. I'm so sorry I'm late," Harriet called out from the hall. I heard the door close and she rushed into the room.

Lorraine stood and wiped her palms on the sides of her pants, her right hand pausing at her pocket.

"Hi. You must be Lorraine. We've spoken on the phone. I'm Harriet. Please sit down. I see Jessica has made you comfortable. I apologize I wasn't here to greet you when you arrived. It's a madhouse over in administration."

"That's okay," Lorraine said, sitting on the edge of the chair.

"Would you both like some tea or coffee?" Harriet asked. "I know I would. There must be some in the kitchen." She left the room as quickly as she'd entered.

"Miss Newmark, would you like some coffee?" I asked.

"Please, it's Lorraine." She smiled. "Nobody calls me Miss Newmark. I wouldn't know to answer to it."

"Lorraine then. You must call me Jessica. Why don't we go into the kitchen and help Harriet find the cups? It'll give you a chance to see where everything is."

We followed the sound of Harriet opening and shutting cabinet doors, and Lorraine seemed to relax at the sight of the homey room. The kitchen looked as if it hadn't been remodeled over the past forty years. Yellow cabinets with green Formica countertops gave it a cheery, if old-fashioned, appearance. The room was immaculate, and I thought either Wes Newmark was a very neat man, or he never cooked for himself. My suspicion was confirmed when I opened the refrigerator to look for milk and saw several take-out cartons on the shelves. I pulled out the bottle of milk, and noted the sell-by date. Letitia Tingwell must have purchased it recently.

"There's regular tea and herbal," Harriet said, pointing to the boxes, "but I can't find any coffee." She opened the freezer and poked around. I saw her glance at a piece of paper.

"Did Wes leave his shopping list in the freezer?" I asked with a chuckle as I took a kettle from the stove and filled it at the sink.

"What? Oh, you're being silly. A label must have come off a package." Harriet stuffed it in her pocket and closed the freezer door.

"Don't worry about the coffee," I said. "Regular tea is fine with me."

"Me, too," said Lorraine.

"Well, that's a blessing," Harriet said. "This herbal tea box has only one tea bag in it."

"Where are the cups, Harriet?" I asked.

"Try the last cabinet on the left."

Lorraine went to the cabinet and took down cups and saucers, comfortable with the familiar task. I opened three drawers before I found the one with the silverware, tossed in next to three decks of cards. After a futile search for napkins, Harriet pulled off three paper towels, and the little table at the window was set for tea.

"I knew Wes wasn't much of an entertainer, so I brought some cake," Harriet said. "Lorraine, if you wouldn't mind, it's in the tote bag I left in the hall."

Lorraine trotted back to the hall to retrieve Harriet's bag. As soon as she was out of the room, Harriet whispered to me, "Have you discussed the funeral arrangements?"

I shook my head. "She hasn't made any yet, and may not have the funds to cover it. And she doesn't have a copy of his will. Do you know where it is?"

"No, but Letitia might. We'll ask her."

Lorraine returned with the tote bag. Harriet pulled out a marble pound cake and cut it into slices, overlapping them in a circle on a round plate. When the kettle had boiled and the tea had been made, we took

our seats at the table, the companionable atmosphere
encouraging conversation. Lorraine and I talked about
favorite cake recipes—I make a mean pecan coffee
roll; Lorraine said her banana cream pie was popular
up north; and Harriet, who didn't bake, praised her
favorite ready-made brand, Pepperidge Farm apple
turnovers. The conversation eventually got around to
Wes, who never cooked at all, according to his sister.
"Cooking was women's work," she said. "My father's
influence again. I'll bet that freezer's full of frozen
dinners."

"It is," Harriet said. "He was obviously a big fan
of macaroni and cheese."

"I imagine there must have been times over the
years when he was sorry he'd never learned to make
himself supper," I said. "Knowing how to cook is part
of what makes you an independent person, not to
mention a healthier one."

"Except that here, he always had the college meal
plan available," Harriet put in. "He was a regular in
the cafeteria."

"When we were young, I used to tease him that
he'd better marry a good cook or he'd starve to
death," Lorraine said. The smile left her face. "But
he didn't do either, did he?" She put down the cake
she'd been nibbling. I put my hand on top of hers and
gave her a little squeeze.

Harriet jumped in to keep the conversation going.
"The college is planning a memorial service for Wes,"
she said. "If it would make it easier for you, we could
combine the memorial service with the funeral. That
would relieve you of the burden of making arrangements, unless, of course, you'd prefer to do it yourself.
Or perhaps you were planning to take his body back
to Alaska."

"Oh, no! He wouldn't know anyone there," Lorraine said. "I mean, no one would know him. No one would come to his funeral up there. No. It has to be here."

"If you want to have the funeral and the memorial service together," I said, "the college has a chaplain who can lead the prayers." I avoided looking at Harriet when I mentioned Pastor Getler.

"And I'm sure I can arrange to have Schoolman advance you any costs of the funeral until Wes's estate is settled," Harriet added. "Do you have a lawyer?"

Lorraine shook her head and stared at her plate, her right hand hovering over her lap.

"Our legal counsel can help you make those arrangements," Harriet said. "I don't know what he charges, but I'm sure he won't take advantage of you."

"You're both being so nice to me," Lorraine said.

"Why wouldn't we be?" Harriet asked.

"Because I have something to tell you, and I don't think you're going to like it."

Harriet sat back sharply and glanced at me, her eyebrows raised.

Lorraine stood and extracted a wrinkled letter from her pants pocket. She sat and unfolded it on the table, smoothing it out with both hands.

"Wes sent this to me a month ago," she said. "As I mentioned, we didn't correspond much, only at the holidays. So I was pretty surprised to receive it."

"What does it say?" Harriet asked.

"Would you like to read it?" Lorraine replied, handing it to Harriet.

Harriet frowned over the paper for a few minutes before tossing it back on the table. "It's totally ludicrous," she said. "He was a big mystery fan, you know. This is just his imagination working overtime.

You should tear this up. It'll just end up being embarrassing for you."

"May I?" I asked.

Lorraine passed it to me.

Harriet tapped her foot impatiently while I read Wes's letter.

Dear Rainey,

I'm writing to you because I've had an argument with— Well, let's just say a colleague here, and it put some things in perspective for me. I think my life may be in danger. I'm not telling you this to upset you. It may come to nothing in the end. But you know as well as I that a man who has power, who holds the reins over others' professional lives, can make enemies along the way. This is not a case of the usual jealousies and misunderstandings. When I looked into those eyes, I saw more than resentment, more than anger. I saw virulent hatred. It rattled me, I admit.

I've done some things in my life I'm not proud of, stepped over the line here or there, but always for a good reason. Now my motives are being called into question and threats are being made. It makes me angry, but it also makes me determined.

All of this is by way of saying that should I die soon of some supposedly natural cause, don't believe it. Investigate it. Like we used to do together. Just in case, I thought you'd like to have the enclosed. When you open my safe, don't be surprised at what's in there. You've been a good sister, and I've provided for you.

Your loving brother,
Wes

"Well, that certainly is distressing, isn't it?" I said, folding the letter and returning it to Lorraine. "You're going to look into this, I assume."

"What are you talking about, Jessica?" Harriet said, her voice rising in anger.

"I have to confess that I had some questions myself about Wes's death," I said to her, "but the autopsy hasn't been done yet. I thought I'd wait to see the report."

"Questions? What questions? You never mentioned anything to me. Why all of a sudden do you have questions?"

"I know I didn't say anything, Harriet," I said, "and I regret it. But you were so overwhelmed with responsibilities that I didn't want to add to your worries."

"That's ridiculous," Harriet said. "I can't believe you're taking that letter seriously. It's nothing but paranoia talking. I knew Wes was acting strange lately, but I didn't realize he'd gone off the deep end. How can you give this any credence? He's a college professor, for heaven's sake, not a titan of industry. Power over people's professional lives, my foot. The department head doesn't hold a lot of power. It's an administrative position. That's all. This is a tempest in a teapot."

"He was afraid for his life," Lorraine said resolutely, waving the folded letter at Harriet. "And then he died. I can't ignore that."

"Well, go ahead and make a fuss. All you'll end up doing is tarnishing the good name of the college—a college, by the way, that gave your brother an excellent opportunity to move up in his career. And not only will you make Schoolman look bad; you'll be making your brother look like a lunatic. No one with any sense is going to believe this. It's not reality. Don't you see? This is fantasy. This is mental illness."

"If he was mentally ill, why did you let him run the English department? You didn't think he was too ill for that—"

"Lorraine," I interrupted, "why don't you wait for the autopsy report before taking this to the police?"

"Police! I can't believe you're thinking of involving the police." Harriet's irritation was palpable. "The man was in a tornado. We found him under a mountain of furniture. If he'd used the brains God had given him, he would have gone to the basement and he'd be alive today."

"Harriet, I know you're upset, but you really should look at this calmly," I said. "It doesn't pay to be emotional when what's needed are facts."

"You're darn right I'm upset. This could ruin us."

"Ruin you? What about my brother? He was killed."

I placed a hand on Lorraine's arm to keep her in her seat, and said to Harriet, "I understand your concern. You're worried about the college's reputation, and that's legitimate. But stop and consider for a moment. You're a reasonable woman. In light of the letter, don't you think it's worthwhile asking some questions about his death? He was obviously afraid that someone was out to get him."

"He was hallucinating. That's what's obvious to me." Harriet turned to Lorraine. "Look, I don't want to upset you by saying unkind things about your brother, but you know he was quirky. He had an overactive imagination and was always immersed in his books. He had practically no life outside those pages, and I'll bet he was always that way, wasn't he?"

Lorraine looked warily at Harriet. "Yes, he always loved books. That's true. From the time he was a little boy. That was the way he learned things—by reading books. But that doesn't mean he couldn't tell the difference between fiction and reality."

"I'm not suggesting that, and I'm sorry if I sounded as if I were," Harriet said. "It's just that Wes didn't have a lot of friends. His life revolved around the classes he taught and the books he read. His monthly card game was the only break from his routine that I ever saw. He rarely went anywhere on vacation, at the most a weekend in Las Vegas. Most of his time off was spent writing. He was very prolific and widely published, which the college likes to see. He lived a life of the mind. It's not unusual in an academic setting, but it *is* insular. So it's not out of the realm of possibility that he began to see traits in other people that he read about in his books. A few people in the English department may be eccentric—Wes was, too— but none of them is mean or vicious. I've worked with these people for years. And Wes had very little influence over their professional lives, other than to assign which classes they taught, order books, and review curricula. When they publish their papers and books, credit automatically goes into their files. Annual reviews include his comments, but they're done by committee, so no one person has an undue influence on the outcome. Sure, if it'll make you feel better, ask around, talk to the police department, but please, I beg you, be circumspect. It's taken a long time to build up a positive reputation for Schoolman, but it will take only a few poorly worded accusations to wreck the years of exemplary service."

Lorraine nodded. "I'll be careful."

Harriet eyed the clock on the wall and rose from

her seat, picking up her teacup and saucer. "I'm sorry
to leave, especially since we haven't really resolved
anything, but I have a five-o'clock meeting with the
buildings department. Maybe we can sit down again
tomorrow and figure out what you'll need for Wes's
funeral. There's only one funeral parlor in town, and
that's Markham's. I'll have my secretary call you with
the number. In the meantime, please stay here as the
college's guest. I'll leave a book of meal coupons for
you with the cafeteria manager, if you'd like to eat
there."

Lorraine and I got to our feet and took our dishes
to the sink. "I'll clean up here," I said, gently elbowing
Harriet out of the way. "Why don't you go off to your
meeting. I'll help Lorraine settle in and then be on
my way."

Harriet dried her hands on a paper towel. Her face
was drawn and pale, a new worry clearly written on
her features. She thanked me and handed her card to
Lorraine. "Here's my number," she said. "Please call
if you need anything. I truly am sorry about Wes's
death. And the college will cooperate with you in any
way we can, both with his funeral and with anything
else that needs to be done."

"I knew I was going to be causing trouble," Lorraine said to me after Harriet had left. "Can I help
you over there?"

"No. Just sit down and keep me company," I said.
"Cleanup will take only a minute."

Lorraine dropped into a chair and sighed. "You
know, everything she said about Wes was true. He was
quirky and absorbed in his books. I always thought he
would become a novelist, not a professor."

"Why didn't he?" I asked, placing the clean cups in
the drainer next to the sink.

"He couldn't stand the rejections. When he was a kid, he said he was going to write a best-seller and make us all rich. He always had some scheme going to make money. He tried three or four times, and each book was sent back with a form letter."

"What kind of books were they?"

She snorted softly. "Mysteries mostly. But after the last one was rejected, he decided that kind of book was dumb anyway and tried nonfiction." She placed her fingers over her mouth. "Oh, I'm sorry. I didn't mean—"

"No apologies necessary," I said. "Go on. I'm interested in the sort of things he wrote."

"He loved puzzles. That's why I was surprised that he didn't stick with mysteries. Mysteries are such wonderful puzzles to solve. When we were kids, we used to hide a prize and then leave clues for each other to find, kind of like a private scavenger hunt."

"Is that what he meant in his letter when he told you to investigate like you used to do together?"

"I guess so. I'd forgotten about that." She paused before saying, "Is now a good time to say I'm an admirer of yours, Jessica Fletcher?"

"That's very kind," I said.

"I'm not being kind," she said. "It's the truth. And I'm not just buttering you up so you'll help me."

"What help are you looking for?"

"What I'm hoping is that you'll help me find Wes's killer, if there *is* a killer."

"We need to find out more before we can make that determination," I said. "Harriet mentioned that he was published widely. Obviously he didn't always receive rejections. What were his successful books?"

"Oh, I don't know all of them. I remember that the first book he sold was an analysis of the work of Daniel Defoe. All his published works are academic treatises of one kind or another."

"Do you know if he was working on a book now?"

"I don't know, but I wouldn't be surprised. It would have been great if he was writing a novel. He always dreamed of writing fiction. Maybe Harriet is right. Maybe the letter is a product of his imagination. I don't know."

"I don't know, either," I said, "but a policeman in New York once told me, 'Just because a guy is paranoid doesn't mean someone isn't after him.' "

Lorraine smiled, as I hoped she would.

"You suggested I wait till after the autopsy before I speak to the police," she said. "What do you think the autopsy will show?"

"I'm not sure," I said. "I'm hoping it will say what killed him. And I don't believe it was falling furniture."

"Can the autopsy tell you that?"

"It can say whether the blow to his head was fatal, and sometimes what the object that hit him was made of, but it may raise more questions than it answers."

"When can we get the report?"

"Tomorrow, I hope. Dr. Brad Zelinsky, the county coroner, is doing the autopsy. He was a friend of Wes's. They played cards together."

"They played cards and he remained a friend?" Lorraine said. "That's a first."

"What do you mean?"

"Wes was a real cardsharp."

"He was?"

"Another of his get-rich-quick schemes. He must have read every book in the library on how to win at cards."

"And did he win?"

"He was pretty good. That's how he earned extra money through college."

"By gambling?"

"Yup. But he didn't keep any friends, not after he took their money playing poker, bridge, canasta, gin rummy, anything he could place a bet on."

"He was in a friendly game with his colleagues. They had a limit on what they could lose."

"I'm surprised he stayed in it. He liked a high-stakes game."

I dried my hands and sat down next to her. "Would you mind letting me see his letter again?" I asked.

"Sure. You can even keep it if you want. This is only a copy. I was afraid she might tear it up."

"Harriet?"

"Yeah."

"I don't think she would have done that."

"You know her. I don't. I didn't want to take the chance."

Lorraine gave me the letter and I reread Wes's message.

"What did he enclose with his letter?" I asked. "Was it a key?"

"This," she said, drawing a chain from under her turtleneck.

"A locket?"

"It's got a picture of us inside."

"May I see?"

She opened the locket to reveal an old, cracked photograph of two little children playing with a kitten. "We must have been around eight and ten when this was taken."

"Do you think he meant it as a keepsake?" I asked.

"Wes was never a sentimental man."

"I wonder why he sent it to you."

"I don't know. I was hoping you'd help me find out."

I sat back and thought of Harriet's angry reaction to my questioning how Wes Newmark died. She was obviously not anxious for his death to be anything more than a freak accident, an act of nature aided and abetted by his poor judgment in not seeking shelter. I certainly didn't want to upset my friend. Still . . .

"I'll help any way I can," I said. "But no jumping to conclusions, no rushing to judgment. Chances are your brother died accidentally."

I looked into her open, honest face and knew I really didn't mean what I'd just said.

"Yes, Lorraine, I'll help you."

Chapter Eight

"Who can tell me who wrote the first classic who-dunit?"

I was happy to see a few hands go up. Classes had resumed at Schoolman College, and it was comforting to take up the routine again. My class had about a dozen students spread out across the room, many with laptop computers on their desks, and some with mini-cassette recorders to record my lecture, certainly a change from my college days, when students who didn't take notes were marked down for not paying attention.

"Eli?"

"Was it from the Bible, Professor Fletcher?"

"There may be some mysteries in the Bible, Eli, but the classic whodunit is a fictional genre. You need to think a bit more modern times, but not too modern, mind you."

"I know," Alice called out. She was parked in a wheelchair, her broken ankle encased in a colorful cast and propped up on the raised leg rest. A pair of wooden crutches was tied to the back of the chair with a bungee cord.

"Tell us," I said.

"Sherlock Holmes."

"No, but you're in the right century, at least. Anyone else?"

A dozen blank faces stared at me.

"I know you've read him in high school." I wrote a name on the blackboard to a chorus of groans. "Edgar Allan Poe," I said. "Now, who knows which of his stories we're talking about?"

The students shouted out titles of familiar Poe stories.

" 'The Black Cat'?"

" 'The Pit and the Pendulum'?"

" 'The Murders in the Rue Morgue'?"

"That's the one," I said. " 'The Murders in the Rue Morgue' is considered the first classic whodunit, and from this mystery classic, in which a crime is committed and then solved—those are the two elements that define the mystery—all other kinds of mysteries have descended."

"What do you mean, 'other kinds of mysteries'?" Tyler said. "How many different kinds of mysteries are there?"

"I'm glad you asked that question," I said. "Mysteries are often categorized by the different elements in the story. When you pick out a mystery, what do you look for? For instance, who is the person who investigates the crime? Is it an officer of the law? A private investigator? A medical examiner? An amateur sleuth?"

"I like the ones where a private investigator is on the case."

"Okay, Tyler. That's one kind of mystery." I wrote *private eye* on the board. "Mysteries may also be grouped by setting. What kind of atmosphere does it have? Does it take place in the city, in the country, or someplace special?"

"I like it when they go back in time and solve a mystery no one ever solved before," said Janine.

"A historical mystery," I said, adding it to the list.

The students caught on to the labeling and began calling out their guesses until we had a list of twelve, having added *cozy, gothic, horror, police procedural, spy, thriller, legal, suspense, forensic,* and *hard-boiled* to our original two.

"You can see that there are many variations on the classic whodunit," I said. "We could come up with more. There are no hard-and-fast rules. For instance, some people group female private eyes separately."

"I like it when a woman solves the crime," Alice said. "Most of the time it's men in the stories. I like to read about women."

"Women sleuths are very popular today," I said as Edgar Poole, the graduate assistant, entered the class and held up a sheaf of papers. "Thank you, Edgar," I said. "Please distribute them, if you don't mind." I'd given him a list of books and articles on mysteries to photocopy, but with the English department temporarily housed in the library, and without its usual complement of equipment, he'd had to beg a favor from another department to accommodate my request.

"While Edgar is handing out your reading list, who can tell me how to classify writers who use humor?" I asked. "Where do they fit in with the list we have on the blackboard?"

Freddie, a gruff young man with a shock of brown hair hanging in his eyes, raised his hand. "Would you make it a subcategory of what we already have? Say 'humorous cozy' or 'comic suspense'?"

"That sounds logical," I said, writing the word *humor* on the board with arrows pointing to the main categories.

"I'm writing a funny, hard-boiled, horror thriller," said Eli, tugging on his earlobe. "With lots of blood."

"Are you?" I said. "How far along are you?"

"I've got about fifty pages done."

Of all my students, I found Eli especially appealing. There was a brightness to his face and walk that was contagious, youthful enthusiasm for everything around him that was hard to ignore. I could have done without the baseball hat worn backward and the impossibly long and baggy pants that rode down on his hips, but cosmetics aside, he was a likable young man.

"Where is your book set?" I asked.

"On a college campus," he replied. "I figured I'd write what I know about."

"Good idea," I said, a vision of Wes Newmark's battered body coming and going in my mind as though someone had put up a slide, and then clicked it off my screen.

"I look forward to reading your book," I said, quickly adding, "when you've completed it and have done all the necessary rewrites."

There were a few groans at the word *rewrite*.

"All good writing is in the rewriting," I said. "And having a solid plot and outline, complete with detailed character sketches and a logical timeline, is crucial. We'll be discussing how to craft a good outline in future classes. For now, let's stick to a discussion of some of the basic elements that go into murder mysteries of all types. It used to be that readers of hard-boiled mysteries rarely picked up a gothic. Fans of cozy mysteries would never be seen reading political mysteries. But today many authors weave mysteries into their works just to fit into the genre. So you get combination genres, like mystery-romance and mystery–science fiction. Even among pure mystery writers, there may be many overlapping qualities, because the definition of a mystery is growing. In the last decade, mysteries have experienced a kind of renaissance, gaining widespread acceptance and filling most of the slots on best-seller lists, so much so that we now have bookstores that sell only mysteries, and Web sites that focus on mysteries in general, or specific mystery writers in particular. We have publishers that specialize in mystery books. Many mystery writers have become celebrities, appearing on nationally broadcast TV talk shows."

"I saw you on the *Today* show once," said Barbara, a petite brunette sitting in the front row.

"I'm flattered that you remember."

Edgar, who'd taken a seat in the back of the classroom, waved his hand. "What's your favorite kind of mystery, Professor Fletcher?"

"I like them all," I said, "but I have to admit a partiality to the amateur sleuth. I like the idea that an everyday person like you or me, without special training or unusual abilities, can be an acute observer of humanity and of daily life, and see things that others might miss. Agatha Christie's Miss Marple is a good example. Dame Christie introduced her in *The Murder at the Vicarage.* And, of course, Arthur Conan Doyle created his brilliant amateur sleuth, Sherlock Holmes, based upon a professor he once had in medical school. Miss Marple and Holmes solved mysteries by being particularly observant of things going on around them."

"What kind of things, Professor?" Tyler asked, typing on his laptop as he spoke.

"Okay," I said. "I'll give you an example. Let's take Eli. What's different about Eli since our last class?"

The students turned in their seats. Eli stood, grinning at me.

"I know," Alice said. "He got a haircut."

Eli shook his head.

Tyler hazarded a guess. "He's wearing new pants?"

"You doofus. I wore these last week," Eli said to his friend.

"You're growing a mustache, right?" Janine said.

"Nope. Thought I could get away without shaving today."

"Maria? Jake? Barbara? Freddie? Anyone have any ideas?"

Eli put his hands on his shoulders and did a slow pirouette.

"I give up," Tyler said, turning in his seat. "There's nothing different about him. He's always been nuts."

"The first order of business if you're going to solve a mystery," I said, "is that you must be observant. You have to notice the little details, so that if there's a change, you'll catch it. People in training to join a police force or the FBI take courses in how to sharpen their observational skills. It's one of the key traits used in mysteries."

"So what's different about Eli?" asked Alicia.

"You're giving up so easily?"

The students looked at Eli and back at me.

"He's wearing an earring," I said.

"So what's the big deal?" Freddie said. "I wear an earring."

"Eli's never worn one to class before," I said. "It's not a major change, but it's a change. Sometimes the smallest detail provides a clue that leads to the solving of the mystery."

"That's so cool, Professor Fletcher. I just got it done

on the weekend." Eli turned to Tyler. "Like it? It's eighteen-karat gold."

"Cool," Tyler said. "Why didn't you tell me?"

"I was waiting for you to notice, man."

"Let's say a murder took place while Eli was having his ear pierced. That would give him an alibi for the time of the murder. Maria, how would you define what an alibi is?"

"It's an excuse, isn't it?"

"That's correct. It's from the Latin word *alius,* meaning 'elsewhere.' Eli was elsewhere, having his ear pierced, at the time of our hypothetical murder. And if a person can present an alibi to the authorities, one that can be confirmed, he or she will no longer be a suspect in the crime. The investigator must look for someone else."

"How do the police decide someone is a suspect?" Maria asked.

"Following a crime, the police start their investigation by asking a lot of questions. Who knew the victim? Who might have wanted that person dead? Who was seen near the crime scene? And little by little they narrow down their list of potential suspects by focusing on those people who fill two requirements." I wrote two words on the blackboard—*motive* and *opportunity.* "There may be several people who have a motive, a reason to kill the victim. But there will be fewer who had opportunity. Where was the suspect at the time of the murder? In our hypothetical murder case, even if Eli has a motive to kill the victim, he also has a firm alibi. Therefore he is removed from the suspect list. Yes, Eli?"

"What happens if there's a death and it looks like an accident but it really isn't?"

"What are you asking?"

"Well, how do they find out it's *not* really an accident?"

"There are several ways that might happen," I said, "but let's put it to the class. What do you think would indicate that a death thought to be an accident is not an accident at all?"

"Ooh, ooh, I know," said Tyler, waving his arm.

"All right, Tyler, start us off."

"The guy is heavy in debt to the mob. That's how they get rid of deadbeats. They make it look like an accident."

"Okay. That's a possibility. If other people have died under similar circumstances, that may cause the police to look a little more closely at this victim. That's when the police recognize a *modus operandi*, or method of operation." I wrote *M.O.* on the blackboard. "Criminals often use the same M.O. from crime to crime."

"Like the Boston Strangler?" Maria said.

"How do you know about the Boston Strangler?" I asked.

"I read about it on the Internet."

"Maria is referring to a famous case," I said. "The Boston Strangler was a serial killer who always chose single women, living alone, as victims. There was never any forced entry, suggesting that either he knew his victims, or he presented a trustworthy appearance. And in each case, he molested them and then strangled them with a piece of clothing. That was his M.O."

"That's disgusting," Alice said.

"Murder is never pretty," I said. "Let's get back to Eli's question. What might trigger a police investigation into a seemingly accidental death? Barbara?"

"What if the police found a clue at the crime scene?"

"Give us an example."

"I don't know, like a button torn off a jacket. I saw that in a TV show once."

"Good. So we have a familiar M.O., and evidence at the crime scene. Anything else? Freddie, did you have something to add?"

"Yeah. What if someone tipped off the cops?"

"An informer. That's another thing the police will take into consideration. Of course, it would be helpful to know the motivation of the informant. Is this person being a good citizen, or is he trying to get someone else in trouble? Any other ideas? No? I've got one. Assuming there's an autopsy, the medical examiner may find something that's inconsistent with an accidental death. And you would want to investigate the nature of the accident itself to be sure there's nothing amiss in how it occurred. Are we answering your question, Eli?"

"Mostly. But what if the police say someone was killed accidentally, you know, like in a tornado, like Professor Newmark was. And what if the guy had some enemies. Not that I'm saying Professor Newmark had enemies or anything. But what if this guy—who wasn't Professor Newmark but was killed in a storm like him—what if he had enemies? How would you know if they had anything to do with his death? It's almost like the perfect circumstances. It looks like he was killed by a tornado. But how can you be sure his death was really an accident?"

"Yeah, Eli, you must've done it," Freddie called out. "Didn't Newmark fail you last year?"

"I'm not talking about Newmark. I'm making up a hypodermic case. Right, Professor Fletcher?"

"I think you mean hypothetical, Eli."

"See?" Eli said to Freddie.

"Sure, you were just making it up," Freddie said.

Eli fell off his chair and grabbed Tyler's sleeve. "I'm innocent, Officer, innocent, I tell you."

There was uneasy laughter around the room.

Tyler pulled away. "Cut it out, dork." He flashed a nervous look at me.

"Anyway, I have the perfect alibi," Eli said, straightening up. "I was in the tornado shelter with Professor Fletcher. Wasn't I, Professor?"

"You were, but I don't see—"

Eli didn't let me finish. "Freddie, you didn't do too great on Newmark's final either, as I remember," he said.

"Hey, don't look at me, Eli. I was right next to you in the shelter."

"No, that was me," said Tyler.

"Then it must have been Edgar," Eli said, pointing to the last row. "He hated the professor, didn't you, Ed?"

"That's not funny, Eli," Edgar said, his face bright red. "A man is dead. That's nothing to make fun of." He grabbed his papers and left the room, leaving the door agape.

"Eli, I think you owe Edgar an apology," I said.

"Aw, I was just playacting."

The other students looked away, silently fidgeting or pretending to read.

Eli looked around and, seeing no support, slipped back into his seat. "Sorry, Professor, lost my cool there a little."

"That was quite a dramatic display," I said. "Are you trying to tell us something?"

"No, ma'am. I'm sorry I disrupted the class."

But he didn't look sorry at all. In fact, he looked pleased with himself.

I cleared my throat. "Let's finish up then," I said, looking at my watch. "We were talking earlier about the two factors that define a mystery—that a crime is committed and a crime is solved. While books have been written on theft, kidnapping, arson, and extortion, the crime that both fascinates and repels us the most is murder." My words seemed to ring in the silent classroom. "For the next class, I'd like you to do a little analysis." I wrote on the blackboard, *Elements of a murder mystery*. "Using your textbook and referring to one of the books or stories on the reading list Edgar has given you, please write down what a novel must contain to meet the definition of a murder mystery."

I listened to the scratching of pencils and pens on paper, keyboard keys clicking, followed by the sound of tape recorders being turned off and laptop cases being closed.

"I'll see you next time," I said.

The class stood and shuffled toward the door. Maria hung her book bag on the handlebars of Alice's wheelchair and steered her friend out of the room. Tyler punched Eli in the arm. "You going to the gym to watch the basketball practice?" he asked.

Eli feinted and pretended to jab at Tyler's jaw. "Yeah."

"Me, too. I'll walk you there."

"Eli?"

He turned to me expectantly.

"I'd like to see you, please."

Chapter Nine

I waited until all the other students had left the classroom.

"Would you like to tell me about that little scene the class just witnessed?"

Eli shrugged.

"I'm curious to know why you raised the subject," I said, stuffing my papers into my briefcase. "It wasn't just a hypothetical case. If you have reason to believe Professor Newmark's death was anything other than an accident, I'd like to hear it."

"He wasn't the most popular guy on campus, you know."

"I *don't* know. I'm here only a short time. What makes you say that?"

"He was a strange-o if ever there was one. Looked like the typical absentminded professor, but he had a mean streak."

"Are you saying that because he gave you a failing grade?" I picked up the eraser and began cleaning off the blackboard.

"He didn't fail me, but it was a close call. Almost lost my scholarship." He levered himself up on my desk and swung his feet back and forth. "And sure did ruin my grade point average. I guess I'll never get into Harvard now. Not that I was thinking about

applying, but still." He grinned. "My buddy Edgar
Poole, now *he* might have had a legitimate chance to
get into a really good graduate program. But Newmark made sure it wouldn't happen."

"How do you know this?"

"Everyone knows. They had a big blowup. Edgar
had asked the professor to let him out of his postgradu-
ate assignment here so he could go back east. I think
he wanted to attend Princeton or some other fancy Ivy
League school. But the professor not only wouldn't let
him out of his duties; he wouldn't give him a good
recommendation, even wrote up a nasty one and
threatened to send it to the grad schools if Edgar didn't
finish out his commitment. Edgar was really pissed—
pardon my language—and they fought about it."

"And you think that was a sufficient motive for
murder?"

"I think that when you're really angry, *really* angry,
it can be a motive for murder for anybody."

"Interesting. Do you think anyone else had a motive
for murder?"

"You mean for murdering Professor Newmark?"

"Do you?"

"Well, there's the ubiquitous Bo Peep Tingwell."

"Why do you call her that?"

"He called her that once, because she was his
shadow. Everywhere Newmark went, Mrs. Tingwell
was sure to follow."

"Well, she is the department secretary, and he was
the department head. Don't you think it's appropriate
to see them together?"

"The other department secretaries don't follow
their bosses around. Besides, she had a heavy crush
on him."

"Now, Eli, how do you know this?"

"I got eyes, don't I? I could see the way she looked at him, all moony and such. Not that he gave a flying . . . uh . . . fig about her."

"No?"

"Nah. He might've liked the attention, but that's all. He was too caught up in himself to care what anyone else was feeling."

"And you think that gives her a motive for murder?"

"You know, 'Hell hath no fury like a woman scorned.' But even if it wasn't her, no matter what others tell you, Professor Fletcher, this was not a nice guy."

"There are always people in the world we don't like, or who we wish would behave in a manner we're more comfortable with. It doesn't mean someone is going to murder them."

"Sure. But they don't show up dead when anyone with a flea's brain knew a tornado was on the way. It just doesn't make sense to me. Does it make sense to you?"

"You're a very observant young man, Eli. That's admirable. But I'd like to see you be a bit more discreet as well."

"What do you mean?"

"Well, let's say someone did kill Professor Newmark—and I'm only putting this hypothetically."

"Yeah, but you're not discounting my theory. I knew you wouldn't."

"I haven't finished, Eli. If—and it's a big if—someone killed Professor Newmark, you don't want to be broadcasting your suspicions in public. First of all, you don't know who the possible killer is, and you don't want to put yourself in danger."

"Don't worry about me. I can take care of myself."

He pushed off the desk and straightened to his full height of six feet.

"Even if that were the case—and I wouldn't underestimate an opponent—you don't want to tip your hand and have the killer go into hiding or disappear. If someone thinks they've gotten away with a crime, they may get sloppy and leave evidence unguarded. But if they think someone suspects them, they're likely to behave flawlessly, and might never be caught."

"I see what you mean."

"If it turns out you have any valid reasons to bring these suspicions to the police, you must be very sure of what you're presenting. The police have no patience with speculation. And if they think you're just making up a story, they won't listen to you again, even if you later turn up something significant. You need proof of the possibility of murder before the authorities will entertain the idea. Otherwise, you'll just be told you have too active an imagination."

"I've already been told that. I guess you have been, too."

"We're not talking about me," I said, smiling.

"No. No. Of course not." He picked up his book bag, flung it over one shoulder, opened the front door of the classroom, and held it for me.

Tyler was lounging in the hall, waiting for his friend.

"Thanks for the advice, Professor," Eli said. He strolled over to Tyler and they walked down the hall to the exit.

"Eli, you got a big mouth, you know that?" I heard Tyler say.

"Yeah, I know."

And I hoped it wouldn't get either of us in trouble. What concerned me most about Eli's suspicions was that I had been thinking exactly the same thing.

Chapter Ten

The Langston Apartments in Sutherland Library had at one time been the on-campus living quarters of the college president. Only two rooms and a bathroom, they were nevertheless the most spacious, elegant, and luxurious rooms on campus, furnished with eighteenth- and nineteenth-century antiques and Persian carpets. A huge tapestry—said to be a copy of one hanging in the Cloisters, a medieval branch of the Metropolitan Museum in New York—covered one wall and almost reached to the carved crown molding that framed the coffered ceiling.

The library had maintained the space for special purposes. The college's board of trustees gathered there each spring, meeting in one room and dining in the other, additional furniture being brought in and out as required. Harriet had been reluctant to allow the English department to use the apartments as a temporary office, but since available space was at a premium, she had relented.

Vernon Foner had ensconced himself in the smaller of the two large rooms and had taken over a massive mahogany desk with three leather cartouches set into the top, each surrounded by inlaid wreaths of laurel leaves in satinwood. I wouldn't have allowed a piece of paper to touch its delicate surface, but Foner was blithely untroubled about it. In addition to several files stacked in a plastic holder, he had arrayed across the desk a stapler, a tape dispenser, a mug of pens and pencils, and a spiral-bound calendar book.

Letitia Tingwell was exiting the room as I entered, an empty cup and saucer in her hand and a frown on her brow. "He has no respect, that man," she muttered. "Resting a coffee cup on that precious furniture. I'll give him what-for when he gets back. And I'm supposed to clean up after him?" She stomped out into the hall, the china pieces rattling against each other.

Four plain teak desks and black office chairs had been brought in to accommodate the other members of the department. Mrs. Tingwell had one to herself in the large room, since she occupied it all day, and the other three were shared by the rest of the faculty, who checked in for messages during a break in classes, but usually found other places to lounge in their free time.

Rebecca McAllister was correcting a pile of student papers when I entered the room. I stopped at her desk. "Hello, Rebecca. How are you?"

"Oh, Jessica, I forgot to get you that article I told you about, the one about your coming to campus. I'll write a note to myself right now. I'm such a sieve-brain these days. Otherwise, I'm fine, thanks."

"There's no hurry," I said.

"There's just so much to do, what with teaching the extra classes. And my paper was accepted by one of the smaller literary magazines. That's good news, actually. I'm just glad someone wants to publish it. But they want me to make changes and I barely have time to breathe." She bent to a paper in front of her. "I'd better get these done, however; my evaluation is coming up," she said.

I crossed to the desk I shared with Manny Rosenfeld. "How greatly do published works really count in your favor as an academic?" I asked, sitting in the steno chair and swiveling to face her.

Rebecca looked up. "Publish or perish? Means the world. We're all expected to keep up with what's happening in modern literature, as well as demonstrate our knowledge of the classics. You can specialize, of course. Larry Durbin, our resident expert on the Bard, has a book out on Shakespeare's lessons for modern life that's getting a lot of attention."

"I'll have to look for it. Do you have a specialty?"

"Twentieth-century women's lit, mostly American," she said, taking up the next paper. "It's amazing what poor spellers these kids are. S-E-S-O-N. That's supposed to be 'season.' How did they ever make it into college? Anyway, where were we?"

"Twentieth-century women's lit," I said.

"Right! I start with the writings of the suffragettes and move forward from there. It's an interesting segment of the American literary canon, the whole women's movement." She scribbled a note on the top of a page.

"Did Wes Newmark specialize, too?" I asked.

"I'd say he focused on eighteenth- and nineteenth-century British. Not too many women there, outside of Jane Austen and the Brontë Sisters."

"Was he working on a manuscript recently?" I asked, trying to get Rebecca back to the topic.

"Probably. He always had some writing going."

"Did he ever discuss what he was working on?"

"Not with me. Probably not with anyone. Why do you ask?"

"He was carrying a briefcase full of papers the last time I saw him, and when his body was found, the briefcase was empty."

"Well, if you listen to Vernon Foner—and I don't—those papers are probably strewn all over campus by now. Ask Mrs. Tingwell. She might have a better idea."

"I'll do that," I said.

The lady in question, having gotten rid of the coffee cup, called to me from the large room. "You had two phone messages, Professor Fletcher. I left them on your desk."

"Thank you, Mrs. Tingwell."

The first call was from Dr. Zelinsky, and I returned it right away. An answering machine told me he was not available but that he could be reached later that afternoon at the same number.

The second call was from one of the dearest people in my life, Seth Hazlitt in Cabot Cove. A country doctor nearing retirement, Seth was a friend of long standing. In addition to his companionship, over the years he had offered immeasurable help to me in writing my books, advising me on medical and psychological matters, and simply being there whenever I needed a calm and thoughtful intellect brought to bear on a knotty problem. I decided to wait to call back Seth when his office hours would be over and when I would have a good hour to spend on the phone. Not that our conversations ever ran that long, but I wanted to be sure that no obligations on either side would interrupt us.

"Professor Rosenfeld left you the preliminary schedule for the memorial service," Mrs. Tingwell said from the door, interrupting my thoughts. "It's in the top drawer."

"Do you know if he's had an opportunity to speak with Professor Newmark's sister yet?" I asked, withdrawing the page and scanning its contents. "She may want to combine this with the funeral arrangements. Have you spoken to her about it?"

"No one told me to run it by her," she said, her tone frosty. "In fact, no one even introduced me to her."

"Surely you knew she was here," I said, looking up from the paper. "You were at Professor Newmark's house when she was due to arrive."

"No one saw fit to invite me to meet her. I'm good for cleaning up but not for introductions." She pulled a tissue from the cuff of her sleeve and dabbed at her nose. "Professor Foner is asked to write a eulogy. Professor Rosenfeld is asked to make the memorial service arrangements. And what am I to do? 'Mrs. Tingwell, will you straighten up Professor Newmark's house for his sister?' I certainly know my worth around here."

Rebecca looked up momentarily, then hunched over her student essays again.

"Mrs. Tingwell, I'm sure that was an inadvertent oversight. Dean Bennett has been so busy with the rebuilding efforts. She must have just assumed you would be in charge of making Lorraine Newmark welcome, as you did for me when I first came to Schoolman. And I apologize if I have offended you in any way. It never occurred to me that you would wait for a formal introduction. Please don't stand on ceremony. Lorraine Newmark is all by herself here; she's in mourning for her brother, as I'm sure you are. The two of you knew Wes Newmark the best. That's something important that you share."

"I only worked for the man."

"Yes, but for many years," I said, surprised that she would hold herself back from helping the sister of the man she'd known for so long and, rumor had it, was in love with. "Nevertheless, I hope you'll extend yourself to Lorraine."

"You really think she needs me?"

"Of course she needs you. How is she to find anything? She won't know where to go for help or information. She doesn't even know where Professor Newmark's will is. Harriet said you might be able to find it. I know she meant to ask you. It can only be that her other responsibilities distracted her."

"I know where most of his personal papers were kept."

"See? She was right. You're the person to help Lorraine."

"Maybe I'll stop by after work and see how she's doing."

"That would be very kind of you," I said.

She looked at her watch. "I could probably run over there now and see if she's free for lunch."

"Don't run anywhere, Mrs. Tingwell," Verne Foner said, rushing into the office and dropping a pile of papers on his desk. "I need you to have these copied for my afternoon class."

"That's Edgar's job," Mrs. Tingwell said, returning to her desk.

"Yes, but I don't see Ed right now. Do you?" Foner called out. "And I need these for my one-o'clock class." He turned to me. "Damned administration won't let us put a copier in here, even if we could find one. Something about it being too hard on the carpeting. Can you believe it?"

"These rugs do look to be quite old," I said.

"It's just going to stand in one place. I'm not going to roll the copier around. It's ridiculous. We've got a department to run." He went next door and dropped a folder of papers on the corner of Mrs. Tingwell's desk. "Ask the librarian downstairs to disconnect the coin operation so you can use that copier," I heard him say. "She'll do it for you. Wouldn't do it for me, the witch." He returned, threw himself in his chair, lifted the telephone receiver, and propped his feet on the edge of the desk, his expensive British-made shoes and the unusual diamond-shaped pattern of their soles staring me in the face. *How rude,* I thought, thinking of the hole in Adlai Stevenson's shoe when he appeared on TV during his presidential campaign against Dwight Eisenhower. Foner dialed a number and proceeded to carry on a loud conversation with the person on the other end.

I could see Mrs. Tingwell through the open door, her lips tight with disapproval, pick up the folder and leave the office.

Foner cupped his hand over the mouthpiece. "By the way, Rebecca, I heard that *Midwest Literature Today* accepted your paper. Congratulations! Although I thought you could do better than that. I forgot to tell you, I finished my next book. I've got a major publisher interested in it already. It's going to be on the influence of George Meredith on Robert Louis Stevenson."

"Goody for you," Rebecca said, gathering up her papers. "I'll see you later, Jessica. I need peace and quiet for this."

Foner laughed. "She's just jealous," he said, returning to his conversation. "I've got to get off," he said to the person on the other end of the line. "I have a class this afternoon. Sure, I'll let you read the manuscript. Anytime you want. Give me a call next week."

I sat at my desk, trying to ignore Vernon Foner. I jotted a note to Professor Rosenfeld about the memorial service arrangements, suggesting he ask Mrs. Tingwell to get involved, and tucked the pink message slips in my briefcase. I planned to stop for lunch in the cafeteria before trying Dr. Zelinsky again.

"Good afternoon, Mrs. Fletcher, Foner, how is everyone today?" said Professor Larry Durbin, who'd just arrived. He stood at his desk across the room from mine and shrugged out of his windbreaker as he scanned his messages.

"I'm well, thanks," I said. "And how are you?"

"Trying to get back into the swing of things," he said, hanging his jacket on the back of the chair. He walked over to the mahogany desk and swung his briefcase at Foner's ankles. "Have a little respect, Vernon. No one wants to see your six-hundred-dollar shoes up on this desk."

Foner dropped his feet to the floor. "What the hell did you do that for?" he said, leaning over and rubbing his ankle. "That hurt, Larry."

"I think you'll live, Verne," Durbin said. He cocked his head in my direction. "Putting one's feet up when a lady is in the room doesn't become our acting department chair, not to mention having so little consideration for this beautiful antique desk." Durbin said to me, "Misery acquaints a man with strange bedfellows, Mrs. Fletcher."

Foner laughed. "Larry here can drop a Shakespearean line at the drop of a hat," he said. "What's that from, Larry, *Hamlet*?"

"Actually, Verne, it's from *The Tempest,* spoken by a

court jester. Translation? Adversity sometimes causes us to have to deal with people we'd rather avoid."

Foner said nothing, but a pout had formed on his lips.

"I'm driving over to the hospital to visit Phil Adler this afternoon and I need Edgar to take over my two-thirty office hours," the corpulent Shakespeare expert said to Foner. "I don't have any appointments, but I need him here in case any of my students show up."

"Ed's supposed to help me with a class at that time," Foner said, sounding like a petulant child.

"You don't really need him, and I do," Durbin said. "This is the only time I can get over there without skipping a class. If you want my good opinion when it comes time to approve a new chairman, you'll accommodate me today."

"I'll think about it."

"Don't think about it, Verne. Just do it. I'm grabbing a bite at the caf and I'm off." He pulled his jacket from the chair and walked out of the room. I gathered my things and hurried after Durbin.

"Professor Durbin, I wonder if I might ask a favor of you," I said, catching up to him.

"You may ask me anything, Mrs. Fletcher, provided you address me as Larry. Only my students call me Professor."

"I'll be happy to call you Larry if you'll reciprocate and call me Jessica," I said, jogging to keep up with his long stride. I was glad I'd kept up my running program since coming to Indiana.

He noticed my gait and slowed down. "My pleasure, Jessica," he said. "I'm on my way to lunch. Would you like to join me?"

"Actually, I would," I said. "And I'd like to hitch a ride to the hospital, too, if I may."

"How fortunate we're both going in the same direction."

"Yes, isn't it?"

We chatted idly over lunch, exchanging histories. Durbin and his wife, Melissa, were originally from Chicago, where he'd taught at a university. They'd moved to Schoolman after their children had finished college and were off on their own. At the time, they'd been contemplating cutting back on obligations and finding a simpler life in a small town. The offer of a post on the faculty at Schoolman had fit right in with their plans.

I told him about my hometown, Cabot Cove, how I began writing for fun, and how, unbeknownst to me, my nephew sent my manuscript to a publisher, who accepted it, starting a whole new career for this former substitute teacher. I mentioned that I'd taught for a while at Manhattan University when I'd lived in New York, and that was where I'd met Harriet Schoolman Bennett.

Durbin was a popular teacher, even though his specialty, Shakespeare, was not an easy one. Several students joined us at lunch to pepper him with questions about the Bard. "I've got an examination scheduled next week," he said, laughing as two more young people sat down. "That's why I'm so popular now."

I waited till we were on our way to the hospital in New Salem to pose the questions I really wanted to ask. I started with: "Are you a close friend of Phil Adler's?"

"Used to be closer than we are now."

"What happened with Phil and his wife, if you don't mind my asking?"

He fell silent.

"If you'd rather not discuss it . . ." I said.

"Oh, no, it's not a problem. Let's see. You want to know about Kate Adler, dear Kate. When she was with him, the four of us spent considerable time together. Kate was from Chicago and knew some of the people we knew. But when she left him about a year ago, Phil became very morose. Wouldn't step foot out of the house, except to go to work, rebuffed every overture we made to get together. Eventually we stopped asking."

"I understand his wife was unhappy with life at a small college."

"My goodness, how long are you here, and you already heard that? Schoolman is such a small town, isn't it? We knew Kate wasn't happy—she was pretty vocal about it. She missed Chicago—bright lights, big city kind of thing. Still, we were kind of hurt that she left without even saying good-bye. It must have been a heckuva fight they had."

"Is that what caused the breakup?"

"According to Phil. He told me they'd been arguing all evening and he finally told her that if she hated it so much here, why didn't she leave. Which is exactly what she did. Never suggest anything you don't really want," he said with a laugh that seemed forced. "At any rate, she packed up that night and was gone by the morning. Really broke him up, poor fella."

"Did you keep up your acquaintance with her?"

"We tried. Melissa sent her a couple of notes, but they were returned with no forwarding address. I guess she really did want to shake the dust of this town off her shoes."

"That's too bad," I said, thinking that the large man behind the wheel was not comfortable discussing what had happened between the Adlers.

"How did *you* get to know Phil?" he asked as we drove through New Salem toward the hospital.

"Actually, I don't know him very well at all. We met when Harriet Bennett came to visit him the other day. I accompanied her."

"And you're visiting him again?"

"I'm not," I said. "I'm hoping to see a doctor at the hospital."

His face turned pink. "I beg your pardon, Jessica. I just assumed. It's none of my business. I didn't mean to pry into personal matters."

"Not at all," I said as he pulled into the hospital parking lot. "I've taken advantage of you under false pretenses. I don't drive, you see. I have a bicycle, but the hospital is a bit too far to pedal over to. When I heard you say you were coming here, I jumped at the possibility of a ride."

"Of course. And you're more than welcome. If you have to get to the hospital another time, I'd be happy to drive you again."

"That's very generous of you, but I'm hoping I don't need to come here too often," I said, letting him think it was a medical problem that had brought me to New Salem Hospital.

"An hour will do it for me," he said as we entered the lobby. "Does that give you enough time?"

"Sounds perfect."

We stopped at the reception desk to get passes and agreed to meet back in the lobby.

I took the elevator downstairs to the laboratory, hoping Dr. Zelinsky would be amenable to a visit rather than a phone call. He'd given me his card, but had been frankly skeptical that he would find anything to support my theory that the cause of death was not accidental. Since I hadn't given him warning that I was on my way, I was concerned that if his call wasn't about the autopsy, I would have made the trip for nothing.

As it turned out, I didn't have to worry.

Chapter Eleven

"Mrs. Fletcher, I was hoping my call had enticed you," Dr. Zelinsky said, standing as I entered his office. He reached across the desk to shake my hand. "Please, sit down."

"You've completed the autopsy, I take it."

"Did it right after you left. A number of tests I sent out won't come back for a couple of weeks, but I doubt they'll change the results." He sat back in his chair, his fingers steepled above his chest, and smiled. "I've been giving a lot of thought to our conversation."

"I'm pleased that you gave my opinion some consideration."

"I have great respect for your opinion. That's what convinced me that we could work well together."

"I'd be happy to cooperate with you in any manner I can, but I'm not certain how you think we can work together. But if my assistance will be helpful in any way, I'm happy to offer it."

He rolled forward in his chair. "Work! Work! What's not to understand about working together? It's easy. What kind of connections do you have in the publishing industry?"

"I beg your pardon?"

"Publishing. You've had many books published.

You certainly must know lots of people in the publishing industry."

"Of course, but I thought your call was about the autopsy."

"We can get to that later. I want to know what kinds of connections you would bring to the party."

"Is that what your call was about? You want to write a book?"

"I believe I may. After all, other medical examiners have had books published. There's Dr. Henry C. Lee, for instance. You know him?"

"The famous forensic scientist? Of course I've heard of him. He consults in a lot of high-profile cases. He was a witness in the O. J. Simpson trial. I believe he was called to testify on blood patterns."

"That's the man. Doesn't he have a book out?"

"Several."

"Precisely. Well, he had to start somewhere."

"And you intend to start now."

"Yes. I figured you'd be able to introduce me to some of your publishing contacts in New York. I could dictate my notes and you could clean them up for me. We might have a best-seller on our hands. Split the profits, eighty-twenty. That's a pretty good payday. What do you say?"

"The eighty would be for you, I assume, and the twenty for me."

"Well, of course. The ideas would be mine, after all. All you'd have to do is write it."

"Would this sudden interest in writing a book have to do with the postmortem on Wesley Newmark?"

He leaned back in his chair again. "You know, after years as a pathologist and especially as county coroner, you get a feeling for a case. It's not anything you can put your finger on. It's more the accumulated wisdom of a man's experience. I can just look at a body and know the cause of death."

"And the cause of death for Wesley Newmark?"

"A blow to the head, of course."

"Yes, I think we knew that."

"Of course, I thought something was fishy when I first saw the body, but I didn't want to say anything at the time."

"Really?"

"No. Can't be too careful with these kinds of things, you know. Don't want to ruffle any feathers, upset the family, not until we have this case locked up, do we?"

"Recognizing that the cause of death raises questions is not the same as solving the crime. It's just step one."

"We leave that to the cops. My job is to enhance their awareness."

"You've obviously found something that leads you to believe Wes Newmark's death was not an accident."

"You know, good science trumps a crime every time."

"I'm eager to hear what you've discovered."

"The body never lies. But it takes a careful patholo-gist to coax the information from the dead." He sounded as if he were already dictating his book.

"Dr. Zelinsky, I'm gratified that you kept an open mind to the possibility of foul play, but please tell me, what makes you think it may have occurred?"

"Carbon."

"Carbon?"

"Not where you would expect to see it."

"In the wound, you mean?"

"Yes!" He grinned. "And that's not all."

"What else?"

"Would you like to see?"

"All right."

"You don't get queasy at the sight of a dead body, do you? Wouldn't want you fainting on the morgue floor."

"I think I can control myself."

We left his office and walked down the hall to the hospital morgue, a tiny, chilly, antiseptic room. Built into the wall at waist height were four refrigerated drawers, their square ends facing out. Zelinsky turned on the overhead light and pushed a stainless-steel gurney out of the way. He grabbed latex gloves from a box on a shelf, drew them on, and unlatched one of the two drawers on the right, pulling it out only far enough to view the head and shoulders of the deceased. He folded back the white sheet and seated himself on a stool he rolled up next to the body. From his pocket, he took out a retractable pointer of the kind used by lecturers. Careful not to touch anything, he explained what the head wound revealed.

"First, notice that the angle of the lesion is not straight. The blow did not come from directly above the victim. The direction of the strike that caused this mark is from lower right to upper left. See? The skin has been pushed to the side."

That would mean whoever hit him was right-handed, I said to myself, *and whatever he was hit with was fairly narrow.* I looked around for another stool, but since there was none, I bent down to see the wound, trying not to let my head block the light. "May I play devil's advocate?" I asked.

"Be my guest."

"What if he were sitting in a chair, leaning over something? Then whatever fell on him could conceivably have provided such a glancing blow."

"Maybe, but here's the interesting part. When the ceiling fell in, a great deal of dust from the collapsing wallboard would have come with it. If the avalanche of debris coming from above had caused this wound, there should be a lot of that wallboard dust in it as well."

"And there isn't?"

"There's some, of course, but it's light and evenly distributed, as if the dust were in the air and settled on everything later."

"But the body was found beneath a file cabinet. Let's say he was sitting at an oblique angle and the cabinet fell on top of him in such a way that the corner of it hit him in the head. Wouldn't the cabinet have shielded the wound from the debris that fell in afterward?"

He looked annoyed. "Whose side are you on?"

"At the risk of being irritating, I'm on the side of the truth. I want to know what really happened."

"What about the carbon?"

"What about the carbon? You haven't told me."

He used the pointer to indicate the crack in the exposed skull. "The bone samples we took from there showed tiny particles of rust and carbon. What does that tell you?"

"It tells me that whatever made that wound is metal, either iron or steel. That supports the filing cabinet argument. But we need to see if the cabinet is rusting, and even more important, if it has any blood along its corner, although, frankly, I can't see how a loaded file cabinet would tip over on its corner anyway. Plus, if a corner hit him, the wound would be triangular, not flat on the bottom, which is what I see." My mind was racing. *I wonder if I can get into Kammerer House to examine that cabinet before the demolition starts. Do we have enough to convince the police to preserve the scene? Maybe I can bring my camera to record any evidence before it's destroyed.*

"Ahem." Dr. Zelinsky cleared his throat, impatient with my silence. "The filing cabinet doesn't account for the carbon, unless someone ran a pencil up and down the side. To my way of thinking, the carbon rules out the filing cabinet."

"Do you know the composition of the carbon?" I asked. "What it might have come from?"

He shook his head, covered up the corpse, and closed the drawer. "Those are the tests that haven't come back yet," he said unhappily.

"We're talking about the aftermath of a tornado. Isn't it possible the wind could have blown carbon into the wound?"

"Anything's possible," he said, locking up the morgue, "but I don't think so."

"Have you notified the police yet?" I asked.

"I'm planning to give Bill Parish a call this afternoon."

We walked back to his office, my mind occupied with what I'd seen and what he'd discovered.

"I thought you'd be delighted," he said. "Why such a long face?"

"I suspected Wes Newmark was murdered, but the truth of it doesn't make me happy. We have a job ahead of us to convince the authorities that what you've found is significant. Not just the police, but the college administration. And there's one thing that worries me more than all the others."

"What's that?"

"Now we know there's a killer on campus."

Chapter Twelve

The yellow police tape surrounding Kammerer House rippled in the breeze as I approached. Keep Out signs every fifteen feet discouraged the curious from trespassing. I stood in front of the damaged building and studied its facade. From this angle, I couldn't see the extent of the destruction that the tornado had wreaked. Behind the building was quite a different picture. There, an observer could see where the twister had torn down three walls of the top floor, and breached the ceiling of the one below.

In the back, it was obvious where rescuers had removed part of a wall below a window to get to Wes Newmark's body. But from the front it looked as if I could just climb the stairs to the door and walk right in. Of course, if I tried, it would be in full sight of people lingering on the quadrangle; most afternoon classes had let out.

I had been warned away once. Lieutenant Parish had let me off with only a scolding. He might not be so tolerant this time. Did I dare cross the police line again?

I walked to where the ribbon dipped low to the ground, gingerly stepped over it, and hurried up the walkway to the stairs. How embarrassing it would be if the door were locked and I had to retrace my steps.

It wasn't. The doorknob turned easily and I stepped into Kammerer House's vestibule.

It was an eerie sight to walk into the front hall, where everything was as it had always been, except for the layer of fine white dust coating the walls, the tops of the furniture, and the floor. I closed the door gently and stood still, absorbing the atmosphere of the old house. The sour smell of dust and mildew assaulted my nose. It hadn't taken long for mold to set in where the remains of the building were not protected from the elements. I could feel a chilly draft coming from the stairs leading to the now-open second floor. I looked down at my feet. I was not the first to enter this way. Several sets of footprints had trodden across the Oriental rugs, disturbing the even layer of dust.

The door to the parlor was open. I walked carefully, trying not to disturb things as I passed. I could see from the threshold the mass of rubble that had poured through a break in the ceiling, almost filling the room. The supports the firemen had put in place to hold up the wreckage while they pulled Newmark's body free were still there. I took out my digital camera and began to snap pictures. I particularly wanted a shot of the rug where the corpse had lain.

Just inside the parlor door stood a wooden desk. Fingerprints on the dusty top showed where someone had braced himself on the corner—probably a policeman or fireman—in order to peer under the debris. I photographed the prints, and contemplated my next move. There was no way around it. If I wanted those pictures of the rug, I was going to have to crawl under the debris and trust that the supports were still solid. The only other alternative was to leave by the front door, walk around to the back where the firemen had dragged Newmark out, pry off the plywood the police had used to cover the hole, and hope a patrol car or security guard didn't show up to chase me away.

I drew a kerchief from the pocket of my running suit, folded it into a triangle, and tied it across my nose like an old-time bandit to avoid breathing in the dust. I looped the camera cord around my neck, took a small flashlight from my handbag, laid it on the floor, and knelt down to plot my course. Too bad I'd forgotten a hat, or better still, a hard hat. Too late for that now. Cautiously I crawled under the heap of broken building materials that had been Newmark's tomb, being especially careful not to brush against the fragile-looking jacks that held up the closest end of the pile. I was surprised at how dark it was when my body blocked the meager light from the opening. I switched on the flashlight and sat back on my knees. Fortunately, the firemen had been taller than I am, and the space they'd cleared was high enough for me to sit up.

I raised the camera and began shooting, starting from my left and taking a new picture every few feet, automatically triggering the flash. *Here's where one of those panoramic cameras would have come in handy,* I thought. I moved on all fours toward where the body had been found, stopping to take shots of the rug. Ahead of me was the file cabinet, lying on its side atop another brace, its top drawer hanging open, the files dangerously close to spilling out. I shined the flashlight along its corner. There was no sign of rust and no hint of blood. But I had expected that. I'd just put down the flashlight and had picked up the camera for another shot when I felt a stiff breeze coming from the direction of the parlor door. *That's odd,* I thought. *I wonder if somebody just came in the front entrance.* Even though I was out of the line of sight for anyone checking under the wreckage, I'd left my handbag by the desk, a sure sign of my presence. I held very still and listened for voices or other sounds of life. Nothing. *Just let me get this picture and I'll be on my way,* I told myself. I straightened up and snapped a shot of the corner of the file cabinet, hoping the camera's auto focus was working properly.

A strange noise made me freeze. Were those footsteps upstairs? I heard a creak, and then a shower of dust rained down on me. *Nuts! Someone is up there,* I thought, brushing the dust off my jacket. *Kids never can resist a place they're forbidden to go.*

There wasn't room for me to turn around, so I began slowly backing out the way I'd come. I paused to shine the flashlight across the narrow confines once more, and a black square behind a wooden joist caught my eye. *What's that?* I started crawling forward again, the light in my hand flickering up to the square and away as I awkwardly made my way on hands and knees toward this new attraction. It was the hearth. I'd forgotten Kammerer House had a fireplace. *And if it has a fireplace, what else would it have, Jessica?*

I reached the fallen rafter, which lay on an angle across the dark cavity. I poked my flashlight over and behind it, and stretched out on the floor so I could see underneath. Lying wedged between the wood and the stone side of the fireplace was a set of three wrought-iron tools, a shovel, a broom, and a poker, all of which had been dislodged from their stand by the avalanche of debris. I pointed the flashlight along the square handles. Could one of these be the murder weapon? It was hard to see if there was any rust, but surely there would be soot, and soot was carbon.

I squinted at the poker. Two hairs caught in the rough edges of the metal three-quarters of the way up the shaft glistened in the beam from my flashlight. I maneuvered to shoot a photograph of the fireplace tools and the fallen stand behind them, but knew that what I really needed was the poker itself. Hopefully the forensic laboratory where the coroner had sent his samples could handle this item as well. He would need to send a sample of hair from the corpse for the lab to seek a match with the hairs on the poker, but that shouldn't be a problem. And a simple spray of Luminol would show whether there was blood on the iron.

I tugged the kerchief from my face and wrapped it around my hand, hoping not to add my fingerprints to whoever's might already be there. I was in an awkward position, lying on the floor, left hand over the lumber, holding the flashlight, my head wedged between the bottom of the wood and the flagstone fireplace floor, the camera under my chin, no room to reach my other hand in to grab the poker. I withdrew my hand, laid the flashlight on the floor, aiming its beam beneath the heavy timber, and wriggled backward, setting off another cascade of dust. Fearful of getting it in my eyes, I shielded my face with one hand and groped with the other, hoping the tool I touched first would be the correct one.

A groan from above triggered another rain of dust, this time with chunks of wood and wallboard. I saw the file cabinet quiver. Someone upstairs was causing the debris to move.

"Wait!" I yelled. "I'm down here."

My fist closed around one of the tools and I yanked it out from under the rafter just as the heavy timber shifted and fell on the floor with a thud. A second earlier and my hand would have been caught beneath its weight.

While my hand had escaped, the rafter had landed on my flashlight, crushing it and leaving me in the dark. But I had my poker—at least I hoped I did. I couldn't see to verify I'd gotten the right tool.

The sound of more movement mobilized me. Suddenly alert to the possibility that the upstairs maneuvering was not just a student prank, I quickly retreated, praying I wouldn't knock into one of the props that kept me from being buried alive. I would have to leave this cave rump first; there was no other choice. Near where I believed I had entered, I reached out my leg, probing with my foot to be sure I wasn't going to hit the jack. All clear. I planted my knee, slid back, and reached out with the other foot.

A hand grabbed my ankle!

"What the hell do you think you're doing? Get out of there right now," an angry male voice said.

"That's just what I'm doing," I said, "if you'll let go of me." The hand released my leg and I backed out into the darkened parlor. The afternoon sun had slipped toward the horizon; its soft light cast a golden glow over the mound of rubble. I sat back on my heels, placed the poker on the floor under the desk to keep from getting more dust on it, and looked up into the furious face of a local uniformed cop.

"I know you weren't expecting anyone to be in the house," I said, "but all your tramping around upstairs could have set off another landslide, Officer. It's a delicate balance under there."

"What are you talking about, lady? I never went upstairs."

"Someone was upstairs," I said, getting to my feet; he made no move to help me. I brushed dust off my jacket. "I heard them."

"There's nobody else in the house, lady, except you, and you're not supposed to be here. Come on. You're under arrest."

"Under arrest? That's preposterous."

"You going to give me a hard time, ma'am?"

"Look, Officer, my name is Jessica Fletcher. I teach here at Schoolman. I realize I probably shouldn't have entered the building, but I was looking for—"

He grabbed my arm and led me outside.

"This is all a mistake," I said. "Please call Lieutenant Parish. I'm sure he'll tell you that—"

"I already did," he said.

"And?"

"And—he told me to bring in anyone found trespassing in this building."

"But—"

"Are you coming peacefully with me, or do I have to cause a scene out here?"

"A scene? No, no scenes."

The small radio pinned to the shoulder of his uniform sounded.

"Jenkins here," he said into it. "Right. Says her name is . . ." He looked at me.

"Fletcher. Jessica Fletcher," I said. "Is that Lieutenant Parish? If it is, I wish to speak with him."

Officer Jenkins removed the radio from his shoulder and held it up to my mouth, his thumb activating the TALK button.

"Lieutenant Parish, this is Jessica Fletcher. I know your officer is doing his job, but there's no need to arrest me. I have a perfectly logical explanation."

"Mrs. Fletcher, I don't care if you're the queen of England. You've broken the law and that means you're under arrest. I'm sure you have an explanation for it, but you can tell it to the judge. Over and out!"

Chapter Thirteen

"Really, Jessica. The last time I had to bail anyone out of jail was when some wags in the senior class hauled Professor Constantine's MG up onto the roof of the Student Union. You can imagine how long ago that was. It's been at least five years since Archie stopped driving, and his last vehicle was a far cry from a sports car."

"Schoolman must have an unusually well-behaved student body," I said.

Harriet and I walked out of the New Salem County Courthouse, where I had spent the last several hours waiting to see the judge. The night was clear and cold enough to prickle the inside of your nose. I still wore the running suit I'd had on earlier, dusty from my prohibited exploration, and not warm enough to shield me from the chilly night air. I looked up at the sky, at the millions of stars, and shivered. I was grateful that Harriet had dropped everything to come to my rescue. Nevertheless, at that moment I wished myself back in Cabot Cove, in my cozy home, warmed by familiar surroundings, with my cherished friends about me. Oh, dear, Seth would be wondering why I hadn't returned his call, and I briefly debated whether or not to give him the full account. He was always sympathetic, but prone to worrying, too.

"I tried to explain to Lieutenant Parish why I'd trespassed," I said, "but he was not in the mood to listen."

"He was just doing his job," Harriet said curtly, her pique evident in her tone.

"Yes, I suppose he was."

Parish had given me the silent treatment from the moment Officer Jenkins delivered me to the town jail, and hours later on the way to the courthouse.

"You're lucky I'm even bringing you here," he told me as he escorted me up the stairs. "I could have left you in jail overnight and been perfectly justified."

"Yes, you could have," I said. "I'm grateful you didn't."

He grunted. "It's only because Judge Coffman's court is open late tonight."

"I wish you'd let me explain," I said. "There's a logical justification for why I was in Kammerer House. Once you understand, I'm sure you'll agree—"

"If you're talking about Brad Zelinsky," he interrupted, "and his harebrained idea that someone murdered Wesley Newmark, I don't want to hear it."

"But there's good reason—"

"Stop right now." He pointed to a bench outside Courtroom B and I sat on it. "I don't know who's more addled," he said, "Brad for wanting to write a book about being 'a brilliant coroner standing in the way of crime,' or you for encouraging him."

Zelinsky's having brought up his book idea when he'd called in the autopsy results to Parish wasn't very prudent. It took away the impact of his report, and cast his findings in a questionable light. It had evidently led Parish to suspect Zelinsky of cooking up a possible murder because it would make for a juicy chapter in his book.

While waiting to come before the judge, I'd considered telling Parish about Lorraine Newmark and the letter she'd received from her brother, but decided to save it for another time, when the news might be received with more interest. A closed mind is not the place to present new evidence.

Frustrated at Parish's refusal to even entertain the possibility of a crime, I was relieved I hadn't shown Officer Jenkins the poker, nor mentioned it to Parish. Until it was tested, there was no proof it was the murder weapon. I'd managed to nudge it farther under the desk with my foot before being taken from Kammerer House. If someone came into the parlor, it would hopefully remain out of sight. The problem was, I realized, that retrieving it would require a return trip, and I was in enough trouble already for trespassing.

"Judge Coffman was willing to release me on my own recognizance," I said to Harriet as we crossed the courthouse parking lot, "but his hands were tied because I didn't have any identification. That's when they let me call you."

"What happened to your wallet?"

"One of the officers at the New Salem jail confiscated my handbag, and forgot to return it when we left. Lieutenant Parish was so annoyed with me, he refused to go back and get it."

"You have it now."

"Another officer kindly brought it to me." I climbed into Harriet's car. "But it wasn't until after you'd already left to come here."

I was thankful the New Salem County judge had

been more patient and understanding than Lieutenant Bill Parish. He also turned out to be a mystery buff. After I'd furnished my identification, offered a slightly skewed explanation for having crossed the police line, called attention to the fact that I'd neither gotten hurt nor harmed the premises, and promised to send him some signed books, Judge Coffman dismissed the charges against me. Since I was the only accused appearing before him that night, he took the occasion to give me a long, convoluted description of the sort of cases he handled day after day, mostly speeding, shoplifting, malicious mischief, and the occasional grand theft auto. He was bored, he told me, and longed for a case that would challenge him, one he'd need to pull out his law books for, one that might even catch the attention of the television court channel. "Know anybody at Court TV?" he asked.

"Ah, yes, I do, but not well."

"Put in a good word for me, will you? Maybe they'd like to do a series on small-town justice."

"I'll see what I can do," I said, thanked him for his courtesies, and left the courtroom.

"I'm sorry to have pulled you away from campus and made you come out here," I said to Harriet, pulling on my seat belt.

"Your adventures here are ending up more interesting than the finance committee's analysis of the cost of repairs." She didn't sound as though she meant it.

"But not nearly as important," I said. "How is it going?"

"Needler has come through," Harriet said, shaking her head. "He's picked up contributions from the Alumni Association, and has pledges from at least two foundations we've been trying to get grants from for years."

"That's wonderful, Harriet."

"Yes, it is. But something about the man still makes me uneasy. Ever since the tornado he's been different, jumpy, more reclusive than ever. I've been watching him closely, and he knows it."

"The two of you may have created a vicious cycle. You think he's paranoid and keep an eye on him. He sees you watching him and becomes paranoid."

Harriet laughed. "You're probably right," she said, driving away from the courthouse and back toward Schoolman.

A black-and-white cruiser pulled out of the lot behind us, and I realized Lieutenant Parish would not have abandoned me at the courthouse if Harriet had failed to arrive. It was a comforting thought. He was not a fan of mine right now, but at least he'd stuck around to make sure that someone drove me home. Perhaps if he had enough time to get over his annoyance at my ignoring the yellow tape and his Keep Out signs, he might unwind enough to listen to my theories. I'd always prefer to assist authorities in their investigations than end up conducting my own.

Someone had struck Newmark on the head. I was convinced of that now. But I couldn't prove it yet, not till an examination of the poker confirmed my suspicions. If it didn't, the case would undoubtedly be closed—"Cause of Death: Accidental." Aside from not wanting to see that happen, I was also beginning to wonder why everyone seemed so anxious to see it end up that way, particularly Lieutenant Bill Parish and Harriet. I understood her motivation, to avoid any hint of scandal at a time when the college was in the process of getting back on its financial feet. But even then, surely covering up a murder couldn't be justified.

If forensic examination showed the poker to be the

murder weapon, I'd have strong evidence to bring to the police. In the meantime, the question to be answered was, *Why* did someone want Newmark dead? If I could figure *that* out, I might be able to come up with *who* it might be.

"I've really got no reason to complain," Harriet said.

"I beg your pardon?" I'd been tuning her out.

"As I said, repairs are going a lot faster than I anticipated. We've already paid for new windows in the Hart Building, and called in an electrical expert to revamp the entire warning system. I even had an arborist examine the oak trees in the quadrangle. You know, those trees are well over a hundred years old."

"They're very beautiful."

"Replacing the three buildings we've lost is the biggest nut, but demolition is now under way on the bursar's office, same with Milton Hall, and we expect to start on Kammerer House next week."

"So soon?"

"Yes."

"Harriet, what if the police want to start a murder investigation? You'll be destroying the scene of the crime and any evidence that remains there."

"The police are not going to start a murder investigation." Her jaw was set, her voice cold and matter-of-fact.

"How do you know that?"

"Bill Parish assured me," she said, sounding confident and pleased. "I know about your suspicions and that you've been poking around Kammerer House. But, Jessica, Wes's death was an accident. I know that, and the police do, too. You write about murders and you've been involved with investigations in the past, so it's only natural that when someone dies in unusual circumstances, you immediately suspect murder."

"Harriet, please don't patronize me. I'm not as single-minded as that, nor so foolish."

"We're a quiet little country college with our share of eccentrics, certainly, but not murderers," she continued as if I'd never spoken.

"I know you want to believe that, but it doesn't make it so."

"We'll get past this terrible tragedy and learn from it. Schoolman is building a reputation as a first-class educational institution, and this will simply be a sad footnote in our history."

"And if I said I could prove it wasn't an accident? Would that convince you to hold up on the demolition of Kammerer House?"

"No."

"No?"

"I'm sorry, Jessica, but we've got to move beyond this."

"Harriet, a man is dead, and even though you won't entertain the idea, you may have a killer on campus. Surely you can see the danger there. Wouldn't it be wiser to do everything in your power to ensure the police have what they need to identify and apprehend this person?"

"I've never gotten in the way of the police. Why do you think I called Bill Parish? I asked him when it would be all right to start on the demolition, and he said, 'Start whenever you like.'"

"I'm going to bring him Newmark's letter to his sister. Surely when he sees that, he'll decide to hold off a bit."

Harriet looked at me and smiled. "Jessica, I've already given it to him."

"When did you do that? I thought we were waiting for the results of the autopsy."

"I went back to Lorraine that same evening, following my meeting. She said the letter was a copy and I could have it. I turned it over to Bill. He agreed with me that Wes was prone to imagining things, that his death was a terrible tragedy but not a crime."

"How would Lieutenant Parish know that about Wes?"

"Because I told him so. It's over, Jessica. Let it go. Wes's death was an accident."

Chapter Fourteen

"Sounds like a murder to me. It's a cryin' shame you have the police against you."

"They're not really against me, Seth. It's just that they're not exactly for me, either."

Seth Hazlitt had listened patiently to my tale and, as he usually did, took my side in the controversy. I looked at my watch. My class was due to start in ten minutes. I'd called him on my cell phone from my empty classroom, after spending a busy morning helping Manny Rosenfeld and Letitia Tingwell make arrangements for the memorial service. This was the first free time I'd found.

"I looked at the photos I took, and they're disappointing," I said. "I got a good shot of the footprint, but the bloodstain looks like dirt. There's something about the footprint that bothers me, but I can't tell you why. And the picture of the filing cabinet is all washed out. The flash was too close."

"Well, hang on to them anyway. You never know if one might come in handy someday."

"The real problem is retrieving the poker—I left it under the desk in Kammerer House. And what do I do with it once I have it?"

"What do you mean?"

"Well, it has to go to a forensic laboratory for exam-

ination. But I can't ask the local police to send it
in. They've already rejected the idea that any crime
took place."

"What about the coroner? Will he do it?"

"I already called him. Apparently Parish came down
hard on Dr. Zelinsky for even suggesting the possibility of murder, and he backed off. He said he doesn't
want to be embarrassed in front of his colleagues. He
told me that if I can get the proof myself, he'll back
me up, but meanwhile he's out of the picture."

"Can you go over their heads?"

"You mean straight to the state police? I somehow
doubt they'd entertain a murder charge if the local
police aren't involved. No. It has to go somewhere
outside of Indiana, somewhere where the results won't
be challenged."

"Mort ought to be able to help you there," Seth
said, referring to our Cabot Cove sheriff. "He's still
got lots of connections in New York City. And he's
already curious about what's taking place at the college. Matter of fact, he rang me up this morning wanting to know what mess you're in now."

"How could he have heard what's happening here?"

"He heard, all right. Seems the police department
in New Salem called him last night, wanting to know
if you had a criminal record."

"Oh, heavens, they didn't."

"Ayuh. They did. You didn't turn up on their na-
tional database, but they thought you might be a
local crook."

"How embarrassing."

"Coulda been a lot worse. It's lucky Mort was the
one to take the call. It would've been all over town
this morning if Phyllis Goad had picked up."

"What's Phyllis doing at the sheriff's office?"

"Temping while Marie's on vacation."

Phyllis Goad had been Charlene Sassi's assistant for years. Charlene owns the bakery in Cabot Cove, featuring the best baked goods and hottest gossip in town.

"That makes it even worse," I said, pacing back and forth in front of the blackboard. "My reputation is teetering on the edge here. Harriet thinks I'm obsessed, and Lieutenant Parish thinks I'm a lawbreaker. If he finds me in Kammerer House again, I won't have a prayer of talking my way out of it. But if I don't get that poker soon, it'll be too late to test it to see if it's the murder weapon. They're planning to start demolition next week."

"Now, don't be going into a pink stink," he said, Maine-speak for what might be considered a blue funk elsewhere in the country. "There'll be some opportunity come along. It always does."

"I hope you're right. Between the letter to Wes's sister, and the angle and nature of the fatal wound, there's every reason to look into his death. And there's also the little detail that it doesn't make sense that a man, recognizing the signs of an impending tornado, wouldn't take pains to protect himself, unless, of course, he couldn't. And another thing I keep coming back to: What happened to his papers? They're missing. He was hugging that fat briefcase so tight when I saw him, whatever it contained must have been very important to him."

"I don't know about that, Jess. Maybe it was just his students' papers. A man wouldn't want to lose those in a storm either."

"You're right, of course. But where did they go? There were no papers under the rubble inside Kammerer House. They couldn't have *all* blown away. If they did, why would there still have been pencils and other items in the bottom of the briefcase? The wind would have taken them, too. And the overturned file cabinet. A drawer is open, but the files are still there."

"That's a puzzlement, I agree."

We continued to chew over the mysteries surrounding Wes Newmark's death in silence, both of us deep in thought. Finally, sounds in the hall jarred me from my reverie. I recognized Tyler's voice saying, "Hey, man, what're you doing?"

"Seth, my class is due to start soon. I'd better hang up now. Thanks for letting me sound off."

"Anytime, you know that. Just be careful, Jess. You're not on home seas there."

"I will."

"And I'll tell Mort he should expect a call from you."

I smiled. "You do that." I pressed the off button and slipped the phone into my purse as the first students entered the classroom.

"Why were you hanging around out there in the hall?" Tyler asked Eli as they took seats together in the back of the room.

"Shh, man," Eli said in a low voice. "I wasn't hanging around. I was waiting for you. You borrowed my tape recorder. Did you bring it back?"

Had Eli overheard any part of my conversation with Seth? Had anyone else? I didn't have time to worry about it. The classroom filled, and the eager faces of my students transported me away from disturbing thoughts for the next hour and a half.

"I was hoping I'd see you again."

"I'm sorry," I said. "Yesterday was a difficult day."

"Letitia came by in the afternoon. She said she'd seen you at lunchtime, but not later on."

"Is she here?"

"Not right now, but I expect her soon. Don't you want to come in?"

"Yes, thanks."

I'd been standing at the front door to La Salle House, trying to decide how I was going to tell Lorraine that the police had dismissed the letter she'd brought with her from Alaska, and that there would be no investigation of her brother's death. She'd opened the door before I even knocked.

"I'm just making myself some tea," she said. "Would you like a cup?"

"Yes. I could use one."

We settled at the kitchen table with two mugs of tea and a plate of cookies one of the faculty wives had delivered.

"Everyone has been so kind," Lorraine said. "I already have a freezerful of casseroles. Even President Needler paid me a condolence call yesterday."

"That was nice of him."

"I thought so, too. He was very complimentary about Wes. He said the board of trustees was considering naming the new English department building after Wes once it's built."

"That would be a lovely tribute to him."

"He wanted to know if he could have the photo of Wes he'd seen once in the study. The college newspaper needed it, he said. I gave it to him. I was planning on taking that home with me. I hope he'll return it. Do you think he will?"

"I would have thought the college would have a photograph on file. And the student newspaper, too, for that matter."

"I guess they don't, if he asked for that one. Anyway, he didn't stay long. He took his books and left."

"What books were those?"

"The books Wes had borrowed."

"He told you Wes had borrowed books from him?"

"Yes. It took him quite a while to find them, too. He went over the shelves pretty carefully, but eventually found them all."

"Do you remember which books they were?"

"Why? Is something wrong? Shouldn't I have let him take the books? They were his, after all. He said he only lent them to Wes."

"Don't fret about it. I just find his timing odd, that's all."

"I think he was afraid I'd pack everything up and ship it off before he could get his books back."

"That must be it."

"I'm sorry, I don't remember the titles. I didn't want them anyway. They were junky books, so dusty and old, the bindings were starting to go. I don't know why he was so anxious to get them back."

"I wonder," I said, sipping my tea, which had gotten cold. "I understand you gave the letter to Harriet," I said.

"Yes. She came back that night and asked for a copy, said she wanted to take it to the police herself. So I gave it to her. That was all right, wasn't it?"

"Of course."

"I know you said you wanted to wait for the autopsy, but I thought the sooner the cops had it, the better. They could start looking into it."

"I'm afraid that's not going to happen," I said, "at least not right away."

"Why not? Wes's letter says he thinks his life is in danger. Isn't that something to investigate?"

"I think so, but Harriet doesn't."

"She didn't give it to the police, did she?"

"Oh, no. She wouldn't lie to you. She gave it to the police as she said she would. But Lieutenant Parish is an old friend of her family's, and he has a great deal of respect for Harriet's opinion. She managed to convince him that Wes was unbalanced when he wrote it, and that it would be futile to investigate what was so obviously a tragic accident."

"And he believed her?"

"He did."

"Maybe if you talked to him . . ." She looked at me hopefully.

"I already have. And so did the coroner. Unfortunately, he didn't believe either of us."

"The coroner? Did he do the autopsy? What did it say?"

"That Wes died from a blow to the head. We knew that already. There are some suspicious findings but nothing definitive." I didn't want to go into details, which would cause her pain. And unless I could get Lieutenant Parish to change his mind, the specific information from the autopsy would only distress her.

"Well, that's it then, isn't it?" she said glumly.

"Maybe, but I'm not sure. Do you have another copy of the letter with you?"

"I have the original."

"Then I have a big favor to ask."

"You want it?"

"I'd like to keep it for a few days if you don't mind."

"I don't mind. You're my only hope for justice for Wes. He said not to accept an accidental death, that it wouldn't be what it appeared to be. 'Investigate it,' he said. I feel like I'm letting him down. I should have listened to you. I never should have given her the copy."

"You did what you thought was best, and no one can fault you for that."

She pushed back her chair. "Let me get the letter for you."

"I'll take good care of it. I promise."

"I know you will," she said. "I trust you."

She went upstairs to the bedroom. A minute later she returned and handed me the letter, her hand trembling.

"I'll photocopy it as soon as I can and return it."

We sat in silence as I reread the letter.

"We found Wes's safe," she said. "It's behind a painting, hanging in the study."

I looked up. Finally some good news. I folded the letter and put it in the zipper pocket of my handbag.

"What was in it?" I asked.

"We haven't been able to open it yet. It's locked, of course, and we couldn't find the combination. We went through every drawer in his desk, and checked every folder in his file cabinet."

"You and Mrs. Tingwell?"

"Yes. Letitia came to introduce herself yesterday. She was very helpful."

"She's a nice lady. Did you show her the letter?"

"No. I figured that until the police made it public, I wouldn't say anything. I didn't want to upset her. She said she and Wes were close friends."

"That was considerate of you."

"She's helping with the memorial service, too."

"I'm happy to hear it."

"The two of us searched for Wes's will yesterday, but we couldn't find it. I think it's probably in the safe. But the combination . . ."

"It wasn't with the letter he sent you?"

"No, just the locket. And before you ask, yes, I looked on the back of the photo, just in case he had written it there."

I smiled. "I see you're a mystery fan, too."

"It was the kind of thing he'd do when we were kids. But there's nothing on or under the photo, or on the other side of the locket. I even examined it under a magnifying glass to see if he'd scratched it on the case."

"Is there a duplicate of the photo somewhere in the house?" I asked.

"I didn't think of that. There's another picture in the study."

We carried our mugs to the study and set them atop a magazine on the desk. The room was small but charming, in a masculine way, with walls painted a deep rust color, a maple desk in front of the window, and a navy plaid love seat against the wall. A laptop computer sat open on the desk. Above the love seat were three oil paintings the college had obviously supplied, and a small shelf on which Wes had placed a glass figure of a cat, a plaster bust of Mark Twain, and a framed photograph of Lorraine posing next to a stuffed polar bear.

"I sent him that one the first year I moved to Juneau," she said, taking down the photo and smiling at the memory. "Alaska was so exotic to me. It was like going to a foreign country. I loved it from the start."

"Do you still feel that way?"

"It's all familiar to me now—the polar bears, the dogsled races, the long winter—but I still love it. Should I check behind this?"

"Can't hurt," I said, and watched her slide off the back of the frame.

"Nothing here," Lorraine said. "I hope the combination wasn't on the back of the photo President Needler took."

"Me, too. Is this the only photo in the house?"

"I haven't seen any others. Wes wasn't a sentimental guy. He'd be more likely to shove pictures in a box than display them. I sent this one of me to him already framed. He probably got the other one that way, too."

"Well, that ends that theory."

"So what do we do next?"

Opposite the love seat were two ladder-back chairs and a wall of bookshelves from floor to ceiling, chockablock with books—upright, stacked, and sideways on top of the standing ones, shoved in wherever space would permit. There were five gaps where Lowell Needler had pulled out books. What Wes hadn't been able to wedge in the shelves, he'd piled on the end of the desk, on a table next to the love seat, and on a little wicker trunk that served as a coffee table.

I picked up a copy of *Kidnapped,* flipped through the pages, and put it back on the stack of books on the desk. "If he tucked the combination into one of his books," I said, "it'll take us a year to find it."

"Letitia and I already checked all the books on the tables," Lorraine said. "No dice."

"Did you check the ones in the living room?"

"I did, but there's nothing there, except Wes had the wrong dustcover on one of the books."

I perused some of the titles on the shelves, *A Child's Garden of Verse, A Tale of Two Cities, The Ordeal of Richard Feverel, The Stories of O. Henry,* books I hadn't read since I was in school. On two shelves were books by Wesley S. Newmark, *Swinburne and the Ros-*

ettis, Poetry of the Pre-Raphaelite Brotherhood, Jane Austen and the Comedy of Manners, Onstage: Voltaire and Congreve, Mark Twain Abroad.

In a section of twentieth-century mysteries, I saw one of my own, *Murder in Spades,* among the eminent names of the genre. I pulled it down and felt a secret pleasure when I discovered the spine was broken, indicating he'd read it.

"It makes sense to me that if he were to hide the combination, it would be somewhere in this room."

"I agree," she said, "but short of shaking out every book on the shelf, I don't know where else to look."

It may come to that, I thought. I asked, "Could I see your locket?"

She undid the clasp. "Here you go," she said, dropping the locket and chain in my palm. She threw herself onto the love seat and lifted her legs onto the little trunk. "If you can find something there, I take my hat off to you."

"You're not wearing a hat," I said, laughing as I sank down next to her.

She laughed, too. "You'd enjoy Alaska, Jessica. Alaskans love to laugh. In the long dark of winter, it helps to have a sense of humor."

"Tell me about this picture," I said. "When was it shot?"

"Golly, I'm not sure." She leaned over to squint at the tiny photo in the locket. "I think we were about eight and ten. That looks like we were at our grandfather's farm. He had cats in the barn. We would adopt one as a pet whenever we went to visit."

"You didn't have a pet at home?"

"No. My father was allergic. Cats made him sneeze. Wes used to say he did it on purpose."

"Wes wanted a cat?"

"Very much so, but it turned out he was allergic, too."

"I noticed that little glass cat on the shelf. He must still have been fond of them."

"Probably. But the only time he had one was when we went to Papa's farm. I remember that little guy now. He was a real cute one, always nuzzling Wes and me."

"What was his name?"

"Aces."

"Aces?"

"Yeah. Wes named him. I told you he loved cards."

"Maybe that's it," I said, jumping up. I pulled my book from the shelf and riffled through the pages, looking for writing or a slip of paper. I shook it upside down, took off the dustcover. Nothing. I put the book back and scanned the shelves for another possibility.

"What are you doing?"

"Looking for another book having to do with cards. The cat's name was Aces. Wes was a big poker player. You said he loved puzzles, all kinds of puzzles. This book I wrote has 'spades' in the title. I thought it was unlikely, but it was worth a shot."

Lorraine got up and joined me perusing titles. There were several books with "hearts" in the title, two with "diamonds," and none with "clubs." We also looked for books with "king," "queen," "jack," "knave," and "joker" in the title.

Half an hour later, Lorraine collapsed on the love seat again. "It was a good idea," she said.

"It's still a good idea," I replied. "Where did he keep packs of cards?"

"I don't know, but there's got to be a deck somewhere." She went around to the back of the desk and pulled open the top drawer on the right. I joined her and opened the drawer on the left. We checked every drawer and every file folder, but found no playing cards.

"I know I've seen them," I said. "I just can't remember where."

"In a closet?"

"No. If he were a passionate player, he'd keep a deck handy, somewhere convenient."

"Like where?"

"The kitchen!" I said. "There was a deck of cards in the kitchen drawer."

We went to the kitchen. Tucked on the side of the silverware drawer were three packages of playing cards, two of them unopened. I took the open pack, sat at the kitchen table, and slid out the cards. "You look at the box. I'll check the cards."

While Lorraine examined the box, checking both flaps and inside in search of writing, I turned over the cards, looking for aces. The first one I found was the ace of spades. There was no writing on the card. I held it up to the light. Turned it over. Nothing.

Lorraine tossed aside the box and took the card from me. "Oh, what a shame," she said, her shoulders slumped. "I was sure you were right."

"So was I," I said, spreading the deck on the table and sifting through it for the other aces. "Don't give up yet. There are three more to go."

Lorraine leaned over the cards, watching intently as I went through the deck, one card at a time. "Look! The ace of hearts. Jessica. Jessica. You did it. There's a number in the center of the heart." She burst into tears.

The number on the ace of hearts was written in a red pen on the red heart, something easily missed by a casual observer. There were also numbers on the ace of clubs and the ace of diamonds, written in ink the color of the suit.

Lorraine whooped, pumped both fists in the air, then pulled out a tissue and blew her nose. She grinned, the tears still streaking down her cheeks. I picked up the three cards and we returned to the study, where Lorraine removed her shoes and climbed on the love seat to reach the center painting. She grabbed one side and swung it open to reveal a silver wall safe. As I read aloud the three numbers, she twirled the dial on the combination lock, turning the knob all the way to the right, back around to the left, and again to the right. It took us four tries, rearranging the order of the numbers, until we came up with the correct combination. The safe door popped open.

"I'm as jumpy as a moose on thin ice," she said, laughing as she lifted a large, heavy green metal box from the safe. A narrow manila envelope was attached to the box with a rubber band. "I can't believe he's got another locked box here. He'll drive me crazy."

We sat on the love seat again. Lorraine placed the box on the wicker trunk and opened the envelope, dumping its contents on her lap. Out fell a tiny silver key and another envelope on which was written, *Last will and testament of Wesley Stanton Newmark*. The key easily fit in the lock of the green box, and Lorraine turned it gently.

"I'm almost afraid of what I'll find," she said, her hand resting on the top of the box.

"Come on," I said. "Let's see what it is."

"What if it's empty?"

"You'll never know till you open it."

Lorraine lifted the lid, let it drop back, and gasped. Inside was a narrow notebook, and beneath it, packed tightly across the bottom of the box, were stacks of one-hundred-dollar bills.

Chapter Fifteen

"What does it come to?"

"Forty-seven thousand, eight hundred dollars." Lorraine wrapped a rubber band around the last bundle. "I guess my brother didn't believe in banks."

"He did sometimes," I said, lifting my head from the file I'd been examining while Lorraine counted the cash. "The bank statements you gave me paint a pretty normal picture. His salary check was deposited directly into his account. Checks were written for all his expenses. He has about twenty-five hundred dollars in checking, four thousand in savings, and an annuity the college contributes to."

"You don't think he robbed a bank, do you?"

"Does that sound like your brother?"

"No. It must be from cards, although I can't believe he won this much playing poker."

"He might have been good enough to win," I said, "but it's doubtful the men he was playing with would be willing to lose that much money. It wasn't a high-stakes game. One of his colleagues in the English department said they played for fifty cents and a dollar. The most anyone was allowed to lose in a night was thirty. After that, they made him leave the table. Plus, they played only once a month."

"At that rate, it would take him a century to amass this much."

"At least."

"What about the notebook that was in the box? Were you able to figure it out?"

"It has notations in it about amounts," I said, "but it's all in code, abbreviations and initials."

"Maybe he had another business on the side."

"It looks that way. And he must not have wanted the government to know about the money, because he didn't put it in the bank."

"He wasn't declaring it on his taxes?"

"Probably not."

"Then I won't get to keep all of this." She looked wistfully at the piles of cash she'd laid out on the desk.

"If he didn't declare it as income, you'll have to pay the tax on it," I said. "You should talk with an accountant and a lawyer. Estate taxes are tricky."

"Jessica?"

"Hmmm?"

"Do you think he was doing something illegal, I mean apart from not declaring the income?"

"I don't know, Lorraine."

"But you're thinking it might be a possibility."

"I have to admit that using a code the way he did would seem to suggest that. He didn't want anyone who came across this book to know what his notations meant. For instance, on this date, it says, 'F dash MS dash one dash twenty M.' And later, it says, 'F dash MS dash two dash ten M.' "

"What do you think it means?"

"Possibly that he collected from someone two times. The Ms have a little line through them, which could be an abbreviation for thousand, twenty thousand, and ten thousand. Here's another. It says, 'N dash fifteen M dash FE.' "

"Who do you think MS or FE are?"

"No one I can think of has those initials. If you don't mind, I'd like to take this with me, too. I'll photocopy it at the same time I copy the letter, and return them both to you tomorrow. Okay?"

"If you can make any sense of that book, you're welcome to it," Lorraine said. "I'd better put this cash away before I get tempted to spend it." She repacked the money in the green box, locked it with the silver key, put the box back in the safe, and twirled the dial. "I'm going to put this key on the locket chain where I can't lose it," she said, climbing down from the love seat and reaching around her neck to undo the clasp. "And I'm going to put those aces back in the deck."

"Good idea," I said. "You'll always remember where they are."

I added the slim notebook to the zipper pocket in my bag, where I'd placed Wes's letter, and looked at my watch. "I'll go to the library right now and use the copy machine."

"You don't have to be in such a hurry."

"I'll feel better once they're back in your possession. Besides, I can study a copy just as easily as the original."

The route from La Salle House, where Wes Newmark had lived, to Sutherland Library took me past the three buildings destroyed by the tornado. The bursar's office had been completely razed, and the demolition of Milton Hall was under way. The yellow tape surrounding both those properties, as well as around Kammerer House, had been replaced in areas where it had started to stretch. It no longer fluttered along the ground, but had been pulled taut, and additional

Keep Out signs had been added. I felt as if the new signs were pointed at me, and Lieutenant Parish probably intended them that way. In addition, he had assigned a patrol car to check on the buildings every so often. As I walked by, I glimpsed a black-and-white cruiser parked on the street behind the former English department office. My heart sped up. That poker inside under the desk was the key to this case. It had to be tested. Maybe I could convince the coroner to call the lieutenant again. Failing that, I could try to talk to the construction foreman and have him retrieve it for me before they began taking down the building. There had to be a way to get it out without my crossing the police barrier.

I hurried past Kammerer House and trotted up the steps to the library door, which opened at my approach.

"Hi, Professor Fletcher. Here to check out a murder mystery? I just did." Eli Hemminger displayed a copy of one of my books as he held the library door open for me.

"That's very nice that you want to read one of my books," I said, stepping inside. "It must mean you've already read the one assigned for class."

Eli followed me inside. "Aw, Professor, I can read more than one book at a time. Can't you? I'll bet you always have three or four going."

I laughed. "And you'd be right," I said. I took the staircase on the left, thinking I'd stop by the English office to see if I had any messages. Eli climbed along with me. "Weren't you just on your way out, Eli?"

"I was, but I have time. I'll walk you to your office. I've never seen the Langston Apartments."

"They're beautiful," I said.

Mrs. Tingwell was locking up when we came to the

door. "Oh, did you want to go in, Mrs. Fletcher? I thought I'd close up early and see if Lorraine New-mark wanted to join me for dinner tonight."

"I'm sure she'll be grateful for your company, Mrs. Tingwell. I can come back tomorrow. Any messages can wait till morning."

"No, no. I won't hear of it." She leaned her tote bag against the wall, unlocked the door, swung it open, placed the iron doorstop in front of it, and switched on the overhead lights. "Here's the key," she said. "Just leave it with the librarian. I'll pick it up tomorrow. Eli, you'll show Mrs. Fletcher where the librarian's office is, please?"

"Yes, ma'am."

"Eli, go ahead in. I need to speak with Mrs. Tingwell for a moment."

I drew the department secretary into the hall. "This is important or I wouldn't hold you up," I said. "I hope you don't mind my asking something about Wes Newmark."

Her body stiffened, but she replied, "Go ahead."

Perhaps she expected a personal question, because she seemed surprised when I asked, "Do you know if Wes Newmark was working on a book before he died?"

"Why do you ask?"

"When I met him outside the Hart Building before Saturday's storm, his briefcase was bulging with something, but when his briefcase was found later, it was empty. I just wondered what papers he might have been carrying."

"I can't tell you that, but I can tell you he usually had some writing project going. What that might have been, I have no idea. For as long as I knew him, he was very secretive about his work. He would take the manuscript with him wherever he went, and the computer disk, too. He didn't want to risk anyone seeing what he'd written before it was published. I always wondered why, but he never told me. It was just one of his quirks."

"So he could have been carrying a manuscript."

"Yes, he certainly could have. But if the tornado blew the pages away, we'll never know. All his work, like his life, gone in a moment. It's such a waste."

I could see that she was struggling to maintain her composure.

"Is that all you wanted to know?" she asked.

"Yes, thank you. I know it's painful for you to talk about him."

"I'll be on my way then." She picked up her tote bag and walked swiftly down the hall.

"These are pretty fancy digs," Eli said as I walked through the main office to the smaller room. "I like that rug on the wall."

"It's a copy of a medieval tapestry, the story of the unicorn," I called back to him as I picked up papers from the in-box on the desk I shared with Manny Rosenfeld.

Eli followed me into the room and whistled. "Who gets to sit here?" he asked, walking around the antique desk and letting his fingers run along the carved edge.

"Professor Foner is using it now," I said.

"Ugh! That phony."

"That's not nice, Eli."

"Sorry if I offend you, Professor Fletcher, but I don't have enough bad things to say about the guy. I could fill three books with what an arrogant you-know-what he is."

"You didn't like Professor Newmark either. I take it you've had Professor Foner as an instructor as well?"

"Once was enough. He thinks so much of himself, he'll only talk to those students he considers brilliant. All the rest of us are 'merely intelligent,' he once told me, not good enough to earn his attention."

"How unfortunate, if that's the case."

"The guy thinks he's so sharp, wearing suits every day now even when everyone else is casual."

I laughed. "Eli, I can't believe you'd dislike someone because of the way he dresses."

He had the good grace to look embarrassed, but not for long. "The clothes are just a symbol," he said. "But he sets himself up as a superior being, and then he can't even remember what he writes in his own books. I actually read one of them and asked him about a passage. He says to me, 'I never wrote that.' I had to go get the book out of the library again and show it to him. He made up some excuse, like his mind is always so busy that he forgets things he did years ago."

"That can easily happen," I said. "When you've written a lot of books, it's not unusual to forget what you said in one. It's happened to me."

"Yeah? When?"

"Once, at an author luncheon. I started talking about a character I'd created, but had ended up discarding in a later draft. You can't always count on a writer to remember everything he's written."

"Well, he was arguing in class against his own philosophy in his book."

"Eli, I think you'll find as you grow older that people change over the years, and their opinions change as well. You're going to think very differently when you're thirty years old than you think now."

"Maybe so. But I don't think I'll take one position, and turn around and take another a year later."

"That's not something to hold against him."

"Oh, that's just one thing. I've got plenty. He's lazy, makes Edgar Poole do all his dirty work. You know what he said to Tyler once?"

"Eli, I appreciate that you feel passionately about Professor Foner, but I don't think this conversation is appropriate. We're talking about a colleague of mine, and he's not here to defend himself."

Eli snorted, and tossed his library book in the air, catching it between his hands and twirling it around. "Okay, let's change the subject."

"That's a good idea," I said, riffling through the papers from my in-box. Mrs. Tingwell had taken a message for me from Harriet. Would I stop by her office? Rebecca McAllister had cut out the article in the student paper that announced my coming to campus and left it for me. I scanned it quickly and folded it, intending to put it in my bag, but a photo on the back of the page stopped me. It was cut off on the side, but there was no mistaking that the face was Wes Newmark's. Why would President Needler have told Lorraine the student paper needed a photograph of her brother when it obviously already had one?

Eli was pacing in front of the antique desk and bouncing the book up in the air like a ball.

"Are you going to the memorial service for Professor Newmark?" I asked.

"Do I have a choice? Everyone on campus is expected to go."

"Who told you that?"

"My dorm adviser. He said Dean Bennett wants a big turnout to impress the prof's sister. That's what I heard. Besides, there's liable to be some press there. Local press anyway. I hope no one throws stones at the coffin."

"Eli!"

"Just kidding, Professor Fletcher. No offense. I'm going to the service. Alice sings with the campus choir. She'd kill me if I didn't show up."

"I think it's time to lock up," I said, putting the rest of the papers back on the desk. "I've got to go make some copies downstairs."

"Professor Fletcher, can I ask you something?"

"That depends. Is it going to be about any of the faculty? If so, I'd prefer you keep the question to yourself."

"Nuts! Well, if that's the way you feel, okay."

"Thank you."

I shut off the lights and locked the door behind us. Eli guided me to the librarian's desk, where I left the key for Mrs. Tingwell with the student on duty.

"Is the copy machine available downstairs?" I asked her.

"Oh, I'm sorry, Professor Fletcher. Mrs. St. Clair is running off a new emergency booklet, and the copier is reserved for the rest of the afternoon and evening. If you'd like to leave what you need copied, I can have it ready for you tomorrow morning."

"Thank you, but I may need to work on it tonight," I said. "I'll come back in the morning."

"Didn't want to leave your stuff with her, did you?" Eli said as we exited the library.

"That's a personal question, Eli."

"Sorry. I'll stop bugging you now. See you later, Professor Fletcher. I've got a paper due for this class I'm taking on writing murder mysteries."

He winked and loped off across the quad, leaving me to wonder what our encounter had really been about.

Chapter Sixteen

My timing was perfect when I walked into Harriet's office; at least it was for her.

"Oh, Jessica, thank goodness. If you hadn't come, I would have had to cancel my meeting with the student government council."

I smiled. "I have a feeling I'm about to be shanghaied again."

"You are, and I hope you won't mind."

She asked me if I would go to Phil Adler's house to wait for a representative from the Visiting Nurse Association. The service was sending someone over to do a "needs assessment" to see how the house could be altered to accommodate the injured man once he was discharged from the hospital.

"It won't be longer than an hour," Harriet said. "I promise. The lady is supposed to arrive at four-thirty. She can let herself out, if you need to leave before she's finished. The house is just off the west campus, not a long walk, but I can get one of the students to drive you over if you'd prefer."

"I have my bicycle," I said. "I just need the keys and directions how to get there."

Phil Adler's house was on a tree-lined street several blocks from the faculty housing where I had an apartment. The white Cape Cod was on a large lot, flanked by a brick-fronted colonial on one side and a Tudor with cream-colored stucco on the other. I wondered which of the two belonged to Larry Durbin and his wife.

Adler had been away less than a week, but there was an air of neglect about the place. The grass, which was turning brown, hadn't been cut for a while. The paint on the door and around the window trim was flaking. A detached garage sat at the end of the driveway, its doors sagging on the hinges.

Inside, I leaned down to pick up the bills, letters, and magazines that had been pushed through the mail slot, automatically sorted them by size and type, and set them on the stairs on my way into the living room. The drapes were tightly closed and the furniture was dusty. I turned on a few lamps, pulled back the drapery, and opened a window to get the musty smell out of the room. I had the impression Adler hadn't been in this room since his wife had left. A fashion magazine, dated a year ago, sat on a table next to the mushroom-colored corduroy sofa. I nudged the magazine with my finger, exposing a portion of the wood where the dust hadn't fallen.

The small dining room was similarly unused, and contained only a cloth-covered table on which sat an empty laundry basket.

I retrieved the mail and went to the kitchen, where I placed it on the round table under the window. The room ran the width of the back of the house, and one side was a family room with a big-screen television on a wheeled cart, and a door to the back porch. Adler probably spent all his time at home in this room, the only one with signs of life. A shirt was draped over the back of a chair. Stacks of magazines, newspapers, and opened mail covered the coffee table in front of a green-and-brown couch against the wall. An empty beer bottle sat on the floor.

Mold had started growing in a coffee cup left in the sink. I washed it out and left the cup upside down in the dish drainer, grateful Phil hadn't left a sinkful of dirty dishes. On the counter next to the refrigerator was a combination telephone–answering machine. The blinking light indicated three calls. Reasoning that Harriet might try to call me here, or that the VNA lady would leave word if she was going to be late, I pressed the messages button. The first call raised goose bumps on my arms. I recognized the voice. It belonged to Wesley Newmark.

"Still have your wife's voice on the machine, Phil? How sweet. You think you're fooling everyone, but you didn't fool me. I'll be at your office at the appointed time. Be there. And make sure you have what we talked about."

The message clearly indicated they had talked before, yet Adler denied knowing what Newmark had wanted to see him about. When I'd questioned him in the hospital, Adler had theorized that Newmark was late keeping the appointment because he couldn't find whatever it was he wanted to show the bursar. But this call sounded like it was *Adler* who was bringing something to the meeting. Before I could contemplate the possibilities, the second message began. This was a voice I didn't know.

"Katy, it's Linda. I can't believe how long it's been since we've spoken. Can you still be so angry? I'm sorry if something I said offended you. I can't even remember now what we argued about. Do you? Katy, we have to resolve this. Think of Mom and Dad. How disappointed they would be. I love you. I don't want to go the rest of my life without talking to you. Please,

please call me back. And Phil, if you get this message first, don't you dare erase it. Let Katy make up her own mind.''

It seemed her husband was not the only one the volatile Kate Adler fought with. She'd been estranged from her sister, and obviously hadn't told her parents about the state of affairs. But if she'd moved back with them in Chicago, it was strange that they didn't know by now. It was also peculiar that Adler had kept his wife's outgoing message on his answering machine. They'd been separated for a year. Larry Durbin had said Phil took her departure hard. *He must still be mooning over her,* I thought.

The third call was from Melissa Durbin, next door. "Phil? Larry told me about your accident. If you can use any help when you get back home, please don't hesitate to call me. I can pick up whatever you need when I do my own grocery shopping. I know you don't like to ask any favors, but I promise you, it'll be no trouble at all. That's what neighbors are for. You know the number.''

I leaned over the telephone, trying to find where the answering machine tape was located. I'd never seen this model before and hoped it wasn't a digital one in which the recording couldn't be removed. I slid my fingernail in a seam on the side of the phone and lifted a small panel, revealing two tiny cassettes, one for the outgoing announcement, the other for incoming messages. If I moved quickly, I could get the tape copied and reinsert it in the machine before Phil was discharged.

Hoping that Linda might have written to Kate in addition to calling, I went to the round table, flipped through the mail I'd left there, and checked the open envelopes on the table in front of the fireplace. There was no personal correspondence of any kind. The visiting nurse was due momentarily, and I felt time getting away from me. Quickly I opened every drawer in the kitchen, starting with the one near the telephone. Surely there had to be a personal address book somewhere. I didn't find one, but what I did discover was the instruction booklet for the telephone, and with it, an extra miniature tape. As I pocketed the tape from the machine as well as the spare, there was a loud knock at the door. I closed the panel on the phone and greeted the nurse.

Marvella Washington was a big-boned woman in a white uniform, a starched cap bobby-pinned to her black curls, who wasted not a moment on small talk and got directly down to business.

"You're going to need help getting him up those stairs," she said, pointing to the two steps leading up to the front door, and making a note on her clipboard.

"Yes, I see that."

"He'll probably be released with crutches, but it would be better if he has a wheelchair to get around."

"Are there places nearby to rent one?" I asked.

"There's one in New Salem. The hospital will direct you."

She pulled out a tape measure and measured the width of the hall, the door to the kitchen, and the front and back doors, while I trailed after her.

"Might have to move some of the furniture around temporarily," she said, pushing a kitchen chair aside. In the dining room, she paused. "No chairs. That's good."

"Actually, I won't be the one taking care of him," I said. "I think Harriet Bennett was the one who called you."

"Doesn't matter to me. I just do the assessment.

The social work department is responsible for the rest." She eyed the stairs to the second floor. "He won't be going up there for a while. You'll need a bed on this floor. Don't let him use the couch. Bad for his back. Order up one of those hospital beds. It's a little difficult to get into, but he'll sleep much better."

"Will you leave a copy of your suggestions?"

"I'll send you a full report. You just have to tell me where."

I gave her Harriet's name and address and she gave me her business card.

"I need to finish my measurements, and if you don't mind, I'll move some furniture so it'll be out of his way."

"I don't mind at all. Will you need my help?"

"No. You'll only get in my way. Why don't you go upstairs and bring down some clothing for him. We can lay it out on the dining room table so he can get to it easily."

"I'll be happy to do that," I said. She had given me the perfect excuse to look around upstairs. It was what I'd been intending to do when she left, but now I could snoop without guilt.

"Use the laundry basket or you'll be making a million trips. Don't pick anything fancy. We may have to cut one leg off his pants to get the cast through."

I collected the laundry basket from the dining room and started up the stairs.

"And don't forget to bring down his shaver and toothbrush," she called after me.

The large master bedroom was simple and neat. A white chenille bedspread was bunched at the end of the bed; a gold blanket had been straightened but not folded back. The pillows had been flattened, Phil's attempt at a made bed. In one corner of the room was a pile of pillows on the floor, which had probably been in that spot since Kate walked out.

The heavy oak dresser with the oval mirror had eight drawers, four on each side. I opened the top one on the right. It contained a profusion of colorful bras and panties, matching sets on one side, unmatched pieces on the other, together with tights and folded panty hose, and balled socks in white and colors. Had Kate left without packing? Had Phil refused to send her clothing? Why, a year later, did he still keep her lingerie in the dresser drawer?

The three remaining drawers on the right were empty, but all the ones on the left were bulging with Phil's clothes, underwear, sweaters, shirts, and T-shirts stuffed in. Why wouldn't he use the empty drawers?

I looked in the closets. One was empty except for some belts that had fallen to the floor. A wire hanger dangled from the bar. The other was tightly packed with his suits, jackets, slacks, robe, heavy sweaters, and jeans. Belts and ties hung from the door.

My mind churning, I laid out a selection of clothes on the bed and went to the bathroom in the hall to gather up toilet articles. It was no surprise to see two toothbrushes in the holder, but it was startling to open the medicine cabinet and face two bare shelves. Perhaps his obsession with her convinced him she would return at any moment, and he wanted to be sure she would know that he had expected her to come back, even leaving her drawers empty so she could replace her belongings where they had originally been.

I carried the laundry basket out of the room and left it on the landing. The second floor contained two small bedrooms in addition to the master bedroom. One was set up as a home office, with a tall file cabinet and an ugly metal desk that looked as if it had been salvaged from a garbage heap. Someone had painted it orange, but dents and scratches showed its original color had been gray. I tiptoed into the office and slid open the top drawer. Under a slew of papers, I found a small address book written in a female hand. I tucked it in my pocket with the tapes, and returned to the hall.

The second bedroom was used for storage. Old furniture—chairs, a bureau, nightstands—was lined up against the walls in no particular arrangement. On the far wall I could see a half door that led to what I assumed was crawl space. I pressed the door back, peeked inside, then ducked into the low room, which was littered with piles of open boxes overflowing with papers, books, handbags, shoes, crockery, linens, and photographs. *It looks as if they'd never finished unpacking,* I told myself. In addition, a rolled-up rug, a lady's dressing table with a cracked mirror, several pieces of luggage, and old stereo equipment had been shoved in willy-nilly. A pair of high heels lay against the dressing table, as if they'd been flung in there and left where they landed.

"What's taking you so long? The man is only going to wear a sweat suit for the next couple of weeks."

"I'm coming now," I called back. I closed the door to the storage room and carried the laundry basket downstairs. Together we laid Phil's clothing along the perimeter of the dining room table within easy reach of a man in a wheelchair. After the nurse left, I locked up and biked back to my apartment. The first order of business was to duplicate the tape and return the original to the answering machine. The second would be to scan the address book and, if my luck held, to find a phone number for Kate's sister. Perhaps she could help answer some questions that were starting to bother me. Why had Kate left so much behind? Why take her outerwear and leave her underwear? Why empty her closet but abandon her shoes and handbags? Had she wanted to start afresh, with no reminders of her life with Phil? Had she planned to send for her belongings, but found her new living quarters too small to accommodate them? And had Phil returned Linda's call to let her know that the marriage had broken up, and that her sister was no longer living at Schoolman?

I hate unanswered questions. And the more I looked into Wes Newmark's death, the more they were piling up.

Chapter Seventeen

"What on earth are you doing here at this time of night?"

"Shhh. Someone will hear."

"Are you in trouble?"

"Not yet! But I will be if you don't let me in."

"This can't wait till tomorrow?"

"No, ma'am. I gotta see you tonight. It's important."

"Well, then you'd best come in." I stepped back from the open door to my apartment.

Eli loped in, his book bag slung across his shoulders, a florist's box under his arm, and a sheepish grin on his face.

Fortunately, I hadn't dressed for bed yet. I didn't fancy the idea of entertaining a student in the faculty quarters at ten o'clock at night in my pajamas.

"You've got a nice place here," Eli said, turning in a circle and nodding his approval of the furnishings. "Way cool."

"You didn't come to admire my apartment, Eli. Why are you here?"

"I brought you this," Eli said, sobering at my tone. He handed me the long white box, and wiped his palms on the sides of his jeans.

I carried the box to the oak table in the corner that

doubled as my desk when I wasn't taking meals at it, and closed the lid on my laptop computer. I'd been reviewing the photographs I'd taken inside Kammerer House, and I didn't want Eli to see them. "This box is a little heavy for roses," I said.

"Yeah. I think you're going to like it, though."

He hung back while I lifted the lid and parted the green tissue paper inside. There, covered in clear plastic and nestled in bubble wrap, was the fireplace poker from Kammerer House.

"I didn't get any fingerprints on it," he said. "Just like the TV shows, I used rubber gloves. I only touched it long enough to put it in the box."

I frowned at him. "You eavesdropped on my telephone call, didn't you?"

"I couldn't help it. You were talking loud, and I was right outside the door."

"I was not talking loudly, and why didn't you come into the classroom?"

"I didn't want to interrupt you."

"Who else was there with you?"

"No one, I swear. As soon as everyone else started coming in for class, I made a lot of noise in the hall so you'd hear me and know."

"This is terrible," I said. "You never should have done it."

"I thought you'd be thrilled. This is an important piece of evidence, isn't it? Now we can prove that Professor Newmark was murdered."

"Don't 'we' me, young man. This doesn't concern you. And furthermore, how could you think I'd be thrilled when you had to cross a police line to get this?"

"I didn't."

"A patrol car has been sitting there all day. You

could have been arrested. I would not have been
thrilled with that."

"But I wasn't—arrested."

"You broke the law, and I feel responsible."

"I didn't."

"What do you mean, you didn't?"

"I didn't cross any lines. That's the best part."

"How could you get into Kammerer House without
going past the yellow tape?"

"There's another way in."

"How?"

"From the basement."

"The basement?"

"It's connected to the library."

"A tunnel!"

"Yeah. From the library basement."

Of course, I thought. Professor Constantine had said
there were tunnels connecting the bomb shelters, and
that he had a map of them. Why hadn't I thought of
that? Where were the other tunnels? What buildings
did they connect?

"Want me to show you the tunnel?"

"Not tonight." I drew the paper back over the
poker and replaced the lid on the box. Eli had packed
it very well, and the box might only need wrapping in
heavy paper to get it ready for shipping. "I'll call Zelinsky tomorrow," I said, thinking aloud.

"Anything I can help with?"

"No."

"There's a mailbox place in New Salem. I can borrow Tyler's brother's car. I'll be very discreet. I won't
tell them what we need it for."

"No. I'm not letting you get more involved in this."

"Look. You wouldn't have the poker if I didn't get
it. Tomorrow I'll show you where the tunnel is. See

how helpful I can be? I'll be the perfect assistant. I'll do whatever you tell me. I won't question anything you ask me to do. I won't say a word to anyone. Please don't shake your head no. There's got to be some way I can help."

"There isn't," I said. "Wait a minute. Yes, there is something you can do."

Eli's eyes lit up with excitement. "Anything. You won't regret it. I'm a great investigator. I'll be Dr. Watson to your Sherlock Holmes."

"Do you have your tape recorder with you, Dr. Watson?" I asked. "The one you use in class?"

"Sure, but what do you need that for?"

"I need to copy a tape. Or rather, I need you to copy a tape for me. Can you do it?"

"Well, sure, but copying a tape is nothing. What do you need it for?"

"You said you'd never question what I ask you to do. Are you reneging already?"

"No! I'll copy a million tapes for you. I won't ask why. Only trouble is I don't have a second recorder with me."

"You can use mine if you have the wire that connects them."

"Yeah, a patch cord. I have that."

"You do?"

"Yeah. The recorder came with it. Earphones and a remote control, too.

I picked up the florist's box with the poker and put it on the floor in a corner, where I wouldn't trip on it, and went to find my recorder and the tapes I'd taken from Phil Adler's house. Eli shrugged off his backpack and emptied half its contents onto the table before pulling out his minicassette recorder and a patch cord.

"One is blank," I said, slipping a tape into my recorder. "Let's make sure you copy the right one." I pressed the rewind button, and then play after the tape was back to the beginning. I kept the volume low and held the recorder to my ear so Eli wouldn't hear Wes Newmark's voice. "This is it," I said, rewinding the tape.

He put the blank tape in his recorder and used the patch cord to connect the two. Moments later I had my copy.

"Okay, what else?" he asked.

"Nothing else. You're leaving now."

"I am?"

"You are. You've been very helpful and you've given me a lot to think about. Now I want you safely back in the dorm. Call me when you get there. Understand?"

"Yes, ma'am. So I guess now that you have the poker and I helped you with the tapes and all, you're not mad at me anymore, right?"

"Wrong! I appreciate that you were trying to help, Eli, but I'm still upset with you. More than that, I'm worried about you. What you did tonight is not the way to investigate a crime."

"A good investigator has to be courageous if he's going to be successful. You said that in class."

"I also said a good investigator always weighs whether the risk is worth the reward. You didn't do that. Instead you took on a tremendous responsibility and didn't even think about the risks."

"What risks? I walked through a tunnel, climbed some stairs, snatched the poker, and ran out again."

"If the unstable mound of debris in Kammerer House had shifted or collapsed, you could have been hurt, or worse. Did you think of that?"

"No, ma'am."

"If the police officer outside had decided to make the inside of Kammerer House part of his patrol, you could have been caught, arrested, and jailed. Did you think about that? What would happen to your scholarship if you were charged with a crime?"

"I don't know."

"Well, I do. You would have lost it, that's what would've happened. And worst of all, if you were followed or seen by the murderer, your life could be in danger. Can you be sure you weren't?"

He didn't answer.

"Think of your parents, your family, your friends, Eli, how devastated they would be if anything happened to you. You can't just act without thinking. You have to know what you're getting into, and you have to consider your responsibility to others. So yes, Eli, I'm still angry at you for taking those chances."

"I'm sorry, Professor Fletcher. I didn't realize."

"I know you didn't. That's what scares me. We're not playing a game, Eli. If the one who killed Wes Newmark is still on campus, he'll go to great lengths to make sure he's not found out."

"Or she."

"This is no time for wisecracking. Don't tell anyone what you did or where you went tonight. Does Tyler know?"

"No, I came right here."

"That's good. Don't tell him under any circumstances. I don't want to scare you—well, maybe I do, a little. If you're not concerned for yourself, keep in mind that you could put in jeopardy the lives of everyone you tell."

I watched as Eli walked out into the night. *Young people have no concept of danger,* I thought. It was ironic. I had chided him for doing in effect what I had done myself. But I had been truthful in telling him that the risks must be weighed. A decision to act made with full knowledge and understanding of the consequences could be justified. But he had dashed into the water without gauging the potential depth. It was a perilous move. Now we would see if he'd created any waves.

Chapter Eighteen

"Did you get a sample of the deceased's hair?" asked Mort Metzger, the sheriff in my hometown of Cabot Cove and a former New York City policeman.

"The coroner said he'll send it separately, along with his autopsy findings to date. A few test results haven't come back yet."

"Are you sure he'll do it, Mrs. F.? Is this Dr. Zelinsky a trustworthy guy?"

"I think so, Mort. I talked to him before I called you. He sounded embarrassed. I think he's sorry that he backed down when Lieutenant Parish dismissed the idea of Newmark's death being a murder. He'd like to show the lieutenant that the coroner's office was correct in its findings, but he's afraid to stick his neck out without the proof. If we can confirm that there's a residue on the shaft that matches Newmark's blood and hair, then we can make a good case that the poker was what killed him. And I think I can persuade Zelinsky to ask for a further analysis of the carbon in the wound to see if it will match the carbon on the poker."

"You'll want the lab to look for fingerprints, too."

Mort had provided me with the name and address of one of the country's foremost forensic laboratories, where I was to send the fireplace poker. He had personally placed a call to the laboratory director, and had authorized the use of his name and his position to get past the strict requirements regarding who was allowed to utilize the lab's services.

"I'm not sure we'll find fingerprints even if the poker proves to be the murder weapon," I said. "I'm concerned that it's been contaminated by so much handling."

"How so, Mrs. F.?"

"When I pulled it out, I used my kerchief. Then it lay under the desk, so I'm sure it picked up some of the fibers from the carpet. At least the hair that was caught on the shaft is still on it. But there may be smudges where the original fingerprints were, assuming the killer didn't wipe them off, because Eli used rubber gloves when he retrieved the poker."

"No kidding. You've got a smart student there. Think he might be interested in going into law enforcement? Tell him to give me a call, if he is. I know a lot of departments that'd like to have a smart one like him on the force."

"He's smart, all right, Mort. After he got the poker, he put it in a plastic bag and sealed it. But I'm not going to praise him just yet. He took a big chance, and I'd never forgive myself if anything happened to him."

"Well, he got the evidence, so send off that box and the experts will take it from there. Even if there's only a partial print, the lab will pick it up. Did you give them all the information you've told me?"

"Yes. I typed up a report and placed it in the box, along with your name and address as a reference. I'm going to ship it later today."

"I expect they'll send both of us copies, but I'll call you when I get mine, just to be sure."

"That's a great load off my mind, Mort. I can't thank you enough."

"We help each other. Always have. Always will. I'm looking forward to sharing a pot of coffee and hearing all the details when you get back."

"Me, too," I said, adding to myself, *I hope the police will realize they have a murder on their hands before then.*

It had started to drizzle when I rode my bike over to Phil Adler's house to replace the tape in his answering machine and the address book in his desk upstairs. I had paged through the book following Eli's nighttime visit, and found two entries that could have been Kate's sister, a Linda under the Ws, and a Linda and Ken under the Bs. No last name was given. After I'd called Mort, I'd tried the Linda W. first and got a recording stating that the number had been disconnected. I hung up and dialed the number for Linda and Ken B. A man answered. His wife was out shopping. Yes, she had a sister Kate, who'd been married to a Philip Adler, and who'd lived in Indiana. But no, they hadn't heard from her. It was sad, really. The two of them hadn't spoken since their parents passed on, something about who got which piece of jewelry. I left my telephone number and asked that his wife call at her convenience.

I pedaled around to the back of Phil's house and pulled the bike up onto the rear porch and out of the weather. It was raining in earnest now. The second key on Phil's key ring fit the kitchen door, and I let myself in. The house looked even gloomier than I'd remembered it.

I put my bag on the counter, rummaged around

inside until I found the minicassette tape with the three messages on it, and went to the telephone. The panel that concealed the tapes was open, revealing the gap where I'd removed the message tape. I replaced the missing cassette, pressed down the panel, and studied the phone. I hadn't left that panel open the last time I was in the house. I was sure I'd closed it.

Not bothering to turn on any lights, I left the kitchen, went down the hall, and trotted upstairs to the little office. I replaced the address book where I'd found it in the orange desk and returned downstairs. There were several envelopes scattered on the rug in the foyer beneath the mail slot. I gathered them up and scanned the return addresses as I walked back into the kitchen.

"Find anything interesting?" said a large figure silhouetted against the open porch door.

I must have jumped a mile. "Larry? Oh, my gracious, you gave me a turn," I said.

"I didn't mean to startle you, Jessica," Larry Durbin said, coming into the room. "Melissa said she saw someone breaking into Phil's back door, and I came over to investigate."

"Well, I'd hardly call it breaking in when I used the key," I said, realizing that I'd foolishly left it in the lock. "You can see it's right there in the door."

"You don't say? I thought you barely knew Phil. How did you get his keys?"

"Harriet Schoolman Bennett gave them to me. She had an appointment she couldn't get out of. She asked me to meet the lady from the Visiting Nurse Association, and help get the house ready for Phil's return." It was only a slight distortion of the truth, since the nurse had already been and gone, but Durbin didn't need to know that. "Do you know when he's coming home?" I asked, adding the day's mail to the pile on the kitchen table.

"I haven't heard," he said.

He was making me uncomfortable. He hadn't moved from the door, and I couldn't see the expression on his face in the dim light.

"There's a light switch to your left," he said, as if divining my unease.

I found it and flipped it up. The glare of the fluorescent fixture cast a harsh light on the dull cabinets and countertop, reinforcing the impression of neglect that permeated the whole house.

"Not exactly *House Beautiful*, is it, Jessica?"

"Not unusual for a man living alone. Many men don't pay much attention to housekeeping."

I could see his face now and relaxed under his wistful gaze. He was dressed in a baggy gray sweatshirt and matching pants; the fabric, strained to accommodate his heavy build, was stretched at the knees and elbows, and had smears of tan paint on it where he'd wiped his fingers. He was a big man but looked more soft than muscular. He moved into the kitchen, pulled out a chair, sat down, and began idly looking through the mail.

"When Kate was still . . ." He hesitated. "When Kate was here, she kept this place just so. She was a very neat, pretty little thing. Loved to dress up. Rings on every finger. She had beautiful clothes. I used to tease her that she came out to the country so she could put on her finery and go dance with the cows." He smiled.

"What kind of marriage did they have?" I asked, taking the chair opposite him.

He scratched the back of his head, further mussing red hair that looked as if he hadn't combed it in a while. "You mean when they weren't fighting?"

"Yes."

" 'If ladies be but young and fair, they have the gift to know it.' "

"*As You Like It,*" I said.

"Aha, the lady knows her Shakespeare. Kate was like many pretty young women: narcissistic as hell. She was a fish out of water here at Schoolman, needed the excitement of the city to bring her alive. She was wasted here. Phil could never see that. He thought if he was happy in the country, she should be happy in the country, too. Stupid ass. He never appreciated her." He chuckled. "Identify this: 'The hind that would be mated with the lion must die of love.' "

I shrugged.

"*All's Well that Ends Well.* If you aim beyond your boundaries in love, you'd better be prepared to suffer for it. Phil suffered plenty."

"What does she look like?"

"Kate? Little, delicate . . . like, I don't know, like a . . . like a little pixie with long blond hair. She used to come crying to me. I would say she cried on my shoulder, but she only came up to here." He put a hand at midchest.

"Why would she be crying?"

"She was begging me to talk to Phil, to convince him to move back north."

"Why did she think he'd listen to you?"

"She said Phil admired me, respected my opinion." He pulled a magazine from the pile and began leafing through it. "I told her I was sorry I couldn't help her, that she should stay here and things might get better. But I wasn't surprised when she went back to Chicago."

"What family does she have in Chicago?"

"I don't really know. She talked about a sister, but they weren't close."

"What about her parents?"

He shrugged. "I never heard her mention them. I assumed they were dead."

"So you never met her sister?"

"No. Why are you interested in her sister?"

"I just wondered where Kate went when she left here."

"Why does it matter?"

"Because she left a lot of things behind."

He looked at me for a long time. "Have you been going through Phil's things?"

"I had to bring down clothing for him," I said. "He won't be able to get upstairs if he's in a wheelchair."

He lumbered to his feet. "Melissa probably knows. Ask her."

As if on cue, Melissa Durbin opened the door. "Larry, is everything okay? You never came back. I got nervous."

"I can't imagine what you're nervous about. Nothing ever happens in Schoolman. That's why we moved here." He pushed past his wife and stepped out to the porch. "There's your housebreaker," he said, pointing at me. "The famous Jessica Fletcher." The harsh tone in his voice put me on edge.

"How do you do," she said, ignoring him. She was a tall woman, almost as big as her husband. She wore a pastel green sweatshirt, a pair of worn jeans, and a baseball cap over her hair. "Larry told me that you were on campus. We haven't had a chance to meet yet." She thrust out her hand and I shook it.

"C'mon, Melissa, I have to change for my class soon. If you want that room finished, don't dawdle."

"Sorry I can't stop and talk," she said, backing out of the kitchen. "We're repainting the den."

"That's all right," I said. "I think it's time I left anyway."

Chapter Nineteen

Edgar Poole gave me a ride into New Salem and dropped me off in front of FedEx, with a promise to return in an hour. I arranged for overnight shipment of the florist's box containing the fireplace poker to the laboratory Mort had recommended. I had no idea how long it would take the lab to analyze the evidence and get back to me, but I urgently needed the results. Any delay, even one day, was of concern now.

The shop also had a copier, and I took advantage of the service to photocopy Wes's cryptic notebook and his letter to his sister, planning to return them to her that evening. I looked forward to seeing Lorraine again. She was the only person in Schoolman, other than Eli, who shared my view that Wes's death should be investigated.

I paid for my copies and shipping charges at the register, and looked at my watch. Edgar would not be back for another fifty minutes.

"Is there a coffee shop or luncheonette nearby?" I asked the clerk. "Somewhere where I can buy a news-paper and sit for a bit?"

"The diner's on the other end of town," she said, "but it's a long walk from here. There's the bakery down the block. They serve cake and coffee. It's across from the hardware store. You can get a paper in the market next door and bring it to the bakery."

I bought a newspaper and stopped at the hardware store to replace the flashlight that had been crushed during my foray into Kammerer House.

The bakery was a charming, old-fashioned shop with polished wood floors and gleaming glass fixtures. A counter ran the length of one side, with a variety of baked goods displayed on top and below. On the other side, maple tables and chairs filled the space, almost all of them occupied. As I looked around for an empty seat, a woman beckoned me. It was Eunice Carberra, from the hospital gift shop.

"Come join me," she said, pointing to the empty chair at her table. "It's hard to find a seat here at lunchtime."

"Thank you," I said, laying my folded newspaper on the table. "I never expected it to be so crowded. I thought they didn't serve lunch."

"They don't, but they have terrific cake. Plus you can order a latte here. New Salem is right up-to-date with the latest coffee trends in the country."

I laughed and made sure to ask for a latte when the waitress arrived to take my order.

"Have a piece of the lemon pound cake, too. Not too fattening, and it's one of their specialties."

I added it to my order and looked at my watch. "I don't have a lot of time," I said. "I got a lift into town with a graduate assistant and he's picking me up in a little while."

"If he's been at Schoolman more than six months, he'll know where to find you."

"What a pretty place," I said. "No wonder the movie people wanted to shoot here."

"I told you about that, didn't I? You have a good memory."

"Most days," I said. "But I have my moments. I just hate it when I enter a room and can't remember what I was looking for."

"Happens to the best of us. I once spent a half hour searching for my glasses, only to find I'd put them in my pocket so I wouldn't lose them. That's when I bought this," she said, fingering the gold chain from which her glasses dangled.

"Solves the problem."

"It does indeed. Everything back to normal at the college? I heard it was a mess over there."

"Pretty much. Three buildings sustained a lot of damage, but the cleanup is going well, and classes have resumed. Were you affected by the storm in New Salem?"

"Not in town," she said. "But the hospital was. The ER saw a lot of action. As soon as the weathermen predicted the storm, we canceled all our public service programs—Mommies and Me, Al Anon, that sort of thing—so we could be prepared to focus on the injured. All the doctors and nurses were called in to be on hand. And then it was mostly bruises and broken bones. Nothing exciting. By the way, we sold three of your books already."

"How nice."

"The signature really makes a difference."

"I'm glad."

"I placed a new order for more of your books. I'm counting on you to come by and sign them."

I laughed. "I'll be happy to sign as many as you get."

She appeared pleased. "So what brings you to town

today, Jessica? Did you come to see Mr. Adler
again?"

"How did you know I visited Phil Adler?"

"Oh, this is a small town, my dear. It's next to impossible to keep secrets. And the hospital is like a
small town within a small town. Phil's going to be
released tomorrow. Marvella Washington told me
Harriet's made arrangements for him to have a private
duty nurse to help him while he's recovering."

"That was considerate of her."

"I told Marvella to make sure the nurse is a pretty
one. He's been so blue since his wife took off. I
thought a pretty nurse would perk up his spirits. But
she told me the nurse they're sending is a man. Can
you imagine? We've women doctors and men nurses.
Quite a change since my youth."

"Mine, too," I agreed, "but it's a good change. It's
nice to see women in positions of authority, and men
who have a nurturing nature."

"Well, I'll never get used it. I remember what a
shock it was when Harriet came back to take over the
college. Never had a woman head the school before,
and the board didn't like the idea at all. Lots of argu-
ments, I heard."

"There are many colleges headed by women these
days," I said. "But Harriet doesn't hold that post. The
president of Schoolman College is a man."

"Don't you believe it. Harriet has always run everything she's ever touched. That man is just a figure-
head. She controls it all."

The waitress interrupted our conversation to place
a cup of latte and a plate with a square slice of cake
in front of me. She returned a moment later to fill
Eunice's cup.

"Tell me how you like the cake."

"It's delicious," I said, after taking a taste.

"It was my great-aunt who gave the recipe to the original bakeshop owner."

"I would love to get the recipe myself. Is it difficult to make?"

"I don't know. I don't bake. It's too bad about that professor who was killed, isn't it?"

"Yes," I said. Eunice reeled from one topic to another like a loose cart on the deck of a rolling ship.

"I thought he and Harriet might make an item, but I guess that's over now."

"They were a couple? I'd never heard that."

"She didn't want anyone to know. Or else he didn't want that secretary to find out. They used to meet at a diner out of town, over by Wabash. But one night the bus for the basketball team stopped to pick up a snack for the boys, and the coach saw them together in a booth. Is that your young man waving at us?"

I looked up to see Edgar peering through the window. He pointed to his watch and to his car, parked at the curb.

I nodded, tucked the newspaper under my arm, took a final sip of my latte, signaled the waitress, and took out my wallet. "It's my treat, Eunice," I said when the waitress put the bill on the table. "It was nice of you to invite me to join you."

"Well, I won't say no. Thanks very much, Jessica. It was a real pleasure running into you today. Don't forget to come back and sign the new books when they arrive." She lowered her voice. "And I'll let Dr. Brad Zelinsky know when you're coming in." She winked at me. "He's a nice fellow," she said, "although how anyone can spend his life cutting up dead people is beyond me."

Chapter Twenty

"In a murder case, the investigator is like a reporter on a news story, looking for the five Ws. Who can tell us what they are? If you've taken any classes in journalism, you would have come across this phrase. Yes, Maria?"

"Who, what, where, when, and why."

"Exactly." I wrote them on the blackboard. "The investigator asks these five questions: Who? What? Where? When? Why?"

It was pouring rain outside. I had checked the TV in the faculty lounge to make sure there wasn't another tornado watch in effect when I'd come in for my class. There wasn't. But the wet weather was enough to keep some of my students away. Eli must have slept in. And Alice may have found it too cumbersome to get around in a wheelchair in the rain, because she was absent as well. The rest of the students were in their seats, but they were fidgety. The room had been abuzz, but when I entered, all conversation had stopped immediately. Still, every time I turned to write on the board, I heard disconcerting whisperings behind me.

"Let's start with the first question," I said. "Who is the victim? Is it a man or a woman? Let's say it's a man. How old is he? What did he look like? What do we know about this person, his occupation, his marital status, his lifestyle?"

"Like, did he have any enemies?"

"Good point, Freddie. Understanding the victim is the first step in investigating the crime. For instance, was this person a criminal himself? Did he have a record? This might lead us in the direction of his criminal associates when we're looking for suspects. Or did this person have a drug addiction? Did he owe someone money, or break up with his longtime lover? Was he fired recently, or did he fire someone else recently? You can see that by finding out about the victim, you develop other avenues for investigation that may lead you to the killer.

"The next question is 'what.' What was it that killed him? Tyler, what do I mean by that question?"

"You're lookin' for the weapon, right?"

"Yes. The weapon, or the means used to kill the victim. Did someone shoot him or stab him or poison him or use something else? How did this person die?" I wrote *means* on the board, and was surprised to hear some giggles behind me. I turned. "Was there a struggle? Was he taken by surprise? What condition was the body in, and what does that tell us about the murder? Yes, Barbara?"

"I know the question for 'where.' "

"Go ahead."

"Where was the body found?"

More giggles.

"I fail to see the humor in this," I said. "Does anyone want to let me in on the joke?"

All eyes were on their desks.

"Okay, Barbara, would you give us the 'where' question again, please?"

"Where was the body found?"

"And also where did the murder take place?" I added. "Sometimes they're not the same. We also want to know what the crime scene looks like. That investigation may take a long time. Don't forget your papers on the crime scene are due next week, so I think we'll hold up talking about that. Janine, do you think you can describe what the 'when' question asks?"

"I think it's: When did the murder take place?"

"That's right, and why is that important?"

"Well, you want to know if it's morning or afternoon or night."

"True, but why do you want to know that?"

Tyler waved his hand. "Ooh, ooh, I know."

"Give Janine a chance to figure it out. What do you think, Janine? Why is it important to know the time of death?"

"Because if someone has an alibi for the time, they couldn't be the killer."

"Very good. Remember what we said in an earlier class. The investigators look for motive and opportunity. We have to know when the victim died to determine who of the suspects had an opportunity to kill him."

"I know the 'why' question."

"Okay, Tyler, tell us."

"Why was the guy killed? That's looking for the motive, right?"

"You are correct. And it's the motive that often leads us to the killer, although sometimes we don't learn the motive until after the perpetrator is caught. Can you give us a motive for murder, Tyler?"

"Sure. How about getting even with someone?"

"You mean revenge."

"Yeah. Like if he did something bad to you and

you want to get him back, like failing someone in a class."

There was a burst of guffaws, and I looked at my students in confusion. "What is going on today?"

Janine gave me the answer. "Tyler thinks Professor Newmark was killed by somebody he gave a failing grade to."

"How did this happen to come up, Tyler?"

"Someone said someone offed Professor Newmark. So I said it had to be somebody he failed because he had a reputation for giving bad marks."

"Everybody on campus is talking about it," Barbara said, "trying to figure out who wanted to kill him. It's a big joke."

"I don't think it's funny," Freddie said. "I actually liked him. His classes were tough but they were interesting."

"Thank you, Freddie," I said. I looked at Tyler. "Where is Eli today?"

He shrugged. "I saw him this morning. I'm kind of surprised he's not here. This is his favorite class."

That perfidious Eli, I thought. *That young man is going to get a tongue-lashing the next time I see him. I specifically asked him not to talk to Tyler or any other of his friends about the murder. Obviously it proved too hard for him to be discreet and follow my instructions.*

"This kind of speculation is very cruel," I said. "Professor Newmark's sister is on campus, and I certainly wouldn't want her to hear talk of this kind. She wouldn't find it funny. Please don't participate in those kinds of discussions. The rumors will go away if no one passes them along."

But I was too late. Harriet was cold when I returned Phil Adler's keys to her.

"I never thought you would do something so under-handed, Jessica," she said sternly. "I've already re-ceived calls from concerned parents today, worrying that there's a killer on campus. Not only that, one of those dreadful tabloids called Roberta Dougherty to ask if you'd been hired to solve the case. How do they hear such things so fast?"

I tried to assure her that the rumors had not started with me, but she remained unconvinced. "You were the only one who thought Wes Newmark's death wasn't an accident—you and Lorraine—and she doesn't have much access to the student body."

"Harriet, I can't tell you how sorry I am that the students are joking about Wes's death, and I promise you I did not start these rumors on campus. In fact, when I found out about it, I pleaded with my class not to discuss Professor Newmark at all, to be consid-erate of his sister, that a man's death was nothing to make jokes about."

"All very laudable, Jessica, but the rumor started somewhere. Can you deny you have talked to me about murder in connection with Wes's death?"

"Well, of course I talked to you about it. And I know you don't agree. But, Harriet, I believe there's proof that Wes Newmark's death was not caused by the tornado. I just need a little more time. Now, whether his murder was premeditated or the result of an impulsive act, I don't know."

Harriet exploded. "Enough, Jessica! I'm gravely dis-appointed in you. You have no idea the havoc you have set off. It's very unprofessional, not to mention inconsiderate and ungrateful. Teaching as one of Schoolman's famous-name professors is a position of great prestige. It is not only an honor, but has pro-vided other writers with a boost to their careers. Now

I'm wondering if I am harboring a Judas. I'm completely disheartened that you took advantage of our program for your own purposes. Is this your way of garnering more publicity for your next book?"

"Harriet, you insult me."

"I'll expect you to finish out the term, and I also expect you not to mention this topic to me again. However, and I say this in all sadness, I won't be inviting you back for another semester."

"I'm sorry you feel that way, Harriet. Nevertheless, it does not alter my convictions. I believe Wes Newmark was murdered, and frankly, I think that should be more of a concern to you than squelching rumors. I'll hope for an apology when the truth is revealed."

I left her office and tried to avoid looking at the shocked faces of her secretary and the other staff members outside the door who'd overheard Harriet's tirade. I was humiliated and infuriated by her assumption that I would use the death of a colleague to promote myself. However, as I'd just told her, I still believed I was right. Now there was even more pressure to prove it.

The rumors of Wes Newmark's murder might be a joke on campus, but they could turn serious at any time, and set off a panic among the students. I understood Harriet's distress, even though I was upset that she could give even the slightest credence to the notion that I would start a rumor to promote my books. She was hanging on to Schoolman's reputation, a laudable goal, no doubt, and I could forgive her for that. But would she sacrifice the truth for it? I was beginning to think she would. Worse, I was beginning to wonder about her relationship with Newmark. Eunice Carberra had said Harriet and Newmark might have been involved romantically, if local gossip could be

believed. Yet Harriet herself had said unkind words
about Wes to me. What was the truth? Until the
blowup in her office, it never would have occurred to
me that Harriet should be included on any suspect list
in Newmark's murder. Now, I sadly realized, she'd
earned a place on that list.

Chapter Twenty-one

Professor Constantine's office was a model of neatness. While it was sorely lacking in adequate storage, he had arranged his materials in stacks of color-coded file folders, arrayed along two deep windowsills, on top of a table, and across the end of his desk. The colorful folders gave the room a cheerful appearance and distracted from the sadly worn furniture and frayed rug.

"Hello, Jessica, what a surprise," he said when I knocked on the frame of his open door. He came around his desk to greet me, leaning on his cane. "Come in. Come in. Sit down. Tell me how you are. I haven't seen you since our tryst in the bomb shelter." He squeezed my hand with his left hand. "The days go by so fast."

"I'm doing all right, Professor Constantine," I said.

"It's Archie, you know. We're old friends now."

He led me to a small wooden chair facing his desk. "How are your classes going?"

"I'm very pleased with them," I said, taking a seat. "The students are attentive and enthusiastic. Their papers have been fun to read. My colleagues have been very gracious and welcoming."

I didn't add that Harriet Schoolman Bennett was furious with me and had declined to invite me back, or that Schoolman had provided me with a mystery to solve that was consuming much of my days and a good deal of my nights, especially if I included the hours of sleep I lost thinking about it. "I'd say everything is going relatively well."

"I'm sure you're being modest, and that your students are as delighted with you as you are with them," he said, slowly moving to the chair behind his desk. "How could they not be with such a knowledgeable and charming professor?"

"You're a flatterer, Archie."

"Not at all. I simply recognize a natural teacher. I knew you would do well as soon as we met. You were so interested in everything around you. It's my theory that you can't be a good teacher unless you have a mind open to learning new things yourself. I was impressed with how eager you were to hear about the history of the fallout shelters while we waited out the tornado. We're lucky to have you on the faculty. I hope the ensuing events haven't soured you on Schoolman. Tornadoes are rare, you know, and fatalities even rarer. You're not anxious about it happening again, are you?"

I wondered if he'd heard the rumors about Wes, but he didn't mention it and neither did I.

"I won't worry as long as I can sit with you in the shelter," I said.

"Aren't you sweet? It will be my pleasure."

"Speaking of shelters, you mentioned that you have a map showing where they're located. I was hoping you'd let me take a look at it."

"Certainly. It's hanging on the wall behind you. You can look all you like. Let me take it down for you."

He started to get up, but I waved him back into

his seat. "I'll get it myself," I said. "It doesn't look too heavy."

"You can put it on this table. The light is good over here."

The map in question was encased in a dusty frame. I lifted it from its hook and held it up while Archie rolled his chair over to a round table at the side of his desk and removed a stack of orange and blue files.

"Let's lay it down flat," he said, grabbing the top of the frame. "One of these days they'll approve my requisition for a five-drawer lateral file cabinet—that's my dream—and then I won't be constantly moving files to make room for other things."

"That doesn't seem like such a lofty dream. Why can't they accommodate you?"

"There's a hold on all extraneous expenses. My file cabinet is low on the list of urgent items to buy."

"I know the tornado put a lot of pressure on the budget," I said, "but it seems to me that before it came through, the college was starting to turn itself around financially. Schoolman has a brand-new gymnasium, doesn't it?"

Archie laughed. "Well, basketball in Indiana will always take precedence over the file cabinet needs of the sociology department," he said. "And for good reason. The alumni will contribute money for the one, but not the other."

"Ah, not so surprising then."

"Sad, but true. Things used to be so different around here. It was a gentler, happier time at School-man when I first arrived, before the current adminis-tration—"

"Yes?"

"Oh, don't listen to me, Jessica. It's just that . . .

well, everything has a hard edge to it these days. President Needler maintains his distance from what's going on on campus every day, not a good thing for a college president, I say."

I nodded. "What about Harriet's leadership?" I asked. "From what I can see, she's a dynamo determined to put things on an even financial keel."

"Financially speaking, yes. No question about that. I suppose we're not unique in having to worship the god of money above all else. A sign of the times. It's just that . . ."

His eyes began to glisten.

"It's just that I revere this small institution and what it once stood for. It isn't the same anymore. No, hardly the same at all."

He rubbed his eyes with the knuckles of his index fingers, forced a bright smile, and said, "Now, Mrs. Jessica Fletcher, about this map. This is the Hart Building, where we were. What exactly did you want to see?"

Chapter Twenty-two

"Do you think I should keep these in the safe?" Lorraine asked when I returned Wes's letter and notebook to her.

"That's probably wise," I said, trailing her down the hall to the study.

"Have you had any luck deciphering his code?"

"It's not so much code as abbreviations, I think. I have some ideas I plan to follow up on."

"I hope you aren't taking any chances, Jessica. One death is enough. I wouldn't want to see you get hurt by becoming involved in this."

"I'm being careful," I said.

"I called you this morning, but you'd left."

"I got a ride into New Salem with Edgar Poole, the graduate assistant in the English department. I don't know if Mrs. Tingwell told you, but he and Wes did not get along."

"Wes could be very irritating, I know. We had some real knock-down-drag-outs when we were kids—even when we weren't kids."

"Was he violent?" I asked. "I don't remember your saying that."

"No. That was an exaggeration, although it wasn't as if I didn't want to sock him sometimes. I did. But he was bigger than me." She smiled. "He was a stub-

born son of a gun. I can see where a student disagree-
ing with him could come away angry. Wes would
never give an inch. The word *compromise* was not in
his vocabulary."

Lorraine slipped out of her shoes and climbed on
the love seat.

"I quizzed Edgar on the ride into town," I said,
taking the chair behind Wes's desk and watching as
she opened the safe and put the letter and the notebook inside. "I asked him where he'd been during the
tornado and just prior to it."

"What did he say?"

"He said he's been waiting for someone to ask him
that question, especially now that the campus is buzz-
ing about the possibility of Wes's being murdered."

Lorraine sat cross-legged on the love seat and
smiled. "I hope you won't be annoyed with me. I
helped start that rumor."

"You did?"

"Yes. I figured that if the police and the college
administration were not going to look into Wes's
death, I'd try to force their hand."

"What did you do?"

"I didn't mention the letter, if that's what you're
worried about. I just said the autopsy was suspicious,
which could be true, right?"

"Who did you say that to?"

"Letitia."

"I didn't think she was the type to spread a rumor."

"She's not, but it was her idea to get the students
to do it for us."

"It was?"

"We were having breakfast in the cafeteria. She was
telling me how she couldn't understand why Wes
didn't go down to the basement when the storm hit.

She was really upset. It was so unlike him to be lacking in judgment, she said. He must have had a heart attack, she said, and that would explain why he was still upstairs when the ceiling collapsed. So I told her that his autopsy was suspicious, and about how you and I wanted the college and the police to look into Wes's death, but they wouldn't, and how frustrated we were."

"And she said?"

"She said sometimes people needed a push. There were some students sitting nearby and she suggested that we talk to each other about the possibility of Wes's being murdered, but raise our voices just enough so we could be overheard. That's all it took. The rumor spread like fire in a dry forest. Letitia phoned to tell me that all the students are talking about it, and that several parents have demanded the administration do something about it immediately. Maybe Harriet will call in the police now."

"Harriet thinks *I* started the rumor."

"She does? Is she mad at you?"

"I'd say that's a bit of an understatement."

"Oh, Jessica. I'm so sorry. I never even thought about what she would think beyond getting her to bring back the police. Do you want me to tell her I did it?"

"Absolutely not. Don't worry about it. I have a tough hide. And maybe your plan will work. If enough parents call the administration, perhaps it will make Harriet rethink her position, even if it's only to ask the police to do a cursory investigation to quiet the rumors."

"Do you think that's possible?"

"I think it's an angle to work on."

"You were talking about the graduate assistant a

moment ago. What did he say when you questioned him?"

"He said he'd seen Wes at Kammerer House shortly before the tornado, and Wes had sent him to the library to do some research. Edgar said he was down in the basement stacks along with about forty others when the storm hit."

"Do you believe him?"

"I believe he was in the basement during the storm. It wouldn't pay for him to lie about that."

"You mean with so many people taking shelter, there would have to be a lot of witnesses."

"Exactly. I'll ask around anyway."

"And before the storm? He could have killed Wes before the storm."

"I don't think he did," I said, half to myself. "Edgar is left-handed. Whoever killed Wes is right-handed."

"How do you know that?"

I realized I'd never told Lorraine that I'd seen her brother's body. I didn't know how she would take it, whether she would consider it an invasion of his privacy. She didn't know about the poker either, and I intended to keep that from her until I had proof that it was the murder weapon. "From the autopsy," I said. "It described the angle of the blow."

"Really? You never said."

"I didn't want to upset you until we knew more."

"Thank you." A shiver passed through her body. "I *don't* really want to know the details."

"I won't tell you then," I said.

"You know that the memorial service is tomorrow."

"Yes. Would you like me to pick you up in the morning? We can walk over together."

"I would appreciate that. There are so few people

I know. If it weren't for you and Letitia, I'd be completely lost."

"I'm glad we can help," I said. "May I tread on that friendship once more?"

"Sure. What do you want?"

"I'd like to examine Wes's computer, see what I can find in his e-mail or in his files."

"Be my guest. Letitia is coming for supper in a little while. Why don't you stay, too? You can work on it together."

"I like that idea," I said, meaning it.

Chapter Twenty-three

The memorial service for Professor Wesley Stanton Newmark had concluded after an hour of homilies by Pastor Getler, eulogies by Vernon Foner and Manny Rosenfeld, hymns sung by the Schoolman College choir, and mercifully short speeches by Harriet Schoolman Bennett and Lowell Needler. Classes had been suspended for the day, and as Harriet had desired, the auditorium seats were filled with students and faculty who waited to file out until the small entourage surrounding Lorraine had made its exit.

"It was a lovely service," she said to me.

"Yes, it was."

"Wes would have been so happy hearing what his colleagues said about him. Professor Rosenfeld's eulogy was very moving."

We moved up the aisle of the Benjamin Harrison Auditorium, named for the Indiana citizen and twenty-third president of the United States. Behind us, Letitia Tingwell, dressed in black, her eyes red and swollen, leaned on the arm of Professor Manny Rosenfeld. My heart went out to her. Of all of us, she mourned Wes Newmark the most, yet had no official place in his life, one that would allow her to be recognized for the sacrifices she'd made for him and the love she bore him that, as far as anyone knew, had gone unrequited.

Outside, the sky was overcast; black clouds rimmed the horizon, a fitting atmosphere for a memorial service. Lorraine stopped at the top of the steps, accepting condolences. A photographer from the student newspaper stood nearby, adjusting his telephoto lens. I moved off to the side.

Vernon Foner stepped away from the group and came up to me.

"Gad, that Getler can go on, can't he? The man just loves the sound of his own voice."

"Lorraine was pleased with the service," I said.

"Yes. Well, Manny did a nice job. He always does. How did you like my eulogy? Did I make Wes sound too saintly?"

"I don't think so."

"Good. Didn't want to lay it on too thick. But with those ridiculous rumors flying around campus, I wanted it known that he was not someone anyone would murder. He was a popular professor."

"Was he?"

"It doesn't matter. The man is dead, after all. Say nice things and get off the stage. We'll all miss him, but life goes on." He tugged on the bottom of his vest. "They'll have to name a new department chairman soon. Other than Wes, I'm probably the most published of the English professors. That should stand me in good stead when they're making their decision. You're a friend of Dean Bennett's. Do you have any idea when she'll be making that announcement?"

"I'm not consulted about such things."

"Well, of course, I know that. But I thought maybe she confided in you."

"If she did, it wouldn't be very nice of me to breach her confidence, would it?"

Foner looked ill at ease. "No, of course not," he said.

"Tell me about your new book," I said. "You sounded very excited when you were telling Rebecca about it."

"Yes. It's going to be wonderful."

"What it's about?"

"The influence of George Meredith on Robert Louis Stevenson."

"I heard you say that the other day. Can't you tell me more than that?"

"It's about their friendship and correspondence. You'll just have to read it," he said, smiling.

"I'd like to do that. Have you been working on it for a while?"

"Oh, I had the idea several years ago, but I didn't have time to complete the research and write it until this summer."

"You must be a very fast writer. I certainly need a lot more than two months to write my books, and they aren't scholarly."

"The research, that takes years, but once I have the vision in my mind, I just sit down and write and write and write. I spent the whole summer on it. It was exhausting, but I got it done."

"Well, congratulations. It's always exciting when a book is accepted for publication. Who's your publisher?"

"I haven't exactly signed the contract yet, so I'm a little superstitious about talking about it. You understand. Don't want to jinx it by using their name. I'll let you know soon."

"Please do. I'm very interested."

"I've been trying to get hold of Larry Durbin. Have you seen him this morning?"

"Isn't that Larry standing next to Lorraine New-mark?"

"So it is. Excuse me."

Foner waded into the crowd surrounding Lorraine, but stopped to talk with a student and never reached Durbin, who left accompanied by his wife, Melissa.

It looked as if the entire campus had turned out for the service. Phil Adler had missed it, of course, but he was due for release from the hospital that morning. Edgar Poole had no such excuse. The English department had been asked to assemble early so that we could all sit together with Lorraine in the front of the auditorium. Edgar's absence had been noted, although not commented on by anyone other than Letitia Tingwell.

"Where is he? He's usually so prompt."

"Maybe he preferred to sit with the students," I said.

"Oh, that's all right then."

But I hadn't seen Edgar among the students, and I'd been keeping watch for him.

There was still a sizable group of faculty members and students waiting to extend their condolences when President Needler emerged from the auditorium, a frustrated look on his face. He pushed through the crowd, elbowed Pastor Getler aside, and took Lorraine's hand. He murmured his sympathies and departed immediately, moving sideways to get through the throng. I caught up with him as he descended the stairs.

"President Needler," I called, "may I speak with you a moment before you leave?"

He hesitated before turning to me. "Will it take very long? I'm leaving for the weekend."

"I wanted to say how much I enjoyed your remarks about Wes Newmark."

"Well, that's very kind of you. Nice to be appreciated."

"And to ask you why you took books and a photograph from his study."

Needler's face turned red; he coughed and cleared his throat. "They . . . uh . . . were . . . uh, books I had lent to him. Yes, I had let him use them for his research and I was merely reclaiming them. After all, they're mine. I don't see why that should concern you." He turned and continued down the stairs, but I kept stride with him. "In fact," he said, when he saw he wasn't rid of me, "that seems to me to be a rather impertinent question, Mrs. Fletcher. You have no business questioning my actions. You're a guest on this campus. That's quite an attitude you have. What have you to say for yourself?"

"President Needler, I'm not a student you can intimidate."

"You'd better have a good reason for this third degree."

He was now on the attack, a tactic I was sure he must have used successfully before. I was taking a chance questioning him, but the time was getting away from me. Kammerer House was to be torn down in a matter of days. If I didn't turn up something soon, the case would die for lack of evidence. I needed to rattle him again and see if I could shake loose some information.

"Wes Newmark died under unusual and frankly suspicious circumstances," I said in a low voice.

"Nonsense," he said. "That's just some student tall tale. I'm surprised you would fall for that."

"The rumor this time is accurate," I said. "An investigation is going to take place. I thought you should know, considering that the police will want to know why you tampered with Newmark's belongings."

Needler was stunned. "Police? I haven't heard that the police were looking into this. When did that happen? And I wasn't tampering. I . . . I . . . I . . . was simply retrieving books that are mine. Wes was going to give them back. He knew they're very precious to me. I didn't want his sister to give them away to a book sale. Why didn't I hear about the police investigation? Why am I being kept in the dark?" His voice was starting to rise.

"Let's walk together," I said. "I don't want us to be overheard." We moved away from people trooping down the stairs and spreading out across the campus. I accompanied Needler in the direction of the Student Union and paused next to one of the bare oak trees in the quad. When I was sure we were alone, I spoke again. "It's all been very hush-hush. Even Harriet doesn't know. You're the first one I've mentioned it to. And you need to keep it quiet."

"Of course, I can be trusted."

"Can you?" I asked, looking hard into his eyes. "Those books were first editions, weren't they?"

He swallowed audibly and nodded.

"You never lend out books from your collection. You told me so yourself. Why did Newmark have those books?"

Needler ran a trembling hand through his white hair, and I felt a momentary pang of guilt for harassing an old man.

"This is not something I want to be made public," he said. "I must have your assurance you will keep it confidential."

"I can't promise you that. If it has something to

do with Wes Newmark's death, the police will have to know."

"It had nothing to do with his death. I've done nothing illegal," he said. "They were simply markers, that's all."

"Gambling markers?"

"Yes. I'd lost a lot of money on . . . well, it doesn't matter what it was on, does it? I was being threatened. It was very frightening. Never happened to me before. I didn't have the money, so I went to Wes. He paid off my debt."

"And you gave him the books as collateral."

"Yes. I would have paid him back the money. I swear. Then, after he died, I couldn't stand the thought that those books might be sent off to some secondhand dealer who didn't know what he had, or sold at some tag sale in Alaska, or worse, thrown out."

"So you took them."

"She had no interest in them. She said they were 'junky.' Can you imagine? One of them was a first edition of Thackeray. It took me years to find it. You won't tell the police about the books, will you?"

"I won't as long as you pay Lorraine fair value for them."

"I will. You have my word."

"How much did Wes give you for them?"

"I . . . uh . . . believe it was several thousand."

"More like fifteen thousand, wasn't it?"

"It may have been as much as that. I'd have to look it up. I've already saved quite a bit so I can repay her."

"Were you the only one Wes Newmark loaned money to?"

"What do you mean?"

"Are you aware of any other people who borrowed from him?"

"I wouldn't know that, although he always had plenty of cash. The guy was an incredibly lucky gambler. He never lost. Not just at our monthly game. We went to Las Vegas a few times. He would clean out the casino. They asked him not to come back."

"Where were you the morning of the tornado? Where were you when Newmark was killed?"

"I . . . I . . . was attending my Gamblers Anonymous meeting in New Salem. It's every Saturday. I'll give you a phone number, if you want. You can call yourself to confirm it."

"I'll keep that in mind. You used the excuse of needing a photograph of Newmark to get into his study and take the books, didn't you?"

He looked confused. "No. No. The student paper needed his photograph for their obituary. I told Miss Newmark and she offered that picture in the frame."

"You're not telling me the truth. The paper had a photograph of him. It appeared in the same edition as the announcement of my coming to Schoolman."

"I'm not lying. Harriet said the campus newspaper needed his photo. She asked me to pick it up when I paid a call on Lorraine."

"Did you give the photo to the student newspaper?"

"No. I gave it to Harriet. She said she'd make sure it went to the proper person."

I was surprised. Harriet had access to faculty records and could have had a photo of Wes Newmark at any time. Why, I wondered, did she want that particular one?

Needler scratched his cheek. "You know, I thought

it was odd that the newspaper didn't have a picture of him. He was a department head, after all. But she said to get it, so I got it."

"Do you always follow her orders?"

He straightened and his expression hardened. "I raise a lot of money for this college. That's what I was hired to do, and I do it. I'm the president! I won't be patronized by you or her or anyone else."

"You're right," I said. "I apologize."

"Is that enough? May I go now?"

"Yes. Thank you for your cooperation."

"I'd appreciate it if you wouldn't mention to anyone about my attendance at Gamblers Anonymous. That's a private matter."

"I won't say anything, but you may want to tell the police yourself, if they question you."

He turned and strode off across the campus, his erect carriage and white hair easily setting him apart from the milling students who stepped aside to let him pass. He was an odd combination of erudition and indiscretion with his love of antiquarian books and his weakness for gambling. But maybe they were more allied than I'd previously thought. Maybe the thrill of purchasing a rare first edition was as much a gamble as betting on a poker hand. He hadn't been entirely truthful, but he'd given me a lot to think about.

Perhaps Wes Newmark had been an underground banker. If so, whoever owed him the most money may have decided not to repay in the usual manner.

Chapter Twenty-four

The library was unusually quiet when I entered the main reading room. Most of the students and faculty had taken off for the weekend, following the memorial service. The tables were empty, the screens dark on the banks of computers.

Administration members and the faculty of the English department would have gone back to La Salle House with Lorraine Newmark for refreshments sent over by the cafeteria staff. Rather than have Harriet's coldness toward me put a chill on the day for the others, I'd told Lorraine I would stop by later on. Instead, I decided, it was an opportune time to explore the passage I'd seen on Professor Constantine's map, the one Eli had taken to Kammerer House to retrieve the poker.

The library's basement housed the stacks for its nonfiction books. Fiction, a more limited collection, occupied the spacious main floor, with its spectacular arching glass skylight. Downstairs, case after case of books with narrow, carpeted aisles between them marched away to the distant walls. The cramped quarters, low ceiling, and fluorescent lighting gave the area a claustrophobic atmosphere despite its substantial size. Only the small signs at the ends of each section signifying the subject matter and its Dewey decimal

numbers gave any indication of where in this vast
room you stood. If there were students here hunting
for books, they were as easily camouflaged as deer in
the woods. It would be impossible to know how many
people had taken refuge here during the tornado. It
was too easy to hide. Claiming to have been here
when Newmark was murdered wouldn't be much of
an alibi for Edgar Poole.

I'd taken the stairs from the main level, which emptied into a corridor that ran the length of the stacks.
Turning to recall which way I'd faced when I'd entered the stairwell, I got my bearings and set out in
what I presumed was the direction of Kammerer
House. At the end of the long corridor, a sign pointing
to the right directed me to the copy center. I turned
the corner; halfway down the hall I passed the room
with the copy machines, two of them churning out
pages in an uneven rhythm. Along the left-hand wall
were several locked doors, none of them giving any
hint of what lay beyond them. I tried twisting each
doorknob, but in the crack between the jamb and the
edge of the door I could see the bolt that spanned
them.

Fifty yards down, I reached the next corner and
paused. If I turned here, I would be going away from
Kammerer House, not toward it. How had Eli found
the tunnel? Was there another set of stairs leading to
them? Maybe I should have let him show me where
it was. Was there someone upstairs who could give
me specific directions?

I walked back in the direction from which I'd come,
trying each of the doors again, to no avail. I stopped
at the entrance to the copy room. Could there be another exit from here?

The copy center consisted of two rooms filled with

large gray machines, the functions of which were obscure except for the two copiers at the entrance. The front room was unoccupied, brightly lit, and noisy. The mechanical clunk and thud of the two machines was deafening in the uncarpeted room, while the only movement visible was the paper as it flew out of the maw of the copiers into twenty separate trays.

"Anyone here?" I called out.

No one answered. I walked through to the back room, which was similarly bright and empty, its machines idle. Metal shelving took up most of the walls. I scanned the room for any sign of a way out, and saw none, but then I spotted a faded sign. Ahead of me, above a shelving unit, painted over and faint, I could discern the old radiation symbol with its three flaring blades in a black circle. Underneath was an arrow pointing to one of the shelving units, which held reams of paper. I peered between the packages and saw the outline of a door. Wedging myself between the wall and the frame, I pushed with both hands and fell forward as the unit moved smoothly away.

Well, that wasn't too hard, I told myself. The door, which had been covered, was unlocked, and opened out into a dark hall, the brilliant interior of the copy room lighting only the first few yards. I fumbled on the wall for a light switch and was rewarded when two bare bulbs, ten feet apart, lit up the beginning of the tunnel. I closed the door and listened. Behind me, the pounding of the copiers was muffled but audible.

Cautiously I moved forward into the damp gray tunnel. Any paint that had covered the concrete walls had long since peeled off. Here and there, delicate flakes clung to a rough surface, the faded curls evidence of the color the walls had once been. The floor was rough and required watching, especially in the pumps I'd worn to the memorial service. Why hadn't I gone home to change? That would have been smart. But my apartment was in the opposite direction from the auditorium and the library. I'd taken the path of least resistance, and hoped I wouldn't regret it.

My decision to explore the tunnel had been last-minute. I'd been curious about it ever since Eli told me he'd gained access to Kammerer House by using the underground passageway. But I hadn't given it much further thought until halfway through the memorial service when it occurred to me that whoever murdered Newmark might well have used the tunnel as his—or her—method of entrance and, more important, as a way to escape in the midst of the storm. Would venturing into the tunnel reveal anything about who that might have been? Probably not. But like people who climb mountains simply because they're there, I felt the tunnel beckon, and I found myself drawn to it like a moth to a summer candle.

By my calculation, the hallway before me stretched out in the direction of the three houses destroyed by the tornado. A short walk showed me that it also branched off into several side passages, none of them marked. I took the first right, twisting a timed light switch I found on the wall. Its rapid ticking reminded me that the light it controlled wouldn't stay on very long. I dug out my new flashlight and forged ahead. The bulb in the wall fixture dimmed just as I came upon another inky hallway that seemed to angle back toward the library.

I know how Hansel and Gretel felt, I thought. *I should have brought bread crumbs.* How had Eli known which passage led to Kammerer House?

Using my flashlight, I retraced my steps to the door of the copy center, the sound of the machines now a comforting beacon, and started out again. This time I decided to see how far the tunnel extended before choosing which side corridor to try.

The tunnel went forward for about two hundred feet when the route angled off to the left, with another corridor to the right. At least there were no other branches on the left side, but I'd counted four on the right, plus assorted doors, none of which I remembered seeing on Archie's map. As I walked, the sound of my footsteps echoed back to me. All else was quiet.

I searched for light switches, but the few I found were either inoperable, or the bulbs in the fixtures were broken or gone. Relying on my flashlight, I reached the end of the tunnel; the way ahead of me was blocked by rubble: slabs of concrete, fallen beams, and shards of metal. I estimated I was near the bursar's office, which had already been razed.

I looked back. Behind me the tunnel was black, the angle of the hall completely obscuring the illumination from the bare bulbs near the copy center door. I shone my flashlight on the wreckage. Spiders skittered away from the light, and I heard a scuffling noise as well. I didn't want to think of what other creatures might be making their home in this subterranean passageway. Casting the beam along the wall, I came across a broken door and stopped to examine the damage. The metal frame had been fractured on the top, possibly by the weight of debris hurled down by the tornado, which put too much pressure on the lintel. I ran my hand down the edge of the door and felt where the lock had previously engaged the frame. A tongue of brass, a short, ineffective appendage, had been wrenched from the faceplate. I pushed on the door and it opened into a room with a sharp squeal, the sound jarring in the surrounding silence. I poked my head through the opening and aimed the flashlight inside. The room was about eight feet by ten feet, small and secure. The ceiling was cement, the walls made of concrete blocks. No rubble had fallen through. I squeezed through the gap and took shallow breaths. There was an odd, acrid odor.

The chamber proved to be another of Professor Constantine's fallout shelters, and was remarkable in that its remote location had kept it from being converted to a storeroom or other practical use. Once abandoned as a shelter, it had been left in its original state of readiness.

Fascinated, I inspected the contents of the room. None of the supplies laid in for a 1960s emergency had been removed. Shelves along the walls held a variety of green canisters and brown cartons with food staples and other provisions. There was a Geiger counter to check for radiation, a pile of folded blankets, a first-aid kit for injuries, a portable radio, and what looked like a well-thumbed civil defense pamphlet. A box marked MADE IN JAPAN held a sanitation unit, which was still sealed in its original packaging. A schematic drawing showed how to set up the commode and attach it to a water source.

Three cots with mattresses were stacked on top of each other, further attesting to plans to use the space as living quarters in the event of an attack. But the only living beings that had benefited from them were mice. In several places the ticking had been chewed through, and stuffing sprouted from the holes. I walked gingerly, trying to avoid the evidence of rodent infestation on the floor.

On the wall was a framed map similar to the one I had pored over with Professor Constantine. The evacuation route had been highlighted with red ink to indicate the safest way out.

Professor Constantine will be delighted with this find, I thought. It was a forty-year-old time capsule. He could bring his students here to demonstrate America's fears of an atomic bomb blast and the precautions some had taken to survive it. I wondered whether the elaborate preparations would have been effective, and was thankful we'd never had to find out.

At the back of the room, I aimed my flashlight at the large and small metal drums that had been stacked to save floor space. The light seemed not as strong as it had been. The batteries were fresh; at least the clerk in the hardware store had said they were. I gave the flashlight a shake and the light strengthened again. Just a loose connection. I focused on what had caught my eye.

One large drum had fallen over and the cover had been dislodged. The word WATER had been stenciled on the outside of the drum but it clearly hadn't been used for that purpose. Spilling out of the crack where the top separated from the drum was the edge of a soiled cloth. *I wonder what they used that for?* I thought as I moved closer to take a better look. Shining my light on the cover of the drum, I put my foot on the edge of the rim and pressed, trying to pry it open more. The lid fell off with a loud clatter, and the cloth tumbled out. But it wasn't just cloth. It was a sleeve. And inside the sleeve was the desiccated arm of a corpse.

Chapter Twenty-five

I backed up to the door and waited for my heartbeat to slow before creeping forward, careful not to touch anything, and aiming the flashlight on the victim.

From the look of the clothing and considering the size of the drum, the person who had been stuffed inside was a small woman. The sleeve had a ruffled cuff. Stiff now, it might have been a gauzy material at one time. There were several silver rings on the skeletal hand. I leaned in to see what I could of the body. A skein of long blond hair was still attached to the skull. The fabric on the bent knees was denim.

I had a sinking suspicion I knew who it was. It was safe to assume that the woman in the drum hadn't died a natural death, and it was highly unlikely that whoever placed her there had been following the deceased's instructions to be interred and left for eternity in an abandoned bomb shelter. In this case, "eternity" had been interrupted by an act of nature, and by what my old friend Seth has been known to call my "unnatural" curiosity.

I couldn't tell how long the body had been there, but the open lid of the drum had exposed it to the air and allowed it to decay. The location of the shelter, which I presumed to be beneath the building that had housed the bursar's office, could not be a coincidence.

No one had spoken to Kate Adler in a year. She hadn't contacted anyone in her family, nor visited any of her friends. Mail sent to her had been returned. And much of her clothing still remained in the home she had shared with her husband, including a pair of high heels flung into a storage room.

Was it Phil who'd killed her—or someone else? Was Wes Newmark's death connected to this one? Was the same person responsible for both murders?

Ignoring the squealing hinges, I pulled back the door and stepped out into the tunnel. Away from the decomposed body and the moldering mattresses, I took a deep breath. The moist air in the tunnel, which I'd barely noticed before, was beginning to become uncomfortable.

I shone my flashlight on the floor ahead of me. There were damp patches on the concrete. The light flickered slightly. I shook the flashlight again, but the beam seemed to be fading. Apparently the batteries I'd purchased were not as fresh as promised. If they failed while I was underground, it would be an unpleasant trip back to the library.

I walked down the corridor, taking care to avoid puddles forming on the floor.

I heard a door slam in the distance. Was it the door to the copy center, or one of the doors to the tunnel? I hurried forward, eager to end this adventure. Finding the access to Kammerer House could wait for another time.

I reached the place where I thought the hall angled back toward the library, but I couldn't see the lights outside the copy center. Had I missed the turn? Perhaps the bulbs were weak, and the light from my flashlight blinded me to them. I pushed the switch to off and was plunged into blackness. I shut my eyes and waited. The air was getting chillier, and goose bumps rose on my arms, despite the warmth of the wool suit I was wearing. I concentrated on my hearing: the only sounds I could discern were the dripping of water and the rustle of my own clothing as I waited restlessly for my sight to adjust to the lack of light. I opened my eyes and squinted. The lights were definitely gone, and I chided myself for leaving the bulbs on while exploring the tunnel. If they were old, they may have burned out quickly.

I switched the flashlight back on, needing the comfort of light. The beam was thin and spasmodic. Should I go back and see if I missed a turn, or move forward and possibly lose my way in the maze of corridors?

Trusting that I hadn't mistaken the turn, I walked swiftly down the hall, hoping the pace would warm me up. The tunnel seemed longer than it had been when I'd first walked its length. Had I gone this far on the way in? I couldn't remember. The flashlight's beam flickered. Shaking it no longer strengthened the light. When the light died completely—a situation that looked likely—I would have to keep one hand on the wall and make my way slowly to avoid stumbling.

The copiers were silent now. I listened for any hint of activity that might assure me I was on the right trail. And then it happened. A breeze caught me from the side, and a tunnel yawned on my right. There had been no tunnels to my left on the way in, and shouldn't have been on my right on the way out.

You've always had a good sense of direction, Jessica, I lectured myself. *Think this through. There has to be a logical way back.* I tried to envision Archie's map, and where it defined the location of the shelters and tunnels. But his plan, he had told me, had been made early in the building process, and hadn't shown the final layout.

I lingered at the entrance to this new tunnel, debating my next move. The flashlight flickered again, and my decision was made. I took the right and entered the new corridor. Three steps later I was in the dark. I gave the flashlight a final shake. No go. *Don't panic,* I told myself. *You can do this.*

The tunnel was about six feet across. If I extended one arm and touched the wall, I needed only a step or two to the side for my other hand to reach the opposite wall. To keep myself from literally bouncing off walls as I walked, I decided to cling to the wall on the right, and use the end of the flashlight as a bumper. At first I walked slowly and dragged the flashlight along the rough surface, but as I became accustomed to the dark and could gauge the distance, I let the flashlight hover near the wall without touching it. Using my hearing, I could "feel" where the wall was. I'd often heard that people who are blind are able to sense when a wall or other large object is in front of them. I was beginning to feel that way, too, and imagined that my hearing was more acute, given my "blindness" in the tunnel.

I'd counted sixty-five steps when I heard a noise that made me halt—something being slammed, a door or a drawer. It was definitely a human noise, not one made by an animal or dripping water. I listened carefully, hoping I'd hear it again. There it was, somewhere up ahead, on the right.

I tiptoed forward, making sure my shoes didn't tap against the concrete and distract me from pinpointing the location of the sound. I switched the dead flashlight to my left hand so I could feel along the wall with my right for the frame of a door or a gap indicating another tunnel. My fingers slipped over a bump and then another ripple before my hand connected with a flat plane. I concentrated on the floor. If it was a door, perhaps I could see a light under the jamb. But there wasn't any light. I tucked the flashlight under my arm and used both hands to feel around the wall. The surface I touched was cold and smooth. The walls were rough. This must be a door. I patted it, felt for the knob, found one, twisted it, and pulled. Nothing happened. I tried pushing instead and the door moved; something was blocking it. I pressed my weight against the door and it budged a few more inches.

"Is anyone there?" I called. "If you're there, please help me open this door."

I stopped pushing to listen for a reply, but when there was none, I stepped back and slammed my shoulder into the door three times till I had moved whatever it was that was blocking the exit enough to squeeze through.

The room I entered was cluttered. I could feel the presence of objects in front of me and to the side. I listened. Did I hear breathing, or was it only my own respiration from the exertion of forcing the door? Gingerly I put out my hands and touched metal. I slid my hand around, feeling a handle. I tugged on it and a drawer slid open. It was a filing cabinet. Oh, if only the flashlight worked. I shook it again, just in case, but it was definitely dead.

I moved around the front of the filing cabinet and, proceeding slowly, slid one foot forward at a time, reaching out with one hand to the side and the other in front of my face to avoid knocking my head against low beams or hanging objects. Something or someone was there. I sensed it. But my hand encountered only metal as I inched along. I counted six cabinets in a row before reaching a wall. Filing cabinets. Could this be the basement of Kammerer House?

As I turned to the right, my foot connected with a hard object. "Nuts," I muttered. I'd bumped into a step. I'd placed my foot on the step when an arm swung around my middle and pulled me tight against a large body.

"Don't you dare move," he said in a growl.

"Who are you? Let me go!" I said, struggling against the arm imprisoning me.

"You're trespassing where you don't belong."

"I was lost, just trying to find my way out of the tunnel. Let go. You're hurting me."

The arm released me, replaced by an iron hand gripping my arm. I heard him reach for something, and then a brilliant light blinded me.

"I might have known it would be you."

I was still blinking rapidly when he let me go and set the torch on the step, its huge beam bouncing off the ceiling and illuminating the room.

"Lieutenant Parish!"

"None other," he said, scowling at me.

"I'm so glad to see you," I said, brushing cobwebs from my sleeve.

"I'm not glad to see you, Mrs. Fletcher."

"I was just trying to find my way out of the tunnel. My flashlight failed, you see." I showed him my dead flashlight, and he pulled it from my hand. *Wouldn't it be just my luck if it worked now?* Fortunately, it didn't.

Parish flicked the switch on and off several times, and nothing happened. "You probably have the batteries in backward," he said. "Wouldn't put it past you."

"Honestly, Lieutenant! I was using it up till about an hour or so ago." I realized I had no notion of how long I'd actually been in the tunnels.

"Well, you managed to find your way to Kammerer House once again, didn't you? Or are you going to insist that being here is just a happy accident?"

"I told you, I got lost."

"What were you doing here to begin with?"

"Professor Constantine showed me an old map of the tunnels and bomb shelters, and I was curious to see them. I was in the copy center in the library and found the entrance. There's nothing against the law in exploring the tunnels, is there? But I made the most shocking discovery. I found a room you'll want to see. Actually, it's a fallout shelter from the fifties or sixties."

"Nice story, Mrs. Fletcher. But then again, that's your business, isn't it, telling stories? Harriet warned me about you."

"Please, Lieutenant, I'm trying to tell you that there's something you must see back there, in one of the rooms—"

"Lady," he interrupted, "you've been a thorn in my side all week long. And you're not getting away with it this time, judge or no judge. You're going to sit in the New Salem jail until Kammerer House comes down. That way I'll know you won't be breaking into this place again." He picked up his powerful light and put a foot on the step. "You're coming with me, Mrs. Fletcher."

I straightened my jacket and looked him in the eye. "On the contrary, Lieutenant," I said, hardening my voice. "This time you're coming with me."

For a moment I thought my stand might cause him to strike out at me. His square face turned red, and there was a visible tremor in his hand. But then he caught hold of himself and said, "What are you talk-ing about?"

"I'm talking about a very dead body in one of the rooms off the tunnels. It's a woman I believe to be Kate Adler. She's been dead a very long time, Lieutenant."

"Are you serious?"

"Why don't you come with me and see."

"You'd better not be playing a game with me, Mrs. Fletcher. I have no sense of humor where you're concerned."

"Murders are not a joking matter, Lieutenant. I hope you'll take both of them seriously. This one and Professor Newmark's."

With our way lighted by his powerful flashlight, we retraced my steps until reaching the room containing the remains of Kate Adler. I stood just outside as he entered the room and did a cursory examination of the corpse without touching anything. When he was finished, he joined me in the tunnel.

"You were right," he said.

"Of course I was right," I said. "Why would you doubt me?"

"Because—"

"And why have you been so adamant about Wes Newmark's death?" I asked. "Why have you and oth-ers refused to even consider that he was murdered? There's enough evidence to at least warrant an investigation."

"You don't understand, Mrs. Fletcher," he said qui-etly. "We have an arrangement with the school."

"Arrangement? What arrangement?"

"We try and keep a lid on things here, to make sure the school doesn't get a bad reputation."

"And this arrangement," I said, "does it even ex-tend to murder?"

He sighed deeply and looked away from me, making it obvious that he was having trouble answering my question. Finally he again looked at me. "Let's just say we've been cooperating with the school for a while to keep things cool, not make a big deal out of students getting in jams in town, things like that."

"I see," I said. "I assume this so-called arrangement began when Harriet returned to take over Schoolman's future."

"Mrs. Fletcher, I—"

"Your cooperation is with her, not the school itself, isn't it? And Harriet, it seems, has convinced you that the school's reputation is more important than the truth."

"When it comes to truth, Mrs. Fletcher," he said, bristling, "I'll take Harriet Schoolman Bennett's word over yours any day. We go back a long time. She was my mother's best friend, and if she says Newmark was a nut and made up stories to make himself look important, I believe her."

"But we're talking about covering up a murder, Lieutenant. Even Harriet couldn't ask you to do that. Could she?"

"Let's go," he said. "I have to report this."

"Are you paid for this cooperation?" I asked, trailing behind as he moved down the tunnel with deliberate speed. I received no answer, which was answer enough. Finally things began to make sense to me. The stonewalling of Newmark's murder was for reasons I could understand, although never agree with. I had wondered how, for so many years, Schoolman had escaped the usual student hijinks that occasionally required police intervention. Harriet was paying off the local police, that was how. Through her young friend Lieutenant Parish, any legal problems that might arise from student misbehavior in town were covered up, and now the same thing was happening to spare the school from possible involvement in a murder. I was making progress.

But the larger question still remained. There were now two murders to be solved.

Who murdered Kate Adler and Wes Newmark? And why?

Chapter Twenty-six

"Jessica, I've been waiting for you. Where have you been?"

"I told you I wouldn't be able to stop by until later, Lorraine."

"I'm sorry. I forgot. It's been such a full house this afternoon, and I kept looking for a familiar face."

"Where did Mrs. Tingwell go?"

"She's upstairs lying down. I insisted. The memorial service was too much for her. Dr. Zelinsky was here earlier, and he gave her some medication."

"That's good. I'm sure she can use some rest."

"You look a little tired yourself. Are you all right?"

"Nothing that a strong cup of tea won't fix."

"I'll put the kettle on right now."

I followed her down the hall. As we passed the front parlor, I glimpsed Vernon Foner and Manny Rosenfeld talking with President Needler. All three held glasses of red wine. Needler had told me he was going away for the weekend. Apparently courtesy toward the dead had detained him. I also spotted Larry Durbin and Rebecca McAllister, standing by a table laden with platters of sandwiches and talking to someone I couldn't see.

Zoe Colarulli and her husband were saying goodbye to Harriet in the kitchen when Lorraine and I walked in. Zoe turned to Lorraine and took her hand. "Miss Newmark, Harris and I are leaving now," she said, "but we wanted to extend our sympathies again and wish you a safe trip back to Alaska."

"Thank you. It was nice meeting you," Lorraine replied, "despite the circumstances." She walked out of the kitchen with them. "Let me see you to the door."

"Hello, Harriet," I said, crossing the room, picking up the kettle, and taking it to the faucet. The sink was piled high with dirty plates and glasses, the drain board filled with china that had already been washed. I shook the kettle, decided I could make do with the water already in it, placed it on the stove, and looked around for a dish towel.

As I waited for the water to boil, I began drying dishes and putting them in the cupboard. Harriet stood next to the small table and fussed with a platter of cookies, taking them from the box and arranging them neatly on the plate. She hadn't said anything since I'd greeted her.

Eventually she cleared her throat. "Jessica, I'm sorry I was so short with you the other day," she said. "Lorraine told me she was responsible for the murder rumor, not you."

"You were more than short, Harriet," I said. "You accused me of behaving irresponsibly and selfishly, and wouldn't let me defend myself. You were so convinced of the rightness of your opinion that you never gave me the benefit of the doubt. You just went ahead and convicted me of the crime, and passed your sentence. No fair trial. No innocent until proven guilty. And certainly no trust between friends. I was very disappointed, I admit."

"You have the right to be angry, Jessica. I acted

irrationally. It's just that—" She stopped when Lorraine entered the room.

"Jessica, you're *not* cleaning up," Lorraine said, pulling the dish towel from my hand and hanging it on a hook under the sink.

"It's no trouble at all," I said. "You're going to need some help here."

"We'll take care of it later." She turned off the flame under the kettle and pulled my arm. "Someone brought a wonderful California wine. Come have a glass with me."

I smiled at her. "Lorraine, are you tipsy?"

"Not yet," she said. "I want to drink a toast to my big brother. Will you do that with me?"

"Of course."

"Everyone thinks they knew the real Wes Newmark, but I don't think any of us did. Not really." Lorraine's sadness was reflected in her eyes.

I put my arm around her shoulder and gave her a squeeze. "Come. I'll bet you haven't had anything to eat all day. Let's have a sandwich. Then we can toast Wes with this fancy wine." I looked back at Harriet, who'd started clearing the table and gathering up paper wrappings from food that had been delivered. "Harriet, why don't you join us?" I said. She looked up at me, a faint smile on her lips, and followed us out of the room.

Extra chairs had been brought into the parlor, and books from the table next to the sofa had been piled on the mantel to clear the surface for a dish of candy and coasters for the drinks. Platters of sandwiches, cheese and crackers, gelatin molds, chopped salads, cakes cut into square pieces, and pies and plates of cookies were spread across the top of a temporary table covered in blue linen that had been set against the wall. Between the extra furniture and the visitors, the usually spacious room was crowded.

Vernon Foner hovered over the dessert portion of the table, eyeing the selections. Rebecca greeted me as she cut a slice of apple pie for him. "Isn't this something? Between the cafeteria and the faculty spouses, Lorraine won't have to cook for a month."

"If she stays that long," I said.

"I'll help her out," Foner said, forking a piece of apple into his mouth. "I'll take home the rest of the pie."

"That's one of the nice things about a small college," Harriet put in as she poured a glass of wine for herself. "Community spirit."

It wasn't until I had filled a plate for Lorraine and turned around to look for her that I noticed Phil Adler sitting in a wheelchair near the window, his leg in a cast pointed at the room, like the barrel of a cannon.

Harriet saw the direction of my gaze. "He missed the service, but insisted on paying a condolence call," she said. "He just got out of the hospital. See what I mean about community spirit?"

I agreed with Harriet about the benefits of community spirit, but I wasn't sure that was what had motivated Phil Adler. He looked much better than when I'd seen him earlier in the week. He was neatly dressed and his hair was washed and combed, but there was still a grayness to his complexion, and new lines on his brow that I hadn't noticed before.

Manny Rosenfeld had moved over on the sofa to make room for Lorraine. I placed a napkin on her lap and the plate in her hand.

"Excuse me for a moment," I said. "I want to say hello to Phil Adler."

Larry Durbin had pulled up a folding chair next to

Phil, and the two were engaged in a low conversation when I approached. "Ah, Jessica," Durbin said, rising. "Would you like to sit down? We were just talking about you. I was telling Phil how considerate you were to come over to his house and make sure his clothing and personal articles would be accessible for him."

"Don't let me interrupt your conversation," I said. "I just came to ask how you're feeling, Phil."

Adler glared up at me. "I'm feeling fine, thank you very much, and I really don't like people going through my house when I'm not there. Who gave you the right to do that?"

The anger in his voice pierced the chatter in the room, and all conversation stopped.

"I did, Phil," Harriet said. She set the glass she'd been holding on the mantel and came to my side. "I had a meeting and couldn't meet the visiting nurse. Jessica was kind enough to fill in for me. Why is that a problem?"

"She snooped around, went through my bureau and medicine cabinet."

"How was she to bring down your clothing if she didn't open your dresser drawers?"

"She listened to the messages on my answering machine. What does that have to do with my clothing?"

Harriet started to answer for me, and I held up my hand to stop her. "I can understand why you're upset," I said. "I only wanted to be sure Harriet or the nurse hadn't called me, but when I heard Wes Newmark's voice, I admit I listened to his message. I found it particularly interesting, since you were supposed to meet him the morning he was killed."

"So what?"

"You told Harriet and me that Wes was going to

show something to you, but his message to you said he expected you to deliver something to him. What were you supposed to bring him?"

"Why do I have to answer any questions from you? What difference does it make?"

"It makes a difference," I replied, "because Wes Newmark was not killed by falling debris. He was murdered."

"That's just a campus rumor," Foner called out from his position by the refreshment table.

"It's not a rumor," Lorraine said, jumping up from her seat. "Wes sent me a letter saying his life was in danger. He was afraid someone was going to kill him—and someone did." She walked to where I stood, physically aligning herself with me.

"I always thought it was odd that he hadn't taken shelter," Manny Rosenfeld murmured to no one in particular.

"I did, too, Manny," I said. "That's why I began looking into his death."

"Why the hell didn't we know about this letter?" Needler said.

Harriet turned to him. "Because I didn't want you to. I thought it was just a figment of Wes's imagination, and I didn't want rumors spread all over campus, upsetting the students and their parents." She paused. "But it happened anyway."

"But as president, I should have been informed."

"Are you sure he was murdered, Jessica?" Rebecca asked. "How do you know?"

"I found the murder weapon, Rebecca." I looked at the faces around the room.

Lorraine looked stricken. "You never told me," she whispered.

"I wanted the proof in hand, Lorraine. It's at a forensic laboratory right now, being examined for evidence. We should hear back any day."

"So you don't know that this so-called murder weapon is that, do you?" Durbin said. "You're just guessing. Maybe Wes wasn't murdered at all. Maybe we're all just victims of your overactive imagination."

"Larry!" Rebecca said. "Why are you being so cruel?"

"We're all hanging on to this fairy tale and she has no proof that Wes Newmark was killed by anything other than a tornado. Murder mystery writers like our esteemed colleague here see villains around every corner, on every page. 'Forbear to judge,' Jessica, 'for we are sinners all.' That's from *Henry the Sixth*, madam, and means you should take stock of your own evil before seeing it in others."

I ignored Durbin's comment and said, "Someone hit Wes Newmark with an iron implement about three-quarters of an inch wide. You can read the autopsy report. Particles of rust and ashes were found in the wound. A fireplace poker from Kammerer House fits that description."

"Where did you find it?" Adler asked.

"The killer had replaced the poker in the stand with the other fireplace tools."

Manny spoke up. "But, Jessica, Wes's body was found under a pile of material and furniture that fell in from the second floor. Was the poker in all that mess?"

"The firemen jacked up the rubble to get Wes's body out," Harriet said.

"And I crawled underneath and found the poker," I said.

"How convenient," Durbin said, his voice heavy

with sarcasm. "You can't tell me that a killer assumed his crime would be covered up by a tornado. Those storms are unpredictable. You never know where they're going to land until seconds before."

"That's true," I said. "But this could be a crime of opportunity. Someone had a grudge against Wes, heard the tornado coming, and took the chance. Or maybe it was just a lucky coincidence that the tornado covered up what would have been recognized as a crime immediately had the storm not occurred."

"But if they heard the tornado coming, how did they have time to get away themselves?" Rebecca asked.

"I know," Manny said. "There's a tunnel off the basement connecting the office to the library. We used to go there during air-raid drills in the fifties and early sixties."

"That's right," I said. "That's how you got into Kammerer House just before the storm, wasn't it, Professor Foner?"

"Me? I didn't kill him. Don't look at me. I was in the library during the entire storm, wasn't I, Larry? You were there, too. So was Edgar. Where is that pipsqueak? Maybe he killed Wes. He hated him enough."

"I saw you for maybe two seconds," Durbin said. "There were dozens of people in the library. I'm not vouching for you or anyone else."

I looked at Foner across the room. "You were in Kammerer House," I said. "Your footprint in blood is on the carpet. I have a photograph of it." I pulled the photo of the shoe print from my jacket pocket. "My guess," I said to Foner, "is that the print in the picture will nicely match up with the soles of those expensive British shoes you're so fond of, with their distinctive diamond-patterned soles. No matter how thoroughly you might have tried to clean off the blood you stepped in, a simple Luminol test will still pick it up."

Foner tucked his feet beneath his chair and said loudly, "Why would I want to kill Wes? What motive could I possibly have?"

"You wanted his manuscript. You took it right out of his briefcase along with the computer disk."

All eyes turned to see who'd made the statement. It was Letitia Tingwell, standing in the doorway. Her eyes were ringed with smeared mascara and her lipstick was gone, leaving her face pale and haggard. But she held herself with dignity and aimed her charge at Foner. "That book you've been bragging about this week was written by Wes, not you."

She sagged against the wall. Having made the accusation, she had nothing more inside to hold herself up. Manny pushed himself up from his seat and went to assist her, but Rebecca was already there. Together they helped her to the sofa.

"You're pitiful. What do you know about my writing? Nothing," Foner said.

Mrs. Tingwell rallied. "You've been getting away with it for a long time, Verne, but not anymore."

"Just try and prove it," Foner said, taunting her. "Wes never talked with anyone about his work, Letitia, and certainly not with you. Wes just used you. Everyone knew that."

"Wes wasn't nice to me; that's true," she said. "And it's also true that he didn't talk about his work with me. But Jessica found some of the books he used for research. They're right down the hall in his study. You didn't know that, did you?" She looked at me and I nodded. "Not only that, we examined Wes's computer

together, and discovered where he kept his duplicate
files. The whole manuscript is in his computer," she
said. "And if the police look at the disk you have,
they'll see the label is written in his handwriting." She
sat back. Tears coursed down her cheeks, but her expression was triumphant.

"It's my book," Foner said angrily. "It's my idea."

"It may have been your idea, but Wes wrote it," I
said. "In fact, you paid him to write all of your books,
didn't you? He was your ghostwriter. He kept a record
of your payments to him in his safe. You paid thirty
thousand dollars for the last one. Does that sound
right?"

"You're lying," Foner said, his face scarlet. "I'm
not talking about this anymore."

"That's too bad. It was just getting interesting."
Lieutenant Parish leaned against the doorframe, his
arms crossed. Our attention had been so focused on
Foner and Mrs. Tingwell that we'd all missed his
entrance.

"Are you finished with your questioning, Mrs.
Fletcher?" Parish asked as I handed him the photograph of the footprint.

"Not yet."

"Well, don't let me interrupt."

I looked at Foner. "You might as well tell the truth
now, Verne," I said. "Lying will only make it worse."

He looked around at his colleagues and smiled.
"Really, ladies and gentlemen, you can see how ridiculous this is. Who is this woman anyway? Merely a
purveyor of popular fiction. She's certainly not a
scholar, like us. What does she know about scholarly
writing?"

" 'One may smile, and smile, and be a villain,' "

Durbin intoned, and not waiting to be asked the line's origin, he said, *"Hamlet,"* sounding pleased to have come up with the right line at the right time.

All eyes stared at Foner. The smile disappeared. He turned to Parish, who was waving the photograph and squinting at Foner's expensive shoes. "I didn't kill him; I swear it. I didn't. He . . . he . . . was already dead when I got there."

"Ah, and when was that?"

"Just before the tornado. I went through the tunnel, into the filing room, and up the stairs to the office. I needed a file I'd left on my desk. I figured I had plenty of time to get back to the shelter before the tornado hit, if it was going to. I walked into the office. He was lying on the rug all bloody. I just turned around and got the hell out of there."

"But not before taking the manuscript," I added. "Lorraine has his briefcase. If we need to, we can examine it for your fingerprints."

"I don't think Vernon is capable of murder," Manny said.

"Thank you, Manny."

"Don't thank me yet," he said. He looked at the policeman. "Vernon may be a thief—I can buy that— but I don't think he's brave enough to kill someone. But if Vernon didn't kill Wes, who did?"

"Let me take a crack at it," said Parish. His eyes bored in on Phil Adler. "I'm guessing it was our favorite college accountant. You could have come through the tunnel, whacked Newmark, and hightailed it back to your office."

All color drained from Adler's face. "That's ridiculous," he said. "I did nothing of the sort."

"Why do you think Phil would kill Wes?" Harriet

asked, having finally accepted that a murder had taken place. "He was injured in the storm, too."

"Maybe he wanted to die," Parish said, knowing that the words still to come would shock. "After killing his second victim."

The room erupted in chaos, everyone talking at once. Two uniformed officers who'd been waiting outside rushed into the room, hands on their holsters.

"Enough!" Parish yelled. "I want it quiet in here." He waved the officers back into the hall.

Adler was slumped in his wheelchair. He raised his head and looked around. "I did want to die," he said. "That's why I stayed there during the storm. But I didn't kill Wes, or anyone else."

"We found the body of your wife in one of the bomb shelters underneath the building that housed your office," Parish said. "She had a crack in her head, too. A coincidence, huh, that they both died the same way?"

"You don't have to tell him anything, Phil," Durbin said to his friend and neighbor. "We'll get you a good lawyer."

"No, Larry, it's over," Adler said. "I've been waiting a year for this to happen, and now I'm glad it finally has."

"How did she die, Phil?" I asked.

He sighed heavily. "She fell down the stairs and hit her head."

I looked at Parish, who raised his eyebrows as if to say, *Likely story,* but remained silent.

"We'd been fighting again," Adler said, his voice weary. "It was pretty loud. She was threatening to leave, and I just . . . I just lost it. I screamed at her to get out. I threw her shoes at her. She threw them back and one hit me in the head. I got so angry I pushed her. She was standing right near the top of the stairs. I saw her start to take a step backward and I made a grab for her. She must've thought I was going to push her again and she moved back—and went down the whole flight headfirst." He shuddered. "I can still hear the sound of her skull hitting the edge of the steps."

"Why didn't you call the police?" Harriet asked. "It was an accident."

"Who was going to believe that? Every neighbor on the block could testify to the fights we'd had. I didn't want to be charged with murder and have my life ruined. Lord knows she ruined it enough."

"Why did Wes want to meet with you?" I asked. "Did he know about Kate's death?"

"I thought he'd found out. All he said was to be there and make sure I had all the financial books ready. I thought he was going to blackmail me, get me to steal from college funds to keep him quiet."

"You assumed that," I said, "but he never actually talked to you about Kate, or demanded money from you, did he?"

"No, but he would have. I know it. I was so relieved when the storm killed him, but I was disappointed that it left me alive."

"How did you get her body down to the bomb shelter without anyone seeing you?" Parish asked.

"I helped him," Durbin said.

Everyone gaped at Durbin.

"You helped him?" some said in unison.

"Not kill her," Durbin said. "I helped get rid of the body, that's all."

"No, Larry. You don't have to do this," Phil said.

"I'm afraid I do, my friend. I helped you get rid of

that wretched woman because she was making your life miserable. Don't misunderstand. I don't advocate murdering those who cause us pain on a daily basis. Divorce would have been far preferable. But since you did the deed, and since it was an accident, I felt it only right for me to lend a hand. As the bard so nicely put it in *The Merchant of Venice,* 'The quality of mercy is not strained. It droppeth as the gentle rain from heaven.' I gave of my own free will, Philip, old chap, and would do it again." He laid a hand on Adler's shoulder and addressed us: "I was the one who told him the cops would never believe it was an accident. My wife and I had heard them fighting. Melissa had even said it sounded like they were killing each other. She made me go over to see if they were all right."

"You didn't answer my question," Parish said.

"We rolled her into a rug and brought her over to the bursar's office the next afternoon," Durbin said. "We did it in broad daylight, figuring if anyone saw us bringing in a rug, it wouldn't look unusual, but if they'd seen us skulking around at night, it would have raised suspicions."

"Is that the rug that's rolled up in your upstairs storage room?"

Adler looked at me sadly, and nodded.

"I've heard enough," said Parish. "You're under arrest, Philip Adler, for your wife's murder. As for you, Professor Durbin, you're facing a charge of accessory to murder."

"Wait a minute, Lieutenant," Manny Rosenfeld said. "We still don't know who killed Wes Newmark." He sat next to Mrs. Tingwell, holding her hand, a parent consoling a child. Rebecca was on the other side of the department secretary. President Needler perched on a side chair chewing the inside of his cheek, while Harriet continued to stand by the fireplace. I took in each of them before turning back to Needler. There was silence as we locked eyes, saying nothing, but our thoughts were as plain as though we had spoken.

"No!" he said suddenly, his face glazed with anger. "I was at my meeting. You promised you wouldn't raise this topic."

"That's right," I said. "You told me you'd been at your Gamblers Anonymous meeting—but you weren't. All meetings of that kind at the hospital were canceled because of the storm. I have that on very good authority," I added, thinking of Eunice Carberra, my friend from the hospital gift shop.

Needler drew up to his full height and assumed a patrician pose. "So I didn't attend my meeting," he said, glowering at me. "You're not my keeper. How dare you challenge my authority."

"I find it interesting," I said, " that whenever you're in trouble, you attack. Where will you say you were now?"

"I drove up north to Lake Michigan."

"You got any witnesses?" Parish asked lazily from the doorway.

"No, I was in my car all day. Never got out, just drove around."

"How do you explain the cobwebs that were all over the back of your coat?" I asked. "No, President Needler, you spent the afternoon in the tunnels, waiting for a time to leave without anyone seeing you."

"That's preposterous."

"Jessica, why would President Needler want to kill Wes?" Lorraine asked.

"Because Wes and Harriet were gathering evidence to oust him. Isn't that right, Harriet?"

"Oh, Jessica, I was hoping against hope that Wes's death had nothing to do with our investigation. Unfortunately, it did."

"What kind of evidence were you gathering, Dean Bennett?" Parish asked.

"He's been using college funds to pay off his gambling debts. Over the years he's cheated Schoolman out of more than two hundred and fifty thousand dollars."

"That's nonsense," Needler muttered.

"Wes was going to get Phil to review the budgets for the last five years," Harriet continued, "to find out how Needler had stolen the money."

"That's a lot of money," Manny said. "Our president doesn't look like a rich man to me."

"That's because he lost it all in poker," I said. "And a good chunk of it in one particular game."

I went to the mantel and picked up one of the books that had been left there. "You may be interested in this," I said, looking at Needler. I removed the dustcover of a popular novel. Under it was an old book with a deep red morocco binding.

"That's mine!" roared Needler, reaching for it.

Parish grabbed him by the arm, and the two other officers rushed in behind to subdue the college president.

"It's mine!" he wailed as they wrestled him to the floor. "He stole it from me, the bastard."

"He won it from you, you mean," I said.

"He deserved to die. I'd kill him all over again if I could. That book is mine."

"What is it, Jessica?" Rebecca asked.

"A first edition," I said. "A very rare first edition."

Chapter Twenty-seven

"I always save the files for my books in two places to be safe," I said. "I figured he would, too."

"What do you mean, 'to be safe'?" Rebecca asked.

"What if my computer crashed or I lost the disk? Then all the work I'd done would be lost. Don't you save the articles you write in two different places?"

"I haven't before, but I will now."

Rebecca and I sat in the Langston Apartments with Letitia Tingwell and Manny Rosenfeld three days after the arrests. I'd put Lorraine Newmark in a limousine to Chicago that morning. She was scheduled to return in a month to settle her brother's affairs.

"You know, Vernon mentioned to me that he'd written the book on his summer break," said Rebecca, "and I never questioned how he could write so fast."

"Not to mention time out for a vacation in Italy," I added.

"That's right! I thought the guy must be a genius, while I'm just a struggling academic trying to get my work published in a respectable magazine. And all the time it was Wes who was the genius while Vernon just coasted along."

"What I don't understand," said Letitia, who had finally asked me to call her by her first name, "is why

Professor Foner didn't report the murder when he came upon it."

"He didn't want to be connected with the missing manuscript," I said. "Since he was aware he'd stolen it, he was sure someone else would notice it was gone if he was the one calling the police."

"My question," said Manny Rosenfeld, "is why Harriet chose Wes to work with in the first place to prove Needler was stealing school funds. Wes didn't know a lot about finances."

"But he knew all about Needler's gambling losses, and how to entice him into a couple of high-stakes poker games. Harriet asked Wes to put financial pressure on Needler to see if they could force him into a compromising situation, make him do something impetuous to cover his losses. She figured Wes would know how to beat him at cards, and that he would enjoy the challenge."

"Isn't that entrapment?" Manny asked.

"If it involved the authorities, it might be," I replied. "Harriet called it a sting. Wes was able to get Needler to bet more and more, and Needler, who had to get money from somewhere, padded the budget, privately selling off Schoolman property and keeping the funds. Initially, his intention was to pay off the markers."

"Pardon my ignorance, but what's a marker?" Rebecca asked.

"It's a promise to pay what's owed," I said. "And Wes was getting quite a few of Needler's markers."

I didn't tell them that when Wes passed along Needler's markers to Harriet, he sometimes made a game out of it, hiding them behind pictures, or putting them in the freezer. There was something unsavory in the way he and Harriet had toyed with the college president. Harriet must have enjoyed the irony of asking Needler to bring her the framed photograph of Wes, because Needler didn't know that one of his markers had been slipped behind the smiling face of Wes Newmark.

"What was that book Lorraine gave to the police?" Letitia asked.

"It was a ledger in which Wes kept track of money paid to him by Vernon Foner for ghosting his books, and money owed to him by Lowell Needler. I have a copy of some of the pages." I pulled out the folded sheets I had spent many an hour poring over and handed one to each of them.

"What's this mean?" asked Rebecca. "It says 'N minus fifteen M minus FE.'"

"I think those minus signs are dashes," I said.

"I bet I can figure it out now," Manny said. He looked over Rebecca's shoulder. "It means Needler dash fifteen thousand dollars dash first edition. Needler must have gambled more than he had, and Wes took books from his collection to cover the value of what Needler lost."

"Exactly," I said. "But Wes couldn't help showing off a little. And that's what sealed his fate. He took Needler to a particularly high-stakes game, and when Needler lost, Wes demanded his most precious book. It was too deep a wound. Needler collected rare books all his life, and Wes had taken away his prize possession in a poker game."

"What was that book, Jessica?"

"A first edition of *David Copperfield*, Rebecca."

"That doesn't sound so rare."

"This one was," I said. "It was a specially bound presentation edition, dated and signed by Charles

Dickens himself. *David Copperfield* was Dickens's favorite book. He considered it his masterpiece. This
one contained an inscription dedicated to another author he admired, Nathaniel Hawthorne. In addition,
inside the cover was a bookplate with the name Theo-
dore Roosevelt on it. It had been a gift to him from
an admirer."

"That's quite a provenance," Manny said. "How
much was the book worth?"

"I don't know what Needler paid for it," I said,
"but I understand in today's market, it could fetch
upward of one hundred twenty-five thousand dollars."

"Oh, my," said Letitia. "I knew the book must have
been important. I saw Wes put the cover of another
book over it. I thought he just wanted to protect it
from the dust or the sunlight. I'm glad I didn't know
what it was worth or I would have been a nervous
wreck leaving it in the house."

"Wes was clever, leaving the book in plain sight," I
said. "Needler never thought to look for it there. He
took several volumes from Wes's bookcase in the study,
but he wasn't able to find the one he really wanted."

"Do you think Dean Bennett will become college
president now?" Rebecca asked.

I shrugged.

"It's already happened," Manny put in. "The board
appointed her acting president this morning."

Then she got what she wanted, I thought, *but at
what price?*

We were about to leave when Eli appeared in the
open doorway, smiled, and waved to me. The group
split up and I joined my student in the hallway, certain
he'd been eavesdropping.

"Hi, Professor Fletcher, got any time to talk with
me?"

"Of course, Eli. I was just going to leave for lunch. You can walk me to the Student Union. Give me a minute."

"Cool."

I gathered my papers, tucked them in the top drawer of my desk, and bade my colleagues farewell.

Eli and I walked downstairs, through the beautiful reading room of Sutherland Library, and out into a sunny Indiana day.

"If you're really good," I said, "I'll treat for lunch."

"That's 'cause you owe me one, right?"

"If you're thinking about the fireplace poker, yes, I do owe you one for that."

"Did they find Needler's fingerprints on it?"

"No. But they did find evidence that it was used in the murder."

"So are they going to have a hard time pinning the rap on the president?"

"I rather doubt it, considering he's signed a confession."

"I bet his lawyers try to have it overturned."

"You may be right."

"I liked working on this case with you."

"My friend, the sheriff of Cabot Cove, says you should consider a career in law enforcement."

"Yeah? I kind of think I'd rather write about solving mysteries instead."

"You have time to make up your mind. You need to finish college first."

"Edgar says he's applying to Princeton's graduate program."

"Good for him."

"He's a really sharp guy. I bet he gets in."

"I hope he does."

"Are you teaching here next semester?"

"No. Dean Bennett asked me to come back, but I miss my friends in Cabot Cove, and I have another book under contract."

"Would you mind if I wrote to you every so often?"

"It would be my pleasure."

"Cool."

We parted after lunch, and I took a long, leisurely walk around the perimeter of the campus. The murder of Wes Newmark had been solved, as had the disappearance of Kate Adler. There was a certain satisfaction to that. At the same time, the idyllic atmosphere of Schoolman College that I'd taken to immediately upon arrival had been replaced by something decidedly less sanguine. Of course, a tornado had the ability to change happiness to terror in the blink of an eye.

But there was an insular quality to life on this campus—probably in most college settings—that seemed to foster excessive introspection, men and women focusing so intently on their own academic passions and need for recognition that larger issues could be lost in the process.

The scandal created by two murders had certainly placed Harriet and the school in the public eye. Whether that would hurt the college's future was conjecture. Chances were it would enhance interest in Schoolman and perhaps even boost enrollment. As the old public relations adage goes, "Say what you want about me, but spell my name right." Such is the state of our society.

The experience of helping solve the murders had taken the edge off my initial pleasure at being there. But that was balanced by the satisfaction I took from my students, bright and ambitious young men and women seeking to carve out their paths into adult life and beyond. I had no doubt that Eli would keep in touch, and that one day I'd receive from him a manuscript, his first murder mystery novel, and that it would be pretty good. At least I hoped it would be. I hate having to respond negatively to young people's early attempts at writing.

I also knew that my relationship with Harriet would never be the same. Oh, yes, we would remain friends while I continued to teach there, and after I'd left, too. But it would be different because we were different people, with different agendas and dreams. Of one thing I was certain: She would accomplish at Schoolman what she intended, to turn it into a financially solvent institution of higher learning of which she, and her staff and the students, could be proud.

I ended my walk back at my small but comfortable apartment, where I made tea and settled in to prepare for the next day's class, which I looked forward to. At the same time, I knew I would not be sad when the semester was over and I would leave Schoolman College. It wasn't that I didn't like it there, even with the complication of two murders. But the contemplation of being back where I truly belonged, Cabot Cove, Maine, made me smile. It always does, no matter where I happen to be in the world.

Al Blevin reared back his head. His shoulder twitched as if he were trying to snap out a punch, but his arms stayed fixed, crossed on his chest. Another spasm rocked his body and he fell backward. His head glanced off a table, knocking over a glass and spilling the remains of Hallie's specialty across the lapels of his immaculately tailored tan jacket and the front of his pristine white shirt.

The club members gasped as their president went into convulsions. His eyes bulged open. His face turned crimson and then blue as his body denied him oxygen, and pink again as the throes of the spasms released their hold on him.

"Come on, everyone, get out of here and make some room for him," Lloyd Burns said, herding people from the train's club car.

They moved cautiously past the prone Blevin.

"Geez, he must have had a snootful."

"I think he's having a heart attack."

"No, it looks like a stroke."

"My cousin had epilepsy. Maybe that's it."

"Did anyone take first aid?"

"Hallie, call for help."

"I did."

"I hope there's a hospital in Whistler."

"How far out are we now?"

"Don't just stand there. Someone help him." Theodora's face was ashen, but she backed away from her husband's prone figure. "Samantha, you're a nurse," she said. "Please do something or he'll die."

"What do you want me to do?" Samantha shouted.

Blevin's body began to tremble again. He arched his back till his body was curved like a bow, only his head and feet touching the floor. His face was drained.

"Give him mouth-to-mouth resuscitation," someone said.

Samantha took a step forward, frowning down at Blevin.

"Don't do it," I said, gripping her arm. "He may have been poisoned."

"I had no intention of putting my mouth anywhere near his," Samantha said, shaking me off and stalking out of the car.

"Poison," Maeve Pinkney gasped and slid down into a faint.

The word triggered a stampede among those who hadn't left yet. They rushed out of the car. Junior leaned over his wife, fanning her face with a railroad map.

Blevin's body shuddered, and he lay limp on the floor. He drew in air through his teeth and color flooded back into his face. Theodora gingerly knelt by his side. She tapped softly on her husband's shoulder and his eyes met hers. "Look what they did to you. Your nicest shirt," she said, wiping the sweat off his brow and then blotting the red stain on his shirt with a napkin. "You're going to be just fine," she said, a quaver in her voice. "You'll see. You just drank too much. Three Bloody Marys, Al. We're going to laugh about this next week." Her son, Benjamin, sat at a table near the bar, staring silently at his mother and stepfather, his arms and legs crossed, his body hunched forward.

"Jessica, what do we do?" my friend Reggie whispered.

"The only thing we can do till medical help arrives," I whispered back, "is keep him warm and quiet. And close the drapes near him. He may be sensitive to light."

"Sensitive to light? How do you . . . ?"

I walked over to where Hallie stood behind the counter, wringing a bar towel. "You said you called for help?" I asked softly.

"I did, I did," she stammered, "but he can't have been poisoned, Mrs. Fletcher. I made his drink myself. No one's ever gotten sick before. Maybe it's just an allergic reaction. I put in a lot of horseradish this time. Do you think that did it?"

"Shh. It's not your fault."

Reggie shrugged out of his jacket and laid it across Blevin's chest.

The waiter who'd been serving hors d'oeuvres only thirty minutes ago rushed into the club car, followed by Jenna, another of the staff, holding a first-aid kit.

"We called for an ambulance," he told Theodora. "There'll be one waiting in Whistler."

"How long will it be?" she asked, adjusting Reggie's jacket over Blevin.

"We're almost there." Jenna propped the first-aid kit on a chair and snapped open the latch.

A long whistle sounded as the train rounded a curve; the shrill squeal of the wheels rent the air. Blevin's body lifted off the floor as another convulsion gripped him. Theodora scrambled away from him and climbed into a chair. The screech of metal on metal reverberated in the car, now emptied of all but a few of the club's delegation.

Jenna and the waiter stared, transfixed, as Blevin's lips curled back in a grotesque grin. His eyes bulged from their sockets and his arms twitched. His skin took on an odd pallor under his tanned complexion, and a blue tinge crept into face.

The train straightened and the wheels ceased their strident sound. But it was too late.

Junior, who'd pulled Maeve up onto a chair and was patting her hand, looked at Blevin and nodded at the two young people. "I don't think that kit's going to do you any good anymore," he said and took a few fast photos of the scene.

Reggie walked to where Blevin lay and gazed into his sightless eyes. He leaned down and pulled his jacket up over Blevin's face. Theodora wailed.

"My God," Hallie cried hoarsely from behind the bar. "He's dead!"